He's her judge, jury and executioner. She's his only chance to truly live.

Savannah Michaels is in desperate need of cash…for all the right reasons. Determined to leave behind her hospital debt and the nightmares of her past, she answers a classified ad to be a paid travel companion in Italy. Of course, she hardly expects her employer to be a tall, handsome and moody vampire.

Luke Evans has a very good reason to seek revenge against the world's greedy souls. After all, greed cost him his wife and mortal life two centuries ago. His latest ploy, classified ads, is working out well. Until he meets Savannah Michaels. She is not what she seems and even worse, hasn't the slightest idea just how different she is.

Suddenly, Luke realizes playing judge and jury over his victims comes at too high a cost, especially when his latest victim may be the love of his life…and the death of his race.

Books by Toni Kelly

Irish Dreams

The Blessed
Blood Eternal

Published by Kensington Publishing Corporation

Blood Eternal

The Blessed, Book One

Toni Kelly

LYRICAL PRESS
Kensington Publishing Corp.
www.kensingtonbooks.com

Lyrical Press books are published by
Kensington Publishing Corp. 119 West 40th Street New York, NY 10018

All Kensington titles, imprints, and distributed lines are available at special quantity discounts for bulk purchases for sales promotion, premiums, fund-raising, and educational or institutional use.

Special book excerpts or customized printings can also be created to fit specific needs. For details, write or phone the office of the Kensington Special Sales Manager:
Kensington Publishing Corp.
119 West 40th Street
New York, NY 10018
Attn. Special Sales Department. Phone: 1-800-221-2647.

Kensington and the K logo Reg. U.S. Pat. & TM Off.
Lyrical Press and the L logo are trademarks of Kensington Publishing Corp.

First Electronic Edition: February 2014
eISBN-13: 978-1-61650-5011
eISBN-10: 1-61650-501-X

First Print Edition: February 2014
ISBN-13: 978-1-61650-758-9
ISBN-10: 1-61650-758-6

Printed in the United States of America

My loving husband and family, your support is endless and I am forever grateful—whether I always show it or not.

a.c. Mason, you've taught me more than you will ever realize. You are immensely talented and utterly inspiring.

Chapter 1

Curst greed of gold, what crimes thy tyrant power has caused.
—Virgil

A biting chill came to Rome early, like it had the year of Victoria's death. This time, Luke Evans sensed the sting and yearned for the crisp wetness, which would have seeped inside his bones if he were human. He pulled the lapels of his coat up out of habit and started across Piazza del Popolo toward Santa Maria di Montesanto. The church and its twin, Santa Maria dei Miracoli, loomed ahead of him, whispering words of warning. This he believed because it made sense damned creatures would not be welcome within their doors.

A young girl hurried toward him. The scent of her hunger and desperation, not unlike that of a beggar, reached him first. Holes laced the cuffs of her thin coat. Her slender form was diminished beneath jeans several sizes too large.

"*Signore*, stop," she said, reached up and tugged the arm of his coat, pleading with her dark eyes. "Please help me. A man has taken my purse. Without it, I have nothing." Her English held a hint of Roman accent. Perhaps a city native?

Luke would bet his immortality she did not have much within her purse. Not that immortality meant much.

"*Signore*?" The girl grasped his hand, her skin warm in comparison to his. "Please."

"Luke." Victoria slipped a hand through his, squeezing it tight. She turned, her pale eyes searching. She was frightened. He needed to soothe her.

No, he thought. *Not real. Not any longer.* Victoria was gone. Eyes closed, he tried to separate reality from the images his mind recreated.

A scream echoed. This time Victoria lay still, cold. Her gray dress reflected the pallor of her skin. A matching handbag rested alongside her, its contents scattered across a growing pool of burgundy. Blood. It encroached upon the cobblestone beneath them.

"Are you okay, sir?" The girl frowned.

"Yes." Luke blinked, letting the image of his dead wife dissipate. The girl shifted with edgy movements. Still, her tale hit too close to home for him to deny her request. He gripped her arm, his firm hold a warning as much as a comfort. "Bring me to where you last saw him."

Her lower lip trembled and her moment's hesitation puzzled him. A possible lie? Perhaps, but curiosity got the better of him. He let her lead him amidst the shadows of an alley. In any case, no predator worse than he awaited them. He scented anxiety, anticipation. Another human being. A male, based on the musk.

"Reveal yourself," he said.

The man's ragged breaths muffled his thumping heart as he stepped beneath a street lamp's orange-tinted halo. Longish, straggly hair covered part of his face. He held a knife, the blade shaky in his tremulous grip. "Give us your wallet."

Beside Luke, the girl backed away. He turned, disappointment a bitter taste on his tongue even as her gaze held regret. "If I refuse?" he asked. "Do you truly believe you could overpower me?"

The man stepped forward. "Leave her alone. Do as I say. We only want your cash." Brows creased, he puffed up his chest. Young, like the girl. Nearly a boy at age eighteen or nineteen, he mistook stupidity for cunning, bravado for courage.

The predator within hungered for an easy kill. He'd gone too long without taking life. His canines lengthened, but he kept them covered. "You know not what you threaten. Do not make the mistake of playing a fool."

The young man squinted, hesitated. His hand lowered slightly as he pressed his lips together. An insecure child pulled within hunger's grasp. The boy shoved back greasy hair. "We need this. Don't try to convince us otherwise. You're free if you give us your money. We don't want to hurt you, but we will if we must."

Damn it. Luke did not have time for children's games. He attacked with a rush of speed, knocked the knife from the boy's hand and seized his neck. "You try my patience." Beneath Luke's thumb, blood pulsed an almost irresistible tune of temptation. It would be easy, quick. Saliva pooled on his tongue but he could sense the three of them were not alone.

An audience of one stood amidst shadows. A heartbeat too slow to be human. Broderick. The halfling possessed impeccable timing. Without easing his grip, Luke turned toward the darkness. "What is it you are hoping for? Do you find fault with my judgment?" His resolve wavered as he waited for an answer. None came. "Selfish men are thieves. Do you not see greed manifests itself here?"

For a moment the weight on his shoulders seemed insurmountable. It was not enough for vampires to drink life's essence. Only a kill would calm the angst consuming him. How he loathed the animal inside him.

"No," the girl cried, tugging at his arm. "We didn't mean any harm. We're hungry, desperate. Leave him alone. Please."

"How touching." He growled and pulled away, tossed the boy against a stone wall. A gush of air left the boy's mouth then he coughed and slid to the ground. The girl came at Luke again and he lifted her, a hand braced against her jugulars. Too thin and delicate. He kept his touch gentle so as not to make a mark. At least she felt regret. "Do you know what I could do? What I should?"

"No, Giulia." The young man coughed again and stretched forward an arm. "Please, don't hurt her. Take me instead." This time, the scent of sweat emanated from him. It flooded the atmosphere, choking Luke with its potency.

Interesting, the boy feared more for Giulia's life than his own. There might still be hope for them. With a sigh, Luke set her down.

She ran to the young man and helped him up, caressing his face, neck and arms in search of injuries. They were in love. Strange how even in the darkest of circumstances, the emotion blossomed.

Luke adjusted the cuffs of his collared shirt. Such luck. In search of wrongdoing, he'd found not true wickedness, but young lovers confined within the depths of hopelessness. Standing before him, they possessed a profound slightness, granted not only by their small stature but through life's cruelty. "Bloody hell."

"Who are you?" the young man asked and pushed Giulia behind him.

Luke hung his head. "I am no one."

The boy opened his mouth as if to say something then backed away, taking Giulia with him.

"Wait." Luke pointed down a shadowed, cobblestone street. "If you go straight, make your second right and you will see a wooden sign for a small hotel. Ask for Francesca and tell her Dante sent you. She will take care of your room and board until you can earn enough wages to pay your own way."

The boy's brows drew together. "Is this some kind of trick?"

"I do not joke regarding favors." He pulled several euro notes from his wallet. "This should take care of you both for the next couple weeks."

"We don't need your charity." The boy snarled.

"I would say current circumstances prove otherwise. What about her?" He nodded at Giulia. "Do you think Giulia deserves this kind of life?"

"She has clothes on her back. We eat enough."

"Her person is frail and such clothes shall not protect you through winter's first week." Luke rubbed his neck, considering. "I too have found myself facing difficult situations, but I warn you once. What you are doing is never the answer. If you insist, you may pay me back through Francesca. She will make arrangements."

"*Grazie, signore.*" Giulia stepped toward him and accepted the money.

"Thanks." The young man came forward.

He faced him. "Do not thank me. I could easily have damaged your person. If you choose a thief's role, be prepared to pay the price. Next time, you might not be so fortunate." He nodded at Giulia. "Take care of her. And take a bath. Several days' stench makes for a terrible lover."

The young man nodded and hurried away, linking his arm with Giulia's.

"Nicely done. Almost Zorro-like," Broderick said. "Dante is it? I'd applaud but you'd call me dramatic."

"Yes, I would." Luke glared as his close friend and private investigator, Broderick Sullivan, left the shadows and leaned against a wall. "Francesca prefers to call me Dante. She has always been fond of *The Divine Comedy.*"

"There is something fitting about it," Broderick replied.

"Believe what you may." Luke preferred not to delve down that path. He was not sure he agreed with Broderick or Francesca. Unlike Dante, his journey did not traverse beyond Hell's realm. "You did not intervene. I know you wanted to. Why resist your urge?"

Broderick stared down the narrow street where the couple had disappeared. "You had everything under control."

"You thought differently." He had heard the uneven skip of Broderick's heartbeat as he held the boy. His friend had not believed him capable of holding out much longer. Difficult to admit, that Broderick might be right. A shiver of unease worked its way through him but he shrugged it away. "Why did you doubt me?"

"You know why. Your problem is you won't admit it."

Luke shook his head. "I would like to think I would not have hurt them. They were young, desperate." Still worth saving.

"They were thieves. Despite what you'd rather think of yourself, you've gone too long between killings. You know feeding is not enough for a pureblood." Broderick stepped closer. "It's not a game whether or not you choose to kill your victims. You don't have a choice. If you keep pushing yourself like this, madness will drive you toward something you regret."

"Something I regret." Luke barked a sarcastic laugh. "Tell me what I do not already know. I choose my victims with a purpose. Are you saying I should let the memory of her die?" He squeezed his eyes shut and swallowed. "Should Victoria have died in vain?"

"Your wife's death happened unexpectedly, an unforeseen tragedy. Not a justification for murder. Especially one that happened over two hundred years ago."

"Murder is never unexpected. Those men knew what could result from such harmful actions. I, however, cannot help what I do."

"Oh yeah." Broderick huffed. "You are what you are."

"What do you expect? Each day, I live her murder like it happened the day before. I am a murderer by nature." And always would be.

"Don't blame nature. You're a vampire. Your premeditation makes you a murderer by choice."

"Enough. I pay you to bring me potential victims, not be their judge and juror. That is my role," Luke said.

"A role you'll fuck up if you don't feed and kill in a timely manner. A vampire with a conscience is anomaly enough. If you want to live as guilt-free as possible, this world's got plenty of scum awaiting your death sentence."

"I'm not searching for a couple guilt-free millennia, I want complete freedom. Do you not understand I need to make a determination whether my victims are evil or not?"

"No," said Broderick. "I don't understand."

"Because you have not been listening."

"I disagree."

"No." Luke closed his eyes and rubbed his temples. "This discussion is over." Broderick's words only grated on his nerves. "What new information do you have for me?"

Broderick hung his head. "Did you get my latest file upload?"

"I did receive the file. Still, I prefer paper. Did you bring it with you?"

"Yes. This is pretty much everything I have on Savannah Michaels." He handed him a manila folder. "You better get with the times. I'm done killing trees for you."

"You are full of sage advice today." Luke accepted the folder and thumbed through the first couple pages.

"Dates wealthy men, volunteers at charity events, which high society women somehow feel obligated to do, and is obviously desperate for money since she answered my ad. This is fairly circumstantial. I have quite a bit of work on this one."

"You don't let me make it easy. If you're looking for justifiable kills, I could bring you convicted felons."

"No." Each killing was as much a test for him as it was for his victim. He might be a monster but he needed to prove he could choose right from wrong, good from bad.

"As you wish." Broderick brushed a hand back through his unruly waves. "People become who they are through experience, upbringing and motivation. Not everyone immediately chooses the wrong path. For some it is thrust upon them." He nodded toward where the young couple had walked. "Like them."

"Exactly why it is important for me to do this."

"You need another purpose beyond revenge. You are strong, but we each have limits. It'll catch up with you sooner or later."

A muscle pulsed along Luke's jaw. "I do not pay you to be my bloody conscience. I am a vampire, for God's sake."

"I haven't forgotten. If anything, I'm reminding you of this fact," Broderick said. "Besides, I'm speaking as a friend, not an employee."

"A friend would understand my motivation." A low blow but he grew tired of their argument. This was not the first time Broderick had expressed concerns. No doubt it wouldn't be the last. Each victim challenged him further. Before long, the lines between good and evil would blend and a primitive part of him would take over. He refused to lose whatever humanity he held without a fight.

The line of Broderick's mouth grew rigid as he met his gaze briefly then turned away. "Ms. Michaels should be en route to your meeting place shortly." He pulled out an iPhone and pushed its Home button. "It's late. Considering your night's distraction, you should leave soon."

Luke paused on a photo in the file. It could only be described as vivid, and Snow White came to mind. He did not believe fairytales, yet something about her warmed the cold crawling along his skin.

"Luke?"

"I have one stop at the church first."

"Fine. Anything else."

"Did you pick up my shipment of blood?" Luke asked.

"It's in my trunk now. I'd recommend a bag or two. It might keep the angst at bay for some time."

He doubted it would help, however, Broderick's intentions remained well placed. "Maybe you are right."

"Of course I'm right."

"Either way, if it gets too difficult, I will call you before I do anything to her."

"Fine."

Beyond the immense doors of Santa Maria di Montesanto, the night's noise died down. As Luke located a pew, he could almost hear Mrs. Thompson say, *the Lord giveth and He taketh away. If you have time to make it to gaming hells, you have time to make it to Mass.*

He smiled at the memory. Despite a fondness for his family's housekeeper, he'd always thought her words the mere poppycock of an old woman. Now... His world was different and the Church had become a vestige of hope. More than two hundred years in Rome, and Catholicism had grown on him. He would not call himself devout, but his interest remained somewhat sturdy, considering his damned status.

After saying a short prayer, he genuflected, made the Sign of the Cross and gathered his black scarf before heading to the back of the church. He smiled at a woman who lit candles, careful not to expose too much fang.

Her mouth curved easily. "*Buona sera, signore.*"

"*Buona sera.*" He wished her good night and strode past.

"*Buona sera, signore. Vada con Dio.*" An elderly lady with gray streaks through her hair greeted him near the front door. A regular, she smelled of incense and dust.

Luke nodded in salutation and hastened into the brusque night. He could have said the damned did not go with God except she seemed a nice lady. Far be it from him to ruin her evening. Besides, there was a certain irony to the fact he concerned himself with religion as an immortal when as a human he'd labeled it a dull, useless waste of time.

He'd seen enough throughout his lifetime to respect the existence of a greater power. Yet he would never understand why this greater power would let a young couple wander through the streets hungry.

Pushing past his thoughts, he picked up the pace. He had an appointment to make. Icy wind whipped through the air and sliced apart a light mist over the near vacant piazza. Late September, and a winter frost tiptoed across Rome.

Chapter 2

*Desperation is the raw material of drastic change. Only those who can
leave behind everything they have ever believed in can hope to escape.*
—*William S. Burroughs*

Savannah Michaels nibbled the fingernails of one hand while she
crinkled a piece of paper with the other. Ninety thousand dollars of debt
and now she was thousands of miles away from home doing only God
knew what. Sure, it had been for necessary expenses. She hadn't planned
the accident and definitely wouldn't have chosen to complete near two
years of physical therapy afterward, but this knowledge didn't soothe the
butterflies in her stomach. A knot tightened her throat. Now was not the
time for cold feet. She massaged her throat and glanced back down at the
internet classified ad she'd printed off.

COMPANION WANTED
*Traveling companion, male or female, between the ages of twenty-five
to forty-five. Requires valid passport and the ability to travel throughout
Italy for four weeks straight. All expenses covered. Will pay handsomely.
Please inquire at immortal1790@gmail.com*

Too good to be true? Savannah released a shuddering breath and
sipped her cappuccino. Steam hit her nose, warming it against the air's
chill. Across a huge expanse of ocean, meeting a complete stranger. She
had to be crazy.

"Your *tartufo*." A waiter leaned forward and placed a chocolate lover's
dream before her. "Anything else, miss?" His gaze questioned beneath a
broad brow.

Rubbing the button holding her pants closed, she smiled. "No, thank
you. Um, *grazie*."

He nodded and turned, attending another table.

Hmm. She planned to eat in Italy and here she sat, content after a sumptuous feast. Of course bread dipped in olive oil, a cappuccino and a heaping plate of capellini al pomodoro slowed her gusto a bit. Aspiring chef or not, a person could only eat so much at one time. Good thing she'd spend four weeks here, although there might not be a plane big enough to carry her back.

She settled further down in her seat, spooned a cold layer of chocolate and cream onto her tongue and let an explosion of cocoa work its magic. The accordion whines of "Quando, Quando, Quando" drifted past her and brought bliss. She'd imagined Italy like this. These tastes and sounds were the reasons her friends oohed and aahed when she'd mentioned this opportunity. Of course they'd also tsk-tsked at the idea of her spending four weeks with a complete stranger. Still, after everything she'd suffered through, what did she have to lose? Bad relationships, no funds, death. She'd pretty much been there and done all of them. Somehow, she stayed afloat, but the exhaustion of life made the thought of sinking deep alluring.

She released a long breath, pushing away any daunting thoughts of her prospective employer. For now, Piazza Navona remained her personal paradise.

Pink and purple painted the evening sky. Groups of tourists hustled into cafes for a warm meal. Passersby stopped to watch musicians and mimes perform for their day's wages. Strange how no matter where one went, it always boiled down to the good old *all in a day's work*. Though not opposed to labor, bartending at Murphy's Irish Pub wouldn't earn enough to pay her debts and establish her restaurant. Not in the near future, anyhow. She pulled out another folded piece of paper, confirmation she moved one step closer to her dreams.

Dearest Savannah,

I am pleased you have decided to accept my offer and I look forward to our meeting in Rome... Once you arrive, you may take a taxi to Piazza Navona—I will reimburse you this expense. After sunset, I will present myself to you outside cafe Tre Scallini.

Cordially,

Luke

Present myself? Who wrote *present* or signed their emails with *cordially*? Technically this was a business deal so the polite tone made sense but this guy came off as an old timer, at least on paper. What would she do with an old guy? Hmm, what did a companion do exactly? She bit her lip. Details, people usually gathered before accepting a job.

Twisting her napkin around her fingers, she shifted in her chair. Evening grew nippy after sunset. With any luck, he wouldn't run late.

"Savannah Michaels?"

She spun toward the man who'd spoken in that deep voice and stilled. Coffee brown eyes, intense brow, sensual lips and definitely off limits in her life right now.

"Yes?" She'd come here to work not admire scenery—no matter how tempting. Wait a minute. She took a breath. This particularly handsome bit of scenery knew her name. He couldn't be him. This man had a strange accent. Not Italian, though familiar. British? Savannah hadn't asked where he was from. "You're not, um, hold on a sec." Her mind blanked and she exhaled loudly, fumbling with the papers in her hand. Several sheets dropped to the ground. "Um, I'm sorry, one moment." Served her right for having expectations of a shriveled old man. He was a man and that's where any similarity to what she'd envisioned ended.

"If your bumbling around is an attempt to ask me whether I am Luke Evans, owner of the companion ad, yes I am." He lifted a thick brow, his face creasing with disapproval.

So much for first impressions. Seemed she was stuck with Mr. Tall, Gorgeous and Grumpy for four weeks. *Suck it up, Michaels, you need this.*

She smiled. "Great, I'm Savannah Michaels." She lifted a hand, silently berating herself for giving him her name when he clearly knew it.

He assessed her half eaten *tartufo* then let his gaze quickly sweep over her. "Follow me." Without a handshake, he turned and headed toward a side street.

What a snot. She dropped her arm and hurried after him, leather backpack swinging off her shoulder as she tugged along a small suitcase. Its wheels clicked along the ground, passing over grooves between cobblestones. Good thing she hadn't packed heavy. He moved incredibly fast. "Wait, I haven't yet paid for my meal."

"I took care of it."

"How did you know what I ordered?" Had he been nearby the entire time?

"I inquired with the waiter. It seems you have quite an appetite." He spoke with his back to her as he paused near a black Audi S6.

She frowned. How embarrassing. Had the waiter mentioned she'd eaten a lot? "I'm a chef in training. I must try things." Didn't mean she had to admit eating nearly every bit on her plate.

He turned and eyed her suitcase. "My email instructed you not to bring anything. I am covering your expenses. Nevertheless, since you did not follow my orders, let me take your bag."

Orders? The man behaved like an ogre. As she stood with her mouth open, he placed her suitcase inside the trunk and opened the passenger door, signaled for her to get in with a graceful sweep of his arm. She'd never understand why he'd bothered. The action was completely at odds with his foul demeanor.

"I only traveled with a few outfits. You never asked my size." She seated herself and inhaled deeply as he shut the door. It wasn't too late, she could still bolt.

As the driver's door swung open, Luke slipped in beside her and met her gaze, his eyes sexy enough to make her squirm. "Having second thoughts?"

Yes. No, wait, the ad said this job would pay handsomely. "No, of course not. Are you?" She couldn't have blown this already.

"No." He started the car and pulled into the late remnants of Roman rush hour. He glared ahead with an expression of disgust.

"Is there something wrong?" she asked.

"No."

Yeah, right. Unsure of how to respond, she twisted her hands together in her lap and bit her bottom lip. What had happened? He couldn't be upset about clothes. Maybe the cafe bill? Guys didn't usually respond negatively to her, at least not those who hadn't seen her scars. She wanted to flip down the car visor and check the mirror for basil between her teeth, but didn't dare chance being caught. As it stood, she might as well have been a goblin, for the attention paid her. "Are you sure you're okay?"

He released a huff of breath. "Why are you here, Savannah?"

"Why am I here—what do you mean? I answered an ad of yours and now you're—"

"I am not referring to your presence here. I mean, why did you answer my ad? Consider this an on the job interview. I want to know you better."

"Oh." He could have asked a bit more politely. She paused and glanced down at her lap. Why was she here? Money, of course. But to say so sounded crude, not exactly interview material. Ugh, she was definitely not prepared for questions. Why hadn't she considered he might want to know more? "I've always dreamt of seeing Italy. Who wouldn't want to travel for four weeks, expenses paid?"

"Why with me? You hardly know me. I could have been a complete psychopath."

Could have been? The idea still held definite possibility and at this point, she didn't need much convincing. "This conversation isn't exactly making me feel comfortable."

"My intention is not to make you uncomfortable." His voice gentled. "Nonetheless, it is important we have open and honest communication. Why with me?"

Better to stick with the truth. Lying could only lead to more trouble. "You said you would pay handsomely."

"I hoped for more." He pressed his lips closed. "I should know better."

"I'm sorry?" Unbelievable. *He* judged her? After she'd decided on honesty? Fiery heat burned on the tip of her tongue. "What exactly are you saying?"

"Take it as you like."

"I don't want to *take* it any way." She gritted her teeth. Why else would someone answer a stranger's ad? After spending ten minutes with Luke, she certainly wouldn't have agreed to meet him due to his charm. "I don't understand."

"All the same," Luke mumbled. "Damn greed."

"Hold on a sec," she said. "I'm not sure what you were *hoping* for, but you haven't even given me a chance. Your ad didn't advertise prerequisites. You don't know me. You should have given this more thought before you flew me several thousand miles to get here. And who runs ads asking for strangers to be their companions, anyway? A question I should have asked myself before answering your ridiculous ad. Either way, if you're going to do such an absurd thing, at least approach it with an open mind."

She gripped the door handle as he swerved around a sharp curve. Her breath caught in her chest, choking. "And stop glancing my way. You'll get us killed if you don't watch the road." After near two years of physical therapy, the last thing she needed was a trip back to the hospital.

"Not likely. And I do not need to know you. I know your type."

"My type?" She'd somehow stumbled onto a caveman. This was more than she could take, even for all the money in the world. "Stop this car. Stop it right now. We're done."

He frowned. "Why? I thought you wanted money."

"Not if it means spending four weeks listening to you," she gritted out. How much did she want this? Hell, it wasn't a want, it was a need. *Think of your restaurant, your dreams.* Damn it, this shouldn't be so hard.

He slowed the car to a stop and rubbed his brow. "I have offended you."

"Really? I'd credit you there with the understatement of the century." She'd shouted but didn't care. "I didn't travel this far and long to be insulted." She could have stayed with Ben for that. Taking a deep breath, she lowered her voice. "I wanted to make some money and see a beautiful country. You know, a good time?"

"And money will give you this good time?"

No, but it would get her debt paid off, allowing her a different kind of life. She rubbed her eyes and shrugged. It would be easy to give up everything but if she hadn't given up two years ago, she wasn't going to give up now. "Money is simply a means to an end. Look, if you've changed your mind and don't want a companion, please drop me back at Piazza Navona. I'll arrange my own accommodations." *Liar.* She was inches away from destitute.

Luke tapped the steering wheel with a thumb, his expression confused and pensive as he remained silent. "Forgive me, my behavior has been inexcusable. I am not myself and I should not have made such inappropriate comments. It does not rectify the situation, however, I must tell you someone attempted to mug me this evening. It put me in quite a distasteful mood."

"Oh God. Mugged." No wonder he was uptight. "Are you okay? Do we need to go to the police? Did they take anything?"

"No, I am fine. Irritated to such a degree, I have noted I am unpleasant company. I am sorry you have taken the brunt of my anger."

She released a long breath. "You should have told me. I would've understood." And not acted a complete brat.

"It is over now and as you can see, I survived minus a bout of ill manners. If you are willing, I would like to start anew and have you hear my proposal."

"Okay." After traveling this far, the least she could do was listen to what he had to say. She settled back against the passenger seat.

"Stay with me for a week in Rome. At the end of it I will give you twenty-five thousand dollars. If afterward you can bear my presence and want to continue with me on to Florence and Venice, you may. I will pay you an additional seventy-five thousand at the end of four weeks. Does this sound agreeable?"

Had she heard right? Did he say one hundred thousand dollars for four weeks? Her insides took a giant leap. It took every ounce of strength to keep calm and collected. "Yes, sounds great." His intense gaze held her motionless. "As long as sex is not a requirement." What had possessed her to say such a thing?

"Believe me." He twisted his full lips into a smirk. "I have no need to force sex on you. I am quite capable of finding my own night companions."

Heat infused her cheeks as a tremor traveled through her body. Yes, Savannah could imagine he had no issues with women. The man was gorgeous, with his old movie-star looks and wide shoulders. Not to mention, she'd seen glimpses of a charmer, despite the moodiness resulting from a recent attack. Alone and vulnerable, anyone would be shaken up. Even if she couldn't picture him defenseless, she'd learned the hard way people were rarely what they seemed.

"Are you cold?" he asked.

"Hmm?" She turned. His eyes glittered below creased brows. The concern in them chipped away at her defenses. "No, why do you ask?" She twisted the hem of her shirt. His question unnerved her. She hadn't had a man worry about her in quite some time, especially not one this handsome.

"You trembled." Luke checked the rearview mirror as he steered the car back onto the road.

"Did I?" She cleared her throat. Despite her efforts, memories of her own helplessness floated to the surface of her thoughts. Night, the cold pavement beneath her, numbness. "I guess I remembered something."

"If I offended you again, I apologize. You did bring up an intimate subject."

"Oh, you didn't. I'm not sure why I made such a statement...you know, about sex. I'm not usually so forward. I guess I wanted things to be clear."

"You are an exceptionally attractive woman," he said, facing her for several long seconds before he returned his attention to the road. "Nevertheless, I will keep my distance whilst you wish it. Now if you were to change your mind, I would of course do my best to accommodate such a request."

"I won't change my mind." Her words had left her in a rush, but didn't seem to bother him. Instead, he tilted his head and curved his lips up in a slight smile. The actions irked and aroused her.

* * * *

Savannah was a conundrum. The captivating green-eyed minx almost convinced Luke she could walk away without any money. She had not reacted to his attitude as expected. Most victims laughed away his insults, maintained a positive mood even when he dangled bait. Only on one occasion or two had previous companions objected. Still, none dared put him in his place or threatened to walk away.

Her reaction should be a breath of fresh air and yet, he could not believe in such a simple outcome. Experience and logic told him she would disappoint him. In two hundred years he had yet to find a victim who'd proved him wrong.

At the edge of his vision, she sat still beside him, staring straight ahead. The photo Broderick had placed in her file did not do her loveliness justice. The ebony waves of her hair framed her pale profile, lending her a sort of classic beauty.

He swiped a hand through his hair, trying to ignore his instant attraction. Her presence left him uneasy. Even after drinking two quarts of blood, Luke's nerves wound tight. Perhaps Broderick's concern was better placed than Luke could admit.

"Here we are." He parked the car and got out. The short walk around to her door provided a much needed respite from her nearness.

She stepped out, blinked and scanned the empty garage around them. "Doesn't anyone else live here? It looks abandoned."

"I like my privacy. Are you frightened?"

For a moment their gazes connected and he sensed her trepidation. His need to taunt her grew with his aggression. How long could he continue to fight this darkness within him? "Come, there is nothing to worry about. I won't let anyone harm you. We will take the elevator." He retrieved her suitcase, led her to a rusty, old-fashioned elevator and pulled aside the door. "After you."

"Uh uh, that doesn't look safe. How old is this place?"

"I recently repaired the elevator and am quite confident it works. If you doubt my abilities," he said, pointing at a door along a far wall, "feel free to take the stairs up eight flights."

Her emerald eyes widened and she stepped inside the elevator. With a jerk, the car started up. In the small space, she huddled like a hunted animal. She had cause to be scared but could not possibly realize why. Yet her fear made the air between them oppressive.

"Almost there." An inexplicable need to soothe her overwhelmed him.

When they reached the eighth floor, he pulled open the sliding door. Savannah straightened and released a long sigh.

"Shocking, you survived." What could have caused the fright he sensed in her? Who exactly had Broderick sent him?

"Despite my being in Italy, I'm not usually a risk taker." She bit her bottom lip and stepped out, leaning along the wall as she walked down the hallway. "This place appears a bit unstable."

"I assure you, the foundation is sound. I have not yet gotten around to beautifying the exterior. My door is the last on the left."

She turned. "Foundation, exterior? Do you mean to tell me you own this building?"

"I do. Actually, I run a real estate company and own quite a few buildings. Pardon me." He slipped past her, brushing along her thin cotton shirt as he took out his key ring. Electricity sparked inside him with the contact and he pulled away quickly. Her hardened nipples drew his gaze for a moment, and he nearly rumbled aloud in appreciation. Amongst her medley of emotions, he grasped arousal. "Follow me, I'll show you your room." Walking through his foyer, he tossed the keys in a bowl on an entryway table and headed toward the kitchen and living room area. "The kitchen is stocked with food. Please make yourself feel at home."

Luke turned but Savannah no longer stood behind him. What now? He returned to the foyer. "Is something wrong?"

She spun slowly, mouth wide like a child's in a candy shop. "It's beautiful."

"Are you not accustomed to fine things?"

She laughed. "Are you always this formal? No, I'm not accustomed to marble floors and cherry wood." She smoothed a finger along the dark finish of an entryway table. "I would be satisfied with being able to pay my bills, let alone buying gorgeous furniture. I'd be lucky to find anything half as nice at Good Will."

He knew nothing of this good will she spoke of. "Are you are willing to be my companion to buy yourself these luxurious items?"

Her eyes met his, and he tensed at the sadness evident there. She felt so strongly it pained him to be near her.

She shook her head. "There is a lot more to life than being wealthy and owning fine things. You're rich. Do you think money buys happiness? I've never found it to be true."

What game did she play? A perceptive question and answer. "Neither have I." The truth left him exposed. He turned away. "If you are ready, I can show you your room." He lifted his wrist, noting the dial of his watch read fifteen minutes past eight o'clock. "You have forty-five minutes to get dressed. Tonight, we shall go out."

Chapter 3

Who is more foolish, the child afraid of the dark or the man afraid of the light?
—Maurice Freehill

Savannah pursed her lips and followed Luke down a softly lit hallway. Despite Luke's formal manner, he'd decorated his home with vibrant colors and combinations. That, or hired help had made it inviting. Peach-colored plaster complimented hardwood floors and Persian rugs. Bold, colorful paintings lined the walls.

"These will be your quarters during your stay here." Luke rolled Savannah's suitcase into a spacious, high-ceilinged room and set her leather bag on a luggage rack. "Towels and sheets are in the armoire along with several gowns. The dresser houses the clothing you will need, and toiletries are in the washroom closet. If you have no questions, I will take my leave now."

Words failed her. A canopy bed. Pale blue wallpaper with an intricate, carved design. Ugh, she'd nearly ruined this. She rubbed her face. If she didn't have everything riding on this one stint as a companion, she would have thrown Luke's ad back at him after he'd insulted her. *The man was mugged.* She was fortunate he still wanted a companion after such a traumatizing experience.

"Shall I take your silence as a sign you have no questions?"

She didn't know what to make of him. He was poised, proper and talked like born royalty, yet there was a rugged side to him. A good night's sleep would do them both good.

"Um, wait. I do have a couple questions. Where are we going? Is there a dress code?"

"An auction. Formal dress." He shuffled in place, performing an odd dance of indecision. "If you require nothing else, I shall leave." Forehead creased, he pivoted and left the room.

She sat on the bed with a huff. A mystery of a man, but she couldn't deny his great taste. Creamy silk curtains framed the tall windows and paintings in this room were of landscapes with soft, muted colors. She smoothed a hand along the dark cherry wood of the bed centered in the room. Who would have guessed a rundown wreck of a building on the outside looked this beautiful within? She yawned. She'd traveled for ten or more hours and hadn't slept in near thirty. The enormous amount of food she'd fed herself hadn't helped either. No relaxing tonight, though.

Italy. She still couldn't believe it. Four weeks seeing centuries old ruins and eating incredible food. Creamy risotto, salty prosciutto, aged parmigiano reggiano. Her stomach whined in protest. "Okay, I get it, you're full."

Better to concentrate on something else. Leaning over, she brushed a pale gold dress lying beside her with the palm of her hand. How had she not noticed it? The gown was stunning, like Luke and his home.

It wouldn't take long for him to see she wasn't accustomed to money, not anymore at least. She fingered the black slacks and blue collared shirt she wore. Hardly a splurge. Otherwise she would have met her potential employer wearing ripped jeans and a tank. Given his formal demeanor, she couldn't imagine that going over smoothly.

Holding the dress, she approached a long, oval-shaped mirror. Simple, yet elegant, the gown had a matching gold belt that dressed it up further. She frowned at her reflection. Becoming a companion for medical bills didn't make her a gold-digger, did it? She didn't want to hurt anybody. Still, his words resonated. She'd let a complete stranger get under her skin.

"I hope you are not practicing your expressions for tonight. I daresay you will not make friends with much ease." The sides of Luke's mouth curved upward as he leaned against the doorframe.

More relaxed than she'd expected, his smile took her off guard. She shook her head and pretended to pick lint off her slacks as she gained composure. "You didn't knock." She stood, smoothed back several locks of hair.

"You left the door open," he said.

"Oh. Guess I was lost in thought."

"You have not washed." He tilted his head but no expression gave away his thoughts.

"I don't take long." She stifled a yawn and hung her dress from a clothing rack next to the mirror. She swore she had barely sat down. Why was he checking on her already? "What time is it, anyway?" How long had she spaced? Dresser, mirror, vanity, lamp...where was a clock when you needed one? "Since I still have to shower, maybe you'd like to join me there also," she bit out then regretted the words as soon as they'd left her mouth.

He combed her with his dark gaze, assessed her. "I have business to take care of before we leave." He entered, holding a rectangular, red velvet jewelry box. "I only came to give you this. And make sure you did not need anything else."

Heat rushed over the surface of her skin, and she bowed her head. She'd behaved a complete shrew but what could he expect? She hadn't slept in over a day. The space which felt enormous when alone, suddenly grew cramped. Barefoot, her height fell near an inch below his jaw. She'd never considered herself a petite woman, but he made her feel small.

"Do not look so disappointed. I can always join you later."

"I didn't actually expect you to accept."

"A shame." Luke held up the velvet box. His expression calmed as if he couldn't see she burned with humiliation and maybe something else she'd rather not admit. "These will complement the dress I left for you."

"Thank you." She pried open the lid and released a soft cry of surprise. Delicate drops of crystals hung intermingled with strands of gold, a necklace and earring set. Her hand hovered over the jewels. "They're beautiful but I couldn't possibly take these." Such gorgeous jewels must have cost a fortune. With his current display of tastes, she couldn't imagine him buying costume jewelry.

"Think of it as a loan. You can give them back afterward."

Ah, of course. The modern day Cinderella story, only she was missing her Prince Charming. She rubbed the pale band of skin around her ring finger and a sharp pang burst in her chest. Who was she kidding? Ben was no Prince Charming. At least she no longer wore his ring. Like a sad and desperate old maid, she'd held onto their engagement long after its expiration, making too many excuses to doctors, nurses and even her friends. Lying had made it worse.

"Is something wrong?"

"Huh?" She lifted her head. "No. I got lost in thought again. I'm sorry. I admit, traveling wore me out a bit."

"I apologize. If it were not for my business, I would not force your attendance, but I cannot leave you here alone."

She fingered the neckline of the dress. "How did you know my size?"

"You are not the first companion I have had, Savannah. I will leave you now to shower and get dressed." He turned and walked out of her room.

"Wait." She brought her hand holding the box down to her side. "You're not answering my question." She followed him but beyond the doorframe, the hallway remained dark and empty. "Hello?"

Not even the click of footsteps echoed amid the shadows.

Chapter 4

Night brings our troubles to the light, rather than banishes them.
—Seneca

Moonlight in a garden. Unusual theme for an auction. Not to mention, this wasn't just any plot of earth and plants. It was a work of art. Savannah couldn't begin to name the many varieties of flowers and foliage cradling the white balcony and steps leading down to the vast lawn. They left her in awe. "Some place for an auction. It's beautiful here."

Luke cleared his throat and said low, "Many believe the environment is near as important as items brought to auction. The right ambiance creates desire to buy."

"I guess I could see the logic behind the belief." She'd never quite understood the fascination of going to auctions. Sure, one could find some unique treasures but they had those at garage sales too. It depended on who was looking.

"Going once, going twice, sold to the beautiful lady in pink." The auctioneer raised his arms in an exaggerated stance and the audience erupted in applause as if the woman had reached the finish line of a marathon. All this for a gold-encrusted mirror that cost twenty-five thousand euro? It was nice but she could have found a comparable look-a-like at a department store for around two hundred euro.

"You do not approve?" Luke bent close, and a shiver rippled through her.

Was she so easy a read? She'd have to be more discrete at displaying her emotions otherwise she would invite questions she didn't want to answer. "Why would you say that?" She brushed her fingertips along the petals of tiny pink flowers on the trimmed hedge beside her.

"Your knit brows, pursed lips. Shall I continue with telltale signs of your facial expressions and body language? Even now you're pretending interest in a bush to avoid my confrontation. Surely you do not believe she should have paid more."

She dropped her hand. She didn't want him to think her cheap, but the auction prices seemed absurd. "I'm not avoiding you. I'm just not a fan of mirrors." Not a complete lie. She hadn't liked them even before her accident. The accident only made them more difficult to deal with—a necessary evil in her book.

"Strange. I assumed a woman of your beauty would be quite fond of her reflection."

Then he hadn't looked close enough, and she hoped he wouldn't anyway. "Ah, but we've already discovered you have a tendency to judge too quickly."

"Well put." He inclined his head and turned toward the auctioneer, allowing her a pleasant view of his strong profile. He was obviously not a native Italian and yet he appeared right at home in a country where Roman gods and goddesses prevailed. A defined jaw and thick brows. The sensual shape of his mouth softened his other features.

As if sensing her stare, he turned. She shivered, sure she could lose herself within the infinite darkness of his eyes.

"What is it?" he asked. "Are you cold?"

She shook her head. "I'm okay for now." Or at least, she hoped to convince herself she was. The night air held a frosty edge to it but the garden atmosphere astonished her with its beauty. Wind whistled through the trees and down toward them, carrying occasional scents of jasmine and lavender. Above them, stars littered the clear night sky. She wasn't searching for a romantic atmosphere but here she'd found it, making her feel more lonely.

She pulled up her shawl around her shoulders and lifted her chin. This wasn't a time to feel sorry for herself. "What's next for bidding?"

"Handcuffs."

He couldn't be serious. "Very funny." Stretching her neck, she tilted her head to get a better view. Beside the auctioneer, a male held up a pair of gold handcuffs. Large emeralds, rubies and diamonds covered the surface. "They're handcuffs."

"As I noted before."

She frowned and rubbed the crease between her brows. "I guess I thought it a strange item to auction. Are those jewels real?"

"Of course. It is not such an unusual piece. Those with money are accustomed to control. Submission is an expected reprieve for some."

Based on what she'd seen so far, he would probably know a thing or two about the rich. "I've never seen this type of display. It's dark."

"It can be, yes."

She swallowed. Those attending the auction didn't appear the types to have whips and chains locked away in their homes—even if they were diamond encrusted—but everyone had their secrets, especially the rich. And this crowd had money. Rich and beautiful. Even Luke possessed a surreal kind of beauty and given his offer of one hundred thousand dollars for four weeks, she didn't doubt he had money.

"And you? Do you like control?" The question was almost a dare and for the life of her, she couldn't figure out why she'd asked it.

He remained quiet, and for an instant she thought he might not answer. "Yes. I would not have it any other way. Surrender requires trust, something I do not easily give."

His words gave her pause. What could have caused him to lose trust? She thought of Ben and his betrayal. Was there no goodness or truth left in their world?

She played with the beads on her purse.

The following auction items included an absurdly priced wooden paddle with an intricate design on one side, a gold chastity belt and a leather whip with a diamond encrusted handle. The last piece sold to a good-looking older man. His distinguished exterior contrasted sharply with the suggestive sexuality of his purchase.

"I don't see what he would use a whip for," Savannah said and brushed the skin along her arms.

Luke shifted beside her. "I can think of quite a few things."

She licked her lips, which had gone dry, and turned to face the platform as gasps of wonder became fevered whispers.

"Ladies and gentleman." The auctioneer's voice rose above the murmurs. "Allow me to present one of our most unique pieces. This painting is called *Mortuaria Benedictus*."

Savannah turned. "What is that?"

The side of Luke's lips lifted in a smirk. "I believe he called it a painting."

She frowned and gave him a slight shove with her elbow. "I heard." Didn't mean she'd ever seen anything like it on canvas. And considering how many art museums she'd dragged Ben to, she'd seen her fill of exotic paintings. A dark background enveloped three nudes: two males and one masked female. This was nothing exceptional, but the males' submissive positions and the female's blood drenched lips and fangs were something to take note of. Vampires? The word alone made her tremble. "I meant, what does it mean?"

"In English the painting is called *Blessed Death*," he said. "What do you think of it?"

"Frightening, dark, lustful, perverse." And at the base of it, oddly sensual, for some reason.

"And?"

What more did he expect her to say? "I'd say it's fairly fantastical. I mean vampires, come on. Although, you could say such fantastical creatures give it an erotic air."

"Maybe," he said. "Sometimes it depends on who you ask."

"Any other bidders?" The auctioneer scanned the room.

Several arms went up, which didn't surprise her, but she hadn't expected Luke's to be one of them. "You're not thinking of getting the painting, are you?"

He lifted his arm again, confirming a higher bid. "Why ever not?"

"I don't know." She turned away, her faced as heated as if she were a teenage prude. "Where would you put it?"

"The living room, above the sofa." He stroked his chin. "It is quite a conversation piece. Do you not agree?"

"Going once, going twice, sold." The auctioneer smacked the wooden gavel down in excitement. "To the gentleman next to the young lady dressed in gold." His gaze lingered a moment on Savannah. "What excellent taste."

"I could not agree more." Luke had spoken so low, Savannah thought she might have imagined the words and yet she trembled as he braced her lower back with a hand. "They will most likely take a break. I must arrange payment and delivery of my purchase, but I have what I came for tonight. Are you ready to leave?"

The women surrounding her stood, tall and willowy, and the men gave off an almost ethereal handsomeness. The view seemed an air brushed backdrop from F. Scott Fitzgerald's *The Great Gatsby*. Beautiful, wealthy people lost inside their own selfish world, too perfect to be true. She should know. She used to be part of such a perfectly arranged scene, but no more. "Yes." She nodded, cupping her yawn. "I'd like to go."

Chapter 5

Society is a masked ball, where everyone hides his real character, and reveals it by hiding.
—*Ralph Waldo Emerson*

Lying back on a living room sofa, Savannah polished off her second bowl of strawberries and cream then licked her fingers. Delicious. At least she'd gone halfway healthy with fruit. She rarely indulged in cream so one day wouldn't hurt. She placed her bowl in the kitchen sink then went down the hallway to her room.

Luke had come around nearly thirty minutes ago to say they would go out again. Unbelievable. Sunset, and he only now woke. The man obviously slept like the dead. She'd spent over a day traveling and now struggled to adjust to a new time zone, yet somehow had managed to wake up at a decent hour. After last night and lazing around today, she needed to clean up.

In her room, she closed the door and stripped off her clothes. Beneath a warm spray of water, she washed, letting the steam seep into her achy muscles. Her body wasn't yet accustomed to travel but the next four weeks would take care of her internal clock.

By the time she'd finished her shower and blown her hair dry, she wanted another bowl of strawberries and a glass of wine. Luke probably wouldn't pay anyone to behave like a slug, but one could dream. She slipped a blue silk dress off its hanger, pulled it over her head and let it shimmy down her body. Next, she took out a box of body tape and laid several strips on the bathroom counter. Once she'd peeled the wax-like paper off one of the double-sided adhesives, she stuck the strip to the inside of one strap and pressed the material against her skin. "One done, many more to go."

A tiresome routine of arranging clothing to hide the most heinous of her scars, but one she'd become adept at over the past two years. Deftly applying a few strips, she secured the dress and glanced at her reflection to inspect her handiwork. A little cover up went a long way. Between the makeup, dress, shawl and layered necklace, most would see her as an attractive woman with pale, flawless skin. Few would catch the pink ridges along her collarbone and none would see the deep purple ones trailing down the sides of her ribs.

She fingered the shadowed areas beneath her eyes. These, on the other hand, were signs of a restless night. Though after last night's strange auction, who could have fallen asleep? With Ben, she'd mingled in her fair share of wealthy circles. Though she'd never attended an event quite like last night's, it didn't surprise her to see such a dark side of high society.

"Good enough." A bit of base and powder beneath her eyes, and she was ready. She stepped back from the glass and opened the bathroom door.

"Luke." Her heartbeat hiccupped then leveled out to a faster thrumming. What was he doing in her room?

"Pardon the intrusion." Luke stood beside her dresser with his back to her and turned as she exited the bathroom. The bottom of his hair curled against the collar of his gray dress shirt and he looked beyond handsome. She couldn't find her voice as his dark gaze glided over her. "Blue is becoming on you."

She nodded, placed a hand to her chest. She should say something back. "You surprised me."

"I heard your shower shut off some time ago. I knocked but it seemed you could not hear me."

"It took some time to get dressed." She adjusted her shawl. Her scars shouldn't be visible but it didn't hurt to make sure. "I'm ready now."

He lifted his arm. "Shall we?"

The drive to the bar wasn't long but having Luke near unnerved her. His presence loomed, masculine, powerful and seductive. Even more so, surrounded by night's silence.

As they got closer to what appeared to be a club district, he turned onto a secluded side street and parked a couple blocks away from the crowds. The glow from the streetlamps highlighted his profile as he walked around and opened her door.

Savannah released a shaky breath and stepped out of the car. An eerie feeling settled in the pit of her stomach. Up ahead, sidewalks overflowed with people waiting to enter a black door at the side of a brick building. She slowed her steps. "Is this another auction?"

These people weren't anything like the sophisticates of yesterday's auction. If anything, she and Luke stood out in this group. Most wore black, their faces covered with heavy masks of makeup. A woman wearing plum-colored latex waved to her and smiled. Savannah swore her eyes glinted red but the woman turned away before she could confirm it.

"No, this is Blood Bar, a club. Watch your step." Luke reached around her hips to guide her past the line of misfits, but she jolted beneath his touch.

"I'm sorry," she said.

"No need to apologize. There is another entrance I prefer to use."

She shivered. If another entrance meant avoiding the characters lining up, she wouldn't object.

"Are you cold?" He stopped before her and tilted her chin so their gazes met. "You seem skittish tonight."

Of course she would be. Almost overnight she'd been thrust into a world of surreal images. Despite his sporadic cheekiness, Luke himself appeared a perfect gentleman. Still, his involvement with this side of society puzzled her. Even last night's crowd seemed unusual. "You don't need to keep worrying about me being cold. I'm from Boston. It's just that those people look different compared to the ones we hung around last night."

"This is a Goth club, but nobody will harm you. Most of them like to believe themselves dangerous. Few, if any, are."

"How can you be so sure?"

"Trust me." He swiped several strands of hair behind both her ears, his obsidian gaze fathomless as it combed over her face and lingered at her lips. For an instant, she thought he might kiss her.

He stepped back, cleared his throat and tugged her hand. "Come." He took her inside, led her to a long bar and ordered drinks. "Do not move from here. I will return shortly."

* * * *

Lorenzo Greco had never seen Luke so unhinged. Luke continued to glance across the room at the human woman he'd brought with him. Despite her dark hair, she possessed an almost angelic fragility. No doubt the young vampire struggled with his decision to make her a meal.

"What did this one do?" Lorenzo asked as he leaned back in his chair and tilted an empty whiskey glass on one rounded edge. His dirty blond hair fell across one eye. He shoved the unruly locks off his face. "Rob a bank? Steal from impoverished orphans?"

"*This* one has a name and it is Savannah Michaels." Luke scowled. "And I do not care to discuss her. What concerns you? Why did you call for this meeting?"

"Do I have to have a reason to see a friend?" Beyond the floor of dancing, writhing bodies, Savannah hugged her drink closer to herself. Her wide-eyed stares at those around her gave away her fear. Such a ripe human, and yet something seemed indescribably different about Luke's latest victim. "Business as usual. Aren't you going to give me a bit of information about this new tasty treat?"

Luke flicked a napkin on the table. "She is a former Boston socialite, ex-fiancee of Benjamin Whitman with Whitman and Hoss. One of Boston's wealthiest men."

"Former? Ex? Better watch this one. She might be a bit desperate. Still, innocent or guilty, you must feed, so either way it doesn't matter. I find it admirable you at least try to rid humanity of its flaws. I certainly couldn't be bothered with such a complicated...diet." He'd never understand how the younger vampire hunted with such complexity. Eventually a lack of consistent kills and food would get to Luke, and he would be there to reap any rewards. Until then, Luke would be a convenient ally.

Monica and a couple other vampires cornered Savannah. They stood out amongst the Goth-like crowd, their perfect coifs copper or gold beneath the dim lighting. Laughter lit their eyes but they were careful. No wide smiles or heads thrown back too far. Masters in predatory manipulation.

"She's a looker. Have you considered turning this one? Might have many uses." His tongue brushed against a fang as he salivated. The sexy gold digger might make an excellent blood slave.

Luke's dark gaze narrowed as he watched Savannah. "I do not turn my victims. Never have, never will. At least, not if I can help it."

Lorenzo laughed. "Oh yes, how could I forget? A mortal sin, right? Or is it a venial sin? I can never get them straight. With the many church visits you've made lately, I'm sure you know what I'm talking about." He leaned forward. "And in regards to whether you can help it or not, what of the kill? How long has it been? Your body is aching for a release." He shrugged, lifting a cigarette. "It will drive you mad." His soft inhalation filled the silence between them.

"I have got it under control," Luke said.

If Luke wanted to believe a lie, he wouldn't stop him. At this rate, the younger vampire was his own worst enemy. "I'm sure you do."

"What is Monica up to?" Luke craned his neck as the blonde slid one crimson red nail down Savannah's arm and whispered in her ear. His concern over the human left him distracted and vulnerable.

Lorenzo waved a hand. "Calm down. No one is going to steal your meal. Monica is fascinated. You know how she is, a dame with a new bauble to fuss over."

Luke rubbed a crease between his brows. "I have no reason to calm down. I am not upset, I merely distrust Monica. I would not be forced into the position of choosing choice victims if it were not for this ailment. Savannah, like those before her, is a quick fix. Still, I would rather choose wisely if I must choose."

"Choose for what? Did you just say what I thought you said?" At times, Luke was too much. Whipping his hair away from his face, Lorenzo took a long drag then coughed out a smoky chuckle. "Only you would see being a vampire as an ailment."

Luke released an exhalation and sipped his blood-infused vodka. The small amount of blood coated his tongue and lips, painting them deep red.

On the dance floor, Savannah's perfect mouth parted as she found herself sandwiched between Monica and a brunette wearing a black tube dress. Her muscles tensed minutely as she tried to slide away, and she heaved a sigh when she found no exit. Her gaze flicked upward, seeking Luke. The air hummed with the electricity between them.

"I ask you again. Why did you want to meet?" Luke now trained his attention back on him.

"I need you to find me another property." Lorenzo said. "And fast." What had started as a small side drug trade was quickly turning into something profitable. Even more than he'd imagined, especially since he'd introduced exotic bloods into the mix.

"What kind of property?" Luke asked.

"For a club."

"You recently built your third club."

"What can I say? They've been quite successful." It wasn't a complete lie, as his clubs generated money. Still, the profit turned wouldn't be enough without the drugs and blood.

Luke remained silent, his expression pensive then said, "Anything particular in mind?"

"I want it near Termini."

The train station. "I have something in Esquilino. Used to be a bar. Interested?"

"I'll take a look at it."

"Fine." Luke rose from his seat.

"Wait." Lorenzo snaked a hand around his wrist.

With the contact, nothing came to him. Luke had constructed a wall around his thoughts in defense. So that was how he wanted to play. Obviously Luke did not trust him enough to leave himself open.

"Is there something else?"

"There's been talk," Lorenzo replied, pushing past the silent insult the other vampire had dealt him. A cloud of smoke wove through the air between them. "Your companion ads are too public, drawing more attention than necessary. The Ancients are becoming suspicious."

"Bollocks. Why would they bother with something so trivial?"

"I don't know, but I'm only protecting your best interests. This is what I've heard."

Luke shook his head "Do you truly want to discuss my companion ads?"

Lorenzo pinched his lips together and rubbed a hand over his face. "If you make powerful enemies, you'll need powerful allies. You can't go it alone against them and still survive." In a softer tone he said, "Believe me, I've tried. Why do you think I surround myself with so much security?"

"I have no quarrel with the Ancients."

"Yet." He would have to work on convincing Luke to create an alliance with him. Otherwise, he would never be free from the accursed, watchful eyes of the Ancients. "Join me. You are powerful but I can teach you so much more. Imagine what a team we'd make. You're a natural entrepreneur and business now couldn't be better."

"I do not do teams. Still, I will take your words under consideration and call you once we can see the property." Luke threw down a few euro notes and left.

Stubborn fool. His obsession with greed and the desire to end his own immortality would be his undoing. Neither was Lorenzo's problem. He nodded to two halfling vampires near the entrance, giving them the signal to follow Luke. Savannah drew his curiosity and he needed to understand her pull.

The iridescent blue of her dress glowed like the bottom of a flame amidst the club's darkness. She leaned beside the bar and put distance between her and the female vamps as Luke crossed the dance floor. Her gaze tracked him as he drew close. "Everything okay?" she asked. The petite human half loved the vampire already. Predictable, and so easily dominated.

Luke placed a hand to her back and guided her to the club exit. "Fine. I apologize for any delay. Let us go. It is late and you are tired."

Lorenzo yawned as they left. He called over a younger halfling, Giovanni.

Giovanni approached. "Yes, sir?"

"Bring me a woman. Human. Oh, and with green eyes if possible. Dark hair too. I don't want to be waiting forever." Yes, green eyes and black hair. Exactly the type of woman a powerful vampire needed.

"Yes, of course." Giovanni nodded and walked away.

Chapter 6

After winter comes the summer. After night comes the dawn. After every storm, there comes clear, open skies.
—Samuel Rutherford

"Where are we going?" Savannah shivered as Luke settled a hand on the small of her back, guiding her outside the bar and into night's humidity. Her heels clicked along cobblestone as they made their way to Luke's car. Why had he mentioned her being tired? Did the bags under her eyes show? She brushed below one eye with a finger, hoping to remove any runny makeup then pulled her shawl tighter and walked faster to keep pace with him. "Who were you talking to?"

"His name is Lorenzo. Do you want my jacket?"

His touch seemed to set fire to her skin, and she shook her head because she didn't trust her voice. Why she'd decided to wear a dress with such a low cut back was beyond her. She was fortunate the cut of the dress hid her largest scars.

"He is different, compared with yesterday's crowd. All of them were." It seemed strange Luke's tastes varied so widely within two nights. And yet he didn't seem to fit in either place. His role playing was impeccable, but something told her there was more to him.

"Yes, his tastes run much more nefarious than the auction crowd's. Get in," he said, suddenly brusque as he opened her door.

She jumped at his tone. Why the rush? Stiff in the passenger's seat, she took a deep breath and waited for Luke to slide in and start the car. Tension hardened the lines of his body, and his midnight gaze darted to the rearview mirror. Something was wrong. "We didn't have to leave. I mean if you wanted to stay, we could have." Perhaps things hadn't gone smoothly with Lorenzo.

He glanced her way. "You are clearly exhausted."

"I'm fine." No way was he blaming anything on her. "Did you finish your business?"

"Enough of it."

Unsure what to say and why he seemed so abrupt, she opened then closed her mouth. Inside Blood Bar, he'd almost been charming. Had she imagined their heated stares at each other across the room?

"You okay?" Despite a concerned tone, he appeared distracted, glanced in his rearview and side mirrors every few seconds.

She nodded, unsure of what he expected.

"Savannah." He gripped the steering wheel and exhaled loudly. "I would like these next few weeks between us to be relaxed and open."

"Me too." She breathed out a pent up breath even as she pushed her hand against the door to keep from swinging with a sharp turn. "But don't you think you should slow down?"

"Not right now." He pressed on the accelerator as they sped through Rome's streets.

This was insane. Was he trying to get them killed? With her heels, she pushed along the floorboard. Her right hand groped for the door's handle. "But you're driving like a madman."

"There are no brakes on your side of the car." Luke glanced again at the rearview mirror. "If police or laws concern you, it is late. Streets are empty."

"Doesn't mean you don't have to obey traffic laws."

"Italians interpret laws more loosely than Americans."

"Judging by your accent, you're not Italian, you're a Brit. Besides," she held onto the sides of her seat as he swerved down a side street, "I was hoping to live past tonight." They raced out of city scenery and onto an unfamiliar narrow neighborhood street. Why the detour? Luke's apartment was located within the city center. "This looks like a quiet neighborhood. Where are we going?"

"Taking a detour." He switched from accelerator to brake to accelerator.

"At three AM?" She took a deep breath and leaned forward, bracing herself against the dashboard. "Can you slow down? I think I'm going to be sick."

"What did Monica say to you?"

"Monica?" He wanted to talk about Monica now? Before she could protest his driving further, Luke slowed the Audi and carefully took the road's curves.

Savannah leaned back and brushed her hair from her face with a shaky hand. "She's, um, different." She laughed awkwardly, suddenly embarrassed to tell him she found his friends frightening. "You have strange friends."

"Monica is not a friend."

"Oh." Why had Monica told her she knew Luke well then? "Okay, your friend who isn't a friend told me if things didn't work with you to give her a call." Savannah removed a card from her purse.

He raised a brow. "Did you tell her you would?"

She frowned. "No. For one, I'm not interested in women and two, she may be gorgeous, but she's also creepy. There's something seriously wrong with her."

Luke stilled abruptly then threw his head back and laughed. The unexpected reaction took her off guard. "It seems you are quite sure of your opinion." His lips twisted into a smirk which showcased a lone dimple on his right cheek.

Caught up with the joy on his face, she let several seconds pass before she answered. "I am." She turned toward the window, trying to focus her thoughts on something other than him. Last thing she needed was a building attraction to her temporary employer. It couldn't possibly lead anywhere, but she didn't need the complication. She had to keep her mind on her dreams.

"Bloody hell."

At his words, her heartbeat, which had recently reached a normal pace, skyrocketed. "What?"

He glanced at the rearview mirror again.

"Why do you keep looking behind us? Is something going on?" She swung forward in her seat as he made a sharp right, heading along a curvy country road. Where the hell were they?

"We have a bit of company. They followed us from Blood Bar."

"Why?" She turned around in her seat. A black sedan tailed them. This couldn't be good. "What are you involved in?" He had mentioned taking care of business. Scenes from *The Godfather* spun through her mind. "You're not mafia, are you?"

"Do not be absurd. I am a Brit, remember? Besides, your eyes were on me all night. Did you see me do anything questionable?"

Heat rose to her face. So he'd noticed her staring. "James Bond was British. An agent, right? Was the ad a ploy?" She could feel herself rambling illogically but somehow her mouth wouldn't heed her mind. "My friends told me this was a bad idea, I should have listened."

"Not an agent," he gritted out from between clenched teeth as he maneuvered the vehicle back onto a city street. "And I highly doubt

James Bond went searching for his Bond girls through newspaper ads. I hope you are not always this irrational when you panic."

The black sedan behind them thrust forward, plowing into their bumper.

"Rational, you want to see rational at a time like this?" Her earlier assumption was correct. The man was insane.

He frowned as if she'd said she'd spotted aliens. "It would help, yes."

Damned if she would spend her last minutes alive pleasing another. Savannah braced herself to keep from smacking the dashboard. "I don't want to die, not like this." She hadn't spent two years fighting to live only to have it end in a high speed car chase. What was it with her and cars?

"You will not die." Then a whisper. "Not like this."

Though she wanted to question his words, she couldn't concentrate beyond trying to keep upright in her seat.

Luke slammed the accelerator then split from the main street onto an access road. Somehow they made their way back into the city. She had no idea how he drove so fast on such narrow streets, but at least he appeared in control. After hitting his first left, he raced down a narrow alley and turned down a ramp into an underground garage. The tires squealed along the smooth surface.

Savannah blinked, trying to adjust to the lack of light. "There are no lights down here. It's abandoned. How will we see anything?"

"Leave seeing to me." He brought the car to a stop. "I know my way around. I will park the car here. We will take the rest on foot. I have a friend who owns a hotel nearby." He shut off the ignition and exited the Audi.

Without headlights on, the garage was pitch black. Silent, except for Luke's shuffling around and her rapid breaths. The car released occasional pops as it cooled. Images of crushed metal and broken glass flashed in her mind. Pain, there had been so much pain. Why had Ben left her alone? She could have died. He'd said he loved her, but now she knew the truth. Love didn't mean anything.

"Savannah. Savannah, snap out of it. Listen to me. We need to go now." Arms of steel slipped around her waist and pulled her from the passenger's side. He'd come back for her.

"You came back," she mumbled. Ben? No, not Ben. Luke.

"What are you talking about? I never left. Can you walk or do you need me to carry you?" Luke asked.

"Of course I can walk." Did he think her a child? She swallowed, her throat dry. "Why wouldn't I be able to?" A moment of terror set in but once her feet hit the ground, she breathed a long sigh.

"You said you could not see." He intertwined his fingers with hers, tugged her along. "There you go, love. Keep going."

Love? They sprinted across the parking garage and down a cobblestone street, leaving the car and images of her past behind them. Her legs trembled with adrenaline and a sharp pain traveled up her shin. Luke's fault: he'd chosen ridiculously dainty heels. *Yes, blame him.* Blame was easier, safe.

She stumbled and Luke caught her before she fell. "Hold onto me. Keep moving." He guided her along a brick wall, carrying most of her weight.

A screech of tires ripped across pavement several hundred feet behind them. The black sedan which had followed them pulled into the entrance of the narrow street.

Savannah tensed, panic choking her chest. "What's going on?" she whispered, scared to give away their position.

"I apologize, pet. You are going to have to trust me." Pushing her into the shadows, Luke pulled her body close, rested his mouth on her shoulder. "I am going to kiss...your neck."

* * * *

Luke would not have thought it possible, but Savannah stiffened even further along the length of him. Her blood, hot and sweet, pumped mere millimeters away from his fangs. Lips against skin.

"Savannah." His fangs descended and it took his complete strength to put several inches between them. Christ almighty, he did not need this.

She gripped his shoulders, pulled him close. "I can hear them. They're coming down the street." She did not tremble like a coward but stood her ground. Her petite, curvy form fit beneath him, soft and inviting.

Luke inhaled deeply and savored her scent of orange blossoms. He hungered for more than the taste of her blood. "Stay close." His voice even sounded strained to him, rough.

"Please hold me," she said.

The air between them trembled. He lifted his hands, hovering over her back and shoulders. Bloody hell.

The woman was frightened, and he thought to possess her in every way. "Do not worry, pet." He could not possibly promise her safety. For once, though, a need to try, even if it meant protecting her against him surged.

Savannah nodded and leaned forward, full lips parted.

He moved closer, kissed the delicate skin of her neck. It tasted sweet, seducing him to take his exploration a step further. As the black sedan drove past, his gut demanded he pull back, but temptation pushed him past reason. The enzymes in his saliva heightened the sensitivity of her skin, preparing it for the pleasure of his bite. She would not notice until too late.

Responding to his ministrations, she groaned and shifted beneath him, causing a thrill to move through the pit of his stomach. He curled back his upper lip, brushed a fang along her skin.

"Luke."

He stilled as his name echoed in the night. Christ, he needed to feed. He did not want to take her yet. Reluctant and confused, he pulled away.

Color flooded her cheeks. "Are they are gone?"

"Yes." He kept his gaze trained on her, willing her to face him and see him for what he was. Had she felt something between them? Had he? "Are you able to walk the rest of the way? It is not far."

Savannah observed her surroundings but avoided looking at him directly. "Yes, I'm fine. Just tell me where to go. Where are we, anyway?"

"We are near Piazza del Popolo, heading north within Rome." He placed a hand on the small of her back, intending only to guide her. "We will go to the end of the street and turn right. Francesca's hotel is on the left hand side."

As if his touch burned her, she turned and moved forward with speed, but favored her right leg.

When had she hurt herself? "What the devil did you do to your leg?" Lifting her left arm around his shoulders, he wrapped his right arm around her waist and supported her weight.

He furrowed his brows, and she exhaled loudly. "What did I do? These damn shoes, that's what. And I didn't choose them, you did. They're one size too big. Do you know how difficult it is to walk around trying to look dignified in uncomfortable shoes?"

Luke opened then closed his mouth. Over two hundred years on this earth and he had not the foggiest idea as to what she referred. "Your shoes?"

"Yes, shoes *you* gave me to put on."

He would have to let Broderick know he'd muddled up her shoe size. Or perhaps, he'd misread the conversion. "Tomorrow we can order more shoes if necessary. For now, those must do."

"Fine excuse, when you're not wearing them." She pushed away and hobbled at a more rapid pace.

Calmness settled within him even as his body missed her nearness. If she possessed enough of her faculties to scold him, her injury must be slight. And she had obviously forgotten their chase.

The rumbling in his chest grew into a full-fledged laugh. She was a sight—gorgeous even in distress—with her black curls in disarray and her lips stained pomegranate.

"Please, wait." He approached and scooped her into his arms. "I must say, you are nothing like what I expected."

"Obviously. Neither are you anything like I expected. Now, put me down. I'm okay to walk."

"I understood you the first time, but I have to disagree, based on your pace. My intention is to reach the hotel before tomorrow night. Francesca should have something to address any injury you have sustained."

She yawned, finally allowing exhaustion to claim her. "Good. Something to look forward to." She stopped struggling and settled in his arms, laying her head on his shoulder. "It's dark now. Reminds me how much I hate night."

Chapter 7

Do not be afraid; our fate cannot be taken from us; it is a gift.
—Dante Alighieri

Luke glanced up and down the dimly lit cobblestone street. The night air clung to his face and clothing. He approached an alcove beneath a painted, hanging sign which read *Pensione di Francesca*. He knocked on the wooden door before him. Almost immediately, it swung wide, revealing a slight woman with salt and pepper hair, big espresso-colored eyes and small red lips.

"Dante." Francesca smiled and opened her arms wide in greeting. "*Buonanotte.* For what reason do I have this pleasure?" The sides of her eyes crinkled like accordions as she rose up on tiptoes and kissed his cheek. "Who is this?" As if only now noticing he carried Savannah, she reached into one of the pockets of her navy skirt and removed a pair of spectacles. "More charity, *Dante mio?*"

"No, *signora.*" He dipped his head, entering her small hotel lobby. "She fell asleep in my arms. It has been a trying night. Would you mind if I let her sleep a bit?"

The older woman shook her head. "Of course not. You may lay her on the bed in my room, as it is closest." She turned and led him to a cozy room with cream colored walls and a double-sized bed covered with a burnt orange quilt. Paintings and relics of the Virgin Mary adorned the walls. He had to credit Francesca's taste. Each painting was startlingly unique with bold colors and a distinct essence of style.

He placed Savannah in the middle of the bed then slid off her shoes. "Perhaps an hour or two will do her some good."

Francesca pushed Savannah's hair back from her face. "To say she is a pretty woman doesn't do her justice." She met his gaze. "She is beautiful. Where did you find her?"

As always, surprised at how comfortable he felt around Francesca, he hesitated. If he did not take care, he would easily tell her everything about himself and most assuredly lose her friendship. "She is visiting Italy from the Americas."

She nodded, placed her hand on Savannah's forehead then slowly pulled away. "Come join me in the living area. We shall let her sleep and you can tell me why you've taken a sudden interest in making me Mother Teresa." She passed a carved hall table with a small crystal lamp, stopping to pick up a mug. "Don't mind me. I was in the midst of drinking some tea."

"Please." He lifted an arm to signal she walk ahead. "I daresay you stretch the truth by referring to Mother Teresa."

Francesca wove over to a large velvet chair, its mauve color faded with wear and tear. She grinned back at him as she placed her mug on a side table, slid off her spectacles and slipped them into her skirt pocket before seating herself in the chair. "I do exaggerate a bit. I quite enjoy the young couple you sent me, Giulia and Paolo. There is hope for them."

He nodded, releasing a long sigh. He was glad to hear he made the right choice in releasing the pair.

"So what brings you to my door tonight, besides the woman? It's been a long time since you've visited or requested a new piece for your collections." She bent and rubbed her knees. "Too long if you ask me. These knees of mine ached less only months ago."

Luke slowly took a seat on a worn sofa next to her. Francesca's dark eyes watched him expectantly as her small lips curled up slightly in a smirk. He imagined she'd been a beautiful woman during her prime. Older, she possessed a sort of frail elegance. "I fear I have missed you."

Francesca laughed, reached over and rubbed his leg. "Always charming, *Dante mio*."

"Some would disagree but I shall accept the compliment regardless."

She scooted forward in her chair. "Is tonight a night of truths, business or pleasantries? Since I heard you recently acquired the *Mortuaria Benedictus*, I must believe it to be either truths or pleasantries." She reached for her tea and sipped from the mug.

Luke smiled and looked down at his hands. Of course Francesca would be informed of his latest purchase. As an art dealer and collector herself, she kept abreast of everything within the art world. "Actually, it can be all three. Art is passion but there is always the right price."

"*Mortuaria Benedictus* is a beautiful piece," she said.

"I agree. Speaking of pieces, have you acquired any new ones?" He scanned the cozy living room. Several Renaissance paintings hung on the walls, their colors rich compared with the faded state of the gold wallpaper. A painting of a woman with golden hair and gray eyes caught his attention. She wore jewels throughout her hair and her dress fell from one shoulder, revealing the swell of a creamy breast. "The oil there is a new one, is it not?" He nodded at the painting of the fair woman.

"Yes," she replied. "The daring in her expression spoke to me. Reminded me of a younger version of myself. But let's get back to your purchase. You changed topics too quickly. I've seen *Mortuaria Benedictus* several times before. It has a special meaning behind it. I'd almost say it's destiny you found it."

"You are not going to start with your fortune-telling rubbish, are you?"

Francesca frowned. "I never tell you rubbish. Just because you don't believe it, doesn't mean it isn't true." She crossed her arms over her chest. "I still insist and will always insist you are my perfect Dante."

Smiling, he shook his head. "Since I met you, you have called me that name. Decades have passed and I fail to see how I am the perfect Dante. Then again, it's been a while since I've read *The Divine Comedy*."

"Well you should spend some time re-reading it." Francesca pushed herself to her feet and came to stand before him. Hands cupping his face, she drew him close. "You'd understand it more when I tell you she will lead you to purgatory and only through her will you find your personal paradise. The woman you brought here is your Beatrice. I can see it clear as day."

He placed his hands over hers, reveling in the aged feel of her skin, as it reminded him of what he would never have. "How I wish I could believe you but I am almost positive you are mistaken. I admit she is different, she makes me laugh, but it will take much more than a few light moments to save me." He bent his head into her hands. If anything, the past few weeks had been more difficult. Each day he refused to kill pushed him further into despair's depths.

She shrugged and backed away, sat back in her chair. "You've always been stubborn, but you shall see for yourself."

Luke lifted his gaze. His thirst overwhelmed him and his eyes must be burning a deep burgundy. They never spoke about what he was. Usually, he preferred to avoid the subject, but tonight was different. "Why is it you have never feared me?" he asked. "I always hesitate to say too much and yet I have the feeling you know everything anyway."

Francesca smiled and shook her head. "Not everything. I've always wondered whether you'd ever ask me that, though. I used to spend hours thinking what I'd tell you."

Stomach churning, he anticipated what she would say. "And?"

"Frankly, I'm too old to care now." She laughed softly. "And I know you. You'd rather take your own life than kill an innocent, but you put yourself in danger going this long without appeasing your hunger. You are a vampire. You must drink blood and you must kill. The predator within demands it as the price for your freedom. You may not believe yourself free but it could be worse."

She was right but the words still were not easy to hear. "You know too much, Francesca. I worry for your safety at times."

"I'm no threat to your kind." She crossed her right leg over her left. "At best I'm an aged meal."

Luke smiled at her bluntness. "More like a fine vintage wine."

"Ah, yes." She laughed. "This I prefer to believe."

He leaned forward, elbows on his knees. "I cannot explain the restlessness inside me. Why does my thirst for blood and death grow stronger? What wrong am I committing?"

Francesca met his gaze. Laughter left her face and her eyes glistened beneath the dim lights. "Surrender. If you can do this, you'll leave an old woman with less sleepless nights."

No doubt she spoke the truth. For as long as he had known her, Francesca had fretted over him. At times, she reminded him of the way a mother should be. His mother had not had a true worried bone in her body. "You should not be losing sleep over me anyhow."

She lifted her chin, a defiant gesture, if he were to guess. "It's my nature to worry."

Luke ran a hand through his hair. Perhaps Francesca was right, but surrender meant trust. Could he learn to trust again? And even if he did, what would he give up? "I will try to do as you ask."

She nodded. "There is hope for you yet."

He stood, lifted Francesca's hand and kissed the top of it. "Tonight was a pleasure. I shall try not to stay away too long this time, but I believe it best if I take her before she awakens."

"Yes, I agree," she said. "I would hate to lie to such a lovely innocent and unless you are ready to reveal yourself, I assume I don't have a choice?"

Francesca tested her boundaries, but he would not let up. He could not afford to reveal himself, not yet, anyhow. And he was not so sure Savannah was the innocent she pretended to be. "I appreciate your understanding."

She bowed her head. "Perhaps there will be another time for us to meet."

"Yes, perhaps," he replied. "For now, please excuse me. Goodnight, Francesca." He turned and left the room.

Chapter 8

Innocence is like polished armor; it adorns and defends.
—Robert South

A loud pounding jolted Savannah awake. "Okay, I'm up." She pushed herself into a sitting position on Luke's living room sofa. One bare leg peeked out beneath a soft white blanket. Strange, she didn't recall changing into her pajamas last night. She didn't recall much after their chase. The chase, how could she have forgotten? And Luke. His lips on her neck, his hands on her. A flutter of electricity moved through her and she knotted her fist in the silky material of her shorts.

Another knock sounded and she bolted up, wrapping the blanket around her as she hurried to the foyer. "Coming." She reached the front door and swung it open.

A pale, dark-haired male smiled and lifted a large rectangular package. "*Buongiorno, signorina. Il suo quadro.*"

She understood good day but he'd lost her with the rest. "I'm sorry, I don't speak Italian."

"Your painting."

Of course. Luke's auction painting from the other night. "Oh, come in. You can put it over here." She walked through an arched entryway and pointed to a large granite island in the middle of the kitchen. Luke could decide what he wanted to do with it when he woke up—if he ever woke up.

The man followed her and slid the painting onto the counter. Turning, he smiled and winked. "Enjoy and *grazie.*"

She felt her cheeks grow heated. Incorrigible Italians. "Thank you."

Once alone, she returned to the painting and smoothed the brown paper, covering it with a finger. Luke probably wouldn't mind if she took a peek at it. She bit her lip. She could always wrap it back anyway.

Mind made up, she took a knife off a wall rack and slid its sharp edge beneath the clear tape holding the paper closed. Peeling back a layer of soft cloth beneath, she released a slow breath. Vibrant colors. From afar, the background had appeared black, but up close, she could tell it was more of a deep plum. Two males lay side by side beneath a masked woman. Their skin held a deep bronze tone, their cheeks were flushed. Both faces were handsome and angular, but she couldn't tell the color of their eyes, as they tilted up in an expression of euphoria. Bodies strained. Their muscular forearms flexed as each dug their large hands into the sheets beneath them. Erotic, and yet the dark colors seemed to signify protection for the males, a comfort with the night. A false sense of security, maybe?

The woman was different. She displayed an almost obvious dominance as she knelt atop the males' torsos. Her skin was pale, translucent almost, and her blond hair combined with the gold mask she wore brought to mind a sense of angelic fragility. Yet somehow Savannah knew with every atom in her body the vampire was far from angelic or fragile. Burgundy dripped from her lips, but her exertion seemed effortless. Her breasts sat full and high, flawless like her entire body. Pure sex, seduction and darkness. The woman's beauty also represented perfection. The kind she would never possess.

Smoothing a hand over her collarbone, she moved it along a raised scar. Down further over the swell of one breast. The skin felt silky, untouched by nightmares of her past. She circled a nipple over the thin material of her camisole. What would it be like to be the woman in the painting, to feel and look so erotic? Floorboards down the hall creaked and she stopped her exploration. The hall remained empty.

Luke? The sun would set in a few hours and he hadn't woken up yet. The mere thought of him made goose bumps surface along her arms. Despite his old-fashioned manners, he had a presence about him, a lethal power riding beneath the surface. It aroused and frightened. How could a man who seemed to guard his emotions so closely touch her with so much passion? His lips against her throat the night before had tingled and warmed, awakening her skin in a way she'd never experienced. She trembled and shook her head. She didn't need any more life complications.

She turned back toward the painting, drew along the gold frame with a finger. The woman was beautiful, yet the crease between her brows seemed to mar her perfection. This was more than a frown. She appeared pained in her ecstasy.

Another creak echoed down the hallway.

Having smoothed the cloth into place over the canvas, she folded the brown paper closed and left the painting on the counter.

Inside her room, she leaned along the door and tried to erase fantasy images of Luke touching her, surrendering to her like the men in the painting. She could only dream. If she kept this up, she'd be in a world of trouble.

She unleashed a resigned breath. A hot shower would make her feel better. If Luke decided he wanted to pay her to stand guard while he slept, this job would be a piece of cake—she hoped.

Peeling off her socks, she hissed through her teeth. The blisters on her feet from last night were raw.

As Luke had carried her through Rome's streets, she'd savored the intimacy of the act. He'd made her feel small and feminine.

After folding her fitted shirt and khaki pants on the bed, she reached behind and undid the clasp of her bra, shimmied out of the rose lace garment and tossed it next to her clothes.

"Who hurt you?" Luke's voice startled her.

She clasped an arm over her breasts and fumbled with the folded shirt before turning to face him. She hadn't heard him open the door, hadn't realized he was awake. "What are you doing? Please leave, I'm going to shower." Probably not an ideal tone to take with her boss but considering her half-naked state, she wasn't ready to invite him for tea.

He shoved off the doorframe and stepped closer as if she hadn't ordered him out of her room. "Answer my question first. Who hurt you?"

What did it matter to him? She made an effort not to tremble beneath the intensity of his stare. "If you haven't noticed, I'm not exactly dressed for a conversation right now."

The lines of his face tightened as the skin along his jaw stretched. "I have seen women in a state of undress. I give you my word I will not hurt you, but I want to know who cut you." He tilted his head. "It is not a knife wound. Something sharp and jagged ripped through your skin. It healed irregularly here." He ran a finger down the side of her ribs.

She sucked in a breath as her skin heated beneath his touch. The instinct to move away froze within her. His voice hypnotized, pushing her beyond reason. She had no interest in talking about her scars or remembering the accident and yet couldn't ignore him.

"Glass," she said. "Glass cut me." In hopes of shaking the fog over her mind, she squeezed her eyes shut. Why was he in her room? She clasped the shirt tighter to her chest. "I'm going to shower." Her voice sounded drone-like.

Luke stepped closer. His dark gaze bored into hers, trailed down over her neck, shoulders and arms. "I did not ask what gave you such scars." His breath tingled along her cheek. "I asked who hurt you."

She couldn't handle this, not undressed and frozen in place, but what could she do? The words she wanted to say stuck to her tongue. Taking a deep breath, she lifted her chin. "I did this to myself. Is that what you wanted to hear? No more mystery to solve regarding Savannah's hideous jigsaw puzzle skin." She exhaled a harsh breath. "No need for you to act a white knight."

He closed a hand around her trembling arm and pulled her to face him. A firm but gentle grip. "I have no illusions of being a white knight and quite frankly, mysteries bore me." Frowning, he traced the pale, raised skin over her collarbone then detoured off the scars and down the slope of her chest. "And you are wrong on another account. Not hideous." He hesitated. "Quite unique, beautiful."

Air expanded through her chest and shuddered through her. What was he playing at? A sarcastic laugh bubbled up in her throat and she broke through the fog of confusion. "Now you've done it. Try telling that to..."

"To?"

"Nobody." She waved a hand and sat on the bed. She wasn't going to take such a dark path again. "Do you mind turning around? If you aren't going to leave, I'd at least like to have some clothes on."

His intense gaze narrowed then he stepped back and turned away. "Did this nobody hurt you?"

Yes, she wanted to scream, but a broken heart was probably not what he referred to. She tugged on her shirt and khakis. Two years later, and it still ached to speak of Ben. "I already told you, I hurt myself." Scooting further back on the bed, she pulled her legs into her chest.

"You do not speak the truth." Luke sat beside her. "Did a man's hand harm you?"

"No." She bent her head, giving up on avoiding him. He obviously wasn't going to stop pushing and she wasn't quite sure she wanted him to. Rubbing her neck, she hunched into herself. "It wasn't anything like that. I argued with my ex." When he didn't say anything and looked at her expectantly, she continued, "I worked in a bar. Still do. He used to drop by after my shift ended so we could spend time together before going home. One night as usual, he came over. We were crowded. I grew tired of standing on my feet all day but he wanted to stay and watch a basketball game."

"You argued about a basketball game?"

"Stupid, huh?" She shrugged, trying hard to pass the memories off as if they meant nothing, resulted in nothing.

A deep crease formed between his brows. "A true gentleman should take into consideration a lady's sentiments."

She laughed bitterly. "Yeah, um, Ben is not exactly your true gentleman. Too bad I didn't realize until too late. I ran from the bar angry and didn't look where I was going. I heard the screech of tires."

"You were hit." He'd stated the words with gravity, his gaze searching hers.

She nodded slowly and bit her lower lip. The room around her blurred. "I froze. I'm not sure if I could've moved fast enough anyway. It didn't hurt at first, even as I bounced off the broken windshield. Pain came later." And seemed to never stop.

"Did he come after you?" Luke asked.

"I don't know, I don't remember much until the hospital," she lied, unable to say what she truly remembered. Nothing could erase the most dreadful and painful days of her life but there was no need to open closed wounds.

"You stayed there for quite a period. In the hospital, I mean."

She attempted a smile she didn't quite feel. "Long enough. If I can help it, I never want to see the inside of a hospital again."

He stood and walked over to the dresser, lifted a bottle of perfume. He turned the small bottle in his hand, as if contemplating his next words. "I apologize for the car chase the other night."

Her intention was not to make him feel guilty. "Don't worry. You couldn't have known—"

"Please, accept my apology. I do not offer them frequently. You had a right to be frightened. I understand why now."

She cleared her throat. "Apology accepted."

"Thank you."

The gravely rasp of his voice sent sparks flurrying through her. Awareness flooded her limbs. She wore a shirt, but without her bra, the tips of her breasts thrust against the thin cotton. Even if she didn't want him there, it was apparent her body did. She hugged her knees tighter.

"You may take your time with your shower and dressing. We will depart after sunset."

"Oh? Where are we going?" And why did he insist on sleeping the days away?

"You know, I have a garden."

She blinked at the topic change. "Did you say a garden?" He could be awkward at times.

"I sense you grow restless during the day. If you continue down the hallway, past my quarters, there you will find a stairwell leading to the roof."

"And there's a garden there? I don't see you as a gardening type."

"There is much you have yet to learn." He turned and headed to the door, then paused. "Working with my hands clears my mind. And I like watching life's cycle. The plants grow, blossom then die. How it should be."

"You mean the way it is," she said.

"Pardon?"

Savannah huffed. "You said *should be* although I'm sure you meant to say *is*. You don't need to speak so formally to me, you know."

He nodded. "I find it difficult to forget my roots. My family was quite formal."

Was? Did he no longer have any family? Though she wanted to ask him, his pensive expression transformed into an impenetrable mask, and she thought better of it.

"I'll leave you now so you can shower. We are going to see a property and then to Blood Bar, the same place we went the other night. Wear the burgundy dress and your citrus perfume."

"Do I have a choice?"

"You always have a choice, Savannah." He slipped out the door.

* * * *

When they left Luke's apartment, Savannah wore a silver halter dress. The sheer act of rebellion put a spring in her step. Luke smiled as she strutted down the cobblestone sidewalk ahead of him. Beneath the moon's light, her pale skin glowed, caressed only by silver silk, which blended with night's shadows. He admired her defiant streak. She walked with her head up, shoulders back. Her dress displayed her elegant shape yet guarded her scars like the painful secrets they were.

Broderick's file said nothing regarding an accident landing her in the hospital for an extended period of time. How could he have missed such a large piece of the picture? There had to be a good reason for such negligence. Either Broderick had blundered or Savannah was the most incredible of actresses. But no. Luke shook his head. He had touched the disfigured skin along her collarbone and sensed the sharp physical pain she experienced. And physical pain was always the easiest to bear, or so life had shown him.

"The past few nights have been beautiful," she said. Her heels clicked along the cobblestones. Light from the streetlamps bathed her form and a light breeze ruffled her hair.

He closed his eyes, letting the scent of orange blossoms brush over him. Lips curved, he inhaled deeply. Her citrus perfume. At least she'd acquiesced to one request. "Yes. Usually, the weather is much cooler at this time."

"How much farther? Aren't you worried with your car back there?"

"No. Besides, I thought you would enjoy the stroll. It is the second entrance from the corner up ahead." He pointed in front of them past several shops and a small bakery. Shadows blanketed the sidewalk every few feet.

"It's so quiet here. Why would Lorenzo want to set up a bar here? I can't imagine a Blood Bar in this neighborhood."

Nor could he, but he did not much care to know what Lorenzo's plans were. He scanned the street for any sign of him, pausing when he caught a smoky musk. "Lorenzo." He turned as the vampire approached behind him. Idiot, he knew better than to use lightning speed when humans were near. "Have you been waiting long?"

Lorenzo's lips curved as he struck a match. His cigarette glowed fiery orange in the darkness. "No." His gaze moved beyond Luke. "Good evening, Savannah."

"Hello." Savannah huddled closer to Luke. "I didn't see you." Her pulse grew erratic as her shoulders gave an involuntary shudder.

"I like to stick to shadows," Lorenzo responded, a cloud of cigarette smoke drifting up into the night air.

Luke cupped Savannah's hip, a silent comfort to her. "Are you ready to see the property?" he asked Lorenzo.

"Lead the way."

Luke walked the last hundred feet to a cherry red door and inserted a key into the lock.

Inside was spacious. Hardwood floors and a long wooden bar. Heavy wooden tables and chairs. Dust covered most surfaces but if Lorenzo searched for a tavern-like appearance, the space would do. Most importantly, the property shared a large loading space with a deli. Either way, it wouldn't matter, as Lorenzo's activities would occur primarily at night or during dawn's early hours.

"What do you think? It will attract a different type of crowd," Luke said.

"I want it to. Target a larger market and you get a variety of tastes." Lorenzo walked beyond the bar and kitchen to a loading area at the back. Moments later, he returned. "There is a stairwell back there."

"Yes. Included in the price are an apartment upstairs and an unfinished basement."

"Space for my office and a cellar. It is perfect. Have you got the papers?"

"Not with me. I will have my secretary, Gina, fax them to your office at Blood Bar. We are headed there shortly."

"Wonderful. I'll let myself out through the back and see you at the club."

As Lorenzo left, Savannah released a long breath. "I think I like your friends at the auction better. I don't see what you have in common with him or why you even do business with him."

"It is quite complicated. Lorenzo helped me during a difficult time." What an understatement. If not for Lorenzo, he might never have found Victoria's murderers and avenged her death. For that, he would always be grateful to the other vampire. "You should not be fooled by the comforts of the rich. Luxury creates the illusion of safety but as you saw the other night, darkness seeps everywhere."

"You're right, I know. He's creepy. I can't explain why he rubs me the wrong way."

For a human, she was intuitive. It made no sense to him why Lorenzo would want real estate in this part of the city. Perhaps he serviced higher-end clients requesting drugs? Pure hypothesis. Lorenzo never discussed side activities with him. That theory could be completely off the mark.

"Come." He cupped a hand at the small of Savannah's back, guiding her to the entrance of the space. "Let us make our way to his club."

* * * *

Blood Bar was packed. The bodies of humans and vampires alike writhed in sync to a pulsing drum and bass rhythm. Luke's only consolation amid the chaos was that they were seated in the somewhat secluded corner Lorenzo reserved for personal use. Velvet curtains added a sense of privacy, but tonight Luke insisted they remain open. Even with a good twenty-five feet between them, he could identify Savannah's scent. Still, he found himself searching out her face every so often. He shoved a hand back through his hair. "Incredible. You would think these types would tire of incessant noise and crowds each night but they do not."

"By the Ancients, you sound like an old man." Lorenzo sat back against a red velvet booth and slipped a pack of MS cigarettes onto the table.

"If I were human, I would nearly be two hundred and thirty years old."

"You're not human." Lorenzo pushed a tumbler full of amber liquor his way. "Why the foul mood? Trouble in paradise?"

"What is it to you?" He grasped the glass of scotch and sipped. Savannah's aversion to Lorenzo seemed to be rubbing off on him. Or his vulnerable state made him more irritable than usual. Lorenzo was no saint, but had no motivation to hurt him and had been asking him to partner with him for years.

"You're the only vampire I know who decides to get personal with dinner. A slight problem. Let me guess, she's not as evil as you first thought?" Lorenzo slipped a cigarette from his pack. "This can't be the first time you've killed an innocent."

Luke lifted his head and met the other vampire's gaze. He could hardly describe what stared back. Ruthlessness. A harsh, barren landscape. His kind never ceased to amaze him. Savannah might not prove innocent. But if she did, he could not go through with taking her life. Her innocence would defeat the purpose of choosing his victims based on their greed.

"Fuck," Lorenzo said. "You truly believe you are dealing justice?" He laughed. "Most times I forget you're only two hundred then you go and say something stupid."

"I have not spoken."

"You didn't have to." Lorenzo leaned forward. "What makes her different than other human scum you've disposed of?"

"A gut feeling."

"Even worse. Use her and be done with it. Don't over think the situation. During the decades you've done this, you've never come across an innocent victim. Humans are conniving, greedy, insignificant rats at best. Sooner you come to realize this, the better off you'll be."

Not easy to believe when every part of her screamed she was a tortured soul. "She has scars covering her. Collarbone, ribs, stomach, hips."

Lorenzo faced the outskirts of the dance floor where Savannah sat and watched them. Her dark curls tumbled over one shoulder, gleamed in the light. "Whatever happened, she appears to have recovered."

"Yes, so it seems." Some, more than others, became adept at hiding the damage done to their person.

The side of Lorenzo's mouth lifted in a smirk. "You've sampled the goods already?"

"No. I am not like you. I do not play with my food." Although the temptation of Savannah weighed on him, getting involved with her would only destroy any objectivity he possessed.

"Unwilling to play, and yet you submit yourself to torture. I suppose the reward after this is worth it. Still, I might make an exception this time around."

Jealousy lanced through him and he ground his teeth. "There is no exception for you to make."

Lorenzo threw back his head and laughed, then narrowed his eyes. "As Shakespeare once wrote, *the devil hath power to assume a pleasing shape*. Perhaps your gut is telling you to take her life and move on."

"Quoting Shakespeare does not make you wiser."

"No, but being your elder does." Lorenzo's brows drew together and his jaw tightened. "It seems you'd rather wallow in your self-inflicted sorrow." He leaned back and lit his cigarette. "This human will be your downfall if you continue to grow attached."

"I understand the risks and would hardly call my concern an attachment."

"Do you truly understand?" He inhaled and blew a steady stream of smoke. "One night's chase is only a taste. You haven't been hunted for centuries."

At no point had he mentioned the chase from the other night. "What did you say?"

Lorenzo let loose a low, gritty chuckle. "Don't stare at me with such wariness. I'm a hunted man. Of course I noticed two watchful, out-of-place vampires in my club. Both left right after you and my guess is, they weren't following you to leave you alone. What do you take me for?"

The tension within him rippled along the lines of his body. Lorenzo spoke the truth. If anything happened in Blood Bar, either he or his goons would know about it. "I guess I have you to thank for the lack of warning."

"You don't actually believe ducking into the shadows with your human chit actually worked, do you?" Lorenzo fisted his free hand on the table. "*My* men led them away from *you*. You *owe me*."

"If your men led them away, perhaps they can tell me what the men following us wanted."

"I told you. The Ancients are onto you. They were hired goons." Lorenzo shrugged. "You should thank me for protecting you and your so-called meal."

Luke was not convinced. "What is it you want in return for this protection?"

Lorenzo puffed another cloudy stream. "A night with the woman might suffice."

"Forget it." His muscles flexed but he remained seated. Never would that happen, if he could help it.

Lorenzo's eyes flashed blood red for a moment before fading to their usual dark amber. He smiled, revealing a sliver of fang, and stood. "Your secretary should have sent the paperwork already. I'll go check my fax and get you your signed contract."

Chapter 9

To dare is to lose one's footing momentarily. To not dare is to lose one-self.
—*Soren Kierkegaard*

Savannah's skin prickled. The blatant stares from those around her gave her the willies. Sure, the silky halter dress was sexy but once again Blood Bar was littered with eerily beautiful people. She hadn't felt so self-conscious in her life. She bent her head. Such a complete lie. She'd always felt uncomfortable and on edge when spending time with Ben's society friends.

Monica, the blonde from the other night, wore a blue one-shouldered mini dress. Lorenzo sat with Luke across the room, his tall, broad form clad in leather pants and a black cotton collared shirt. Both he and Monica could have walked right off the set of some nighttime bounty hunter soap opera.

Something about them haunted her. Even Luke gave off an aura. Beyond their eerie beauty, they possessed an ethereal grace and authority. Stunning yet frightening at the same time.

"Have you slept with him yet?" Monica's icy blue eyes sparkled with mischief. Their color was so light it seemed otherworldly.

"Excuse me?" Savannah coughed out the lime slice she had been sucking on and wiped her mouth with her wrist. "Do you mean Luke?" She glanced to where he sat talking to Lorenzo, relieved he didn't appear to have heard Monica's comment or noticed her embarrassing reaction.

One blond brow lifted and she thrust a napkin toward her. "Are you seeing other men too?" Her husky Italian accent lingered over *other*.

"Of course not. It's not like that between Luke and me." She almost mentioned he was her employer but thought better of it. Maybe it was the sex-kitten looks or Monica's daring attitude. Whatever it was, she didn't trust her.

Toni Kelly

"There doesn't have to be *anything* between you. Sex can be casual."

"Maybe you Italians do things a bit differently but I don't sleep with anyone casually, I barely know—"

"No lying." She tsk-tsked. "Not Italians. Our nationalities aren't what make us different." She tilted her head.

A shiver skipped up Savannah's spine. The way Monica emphasized her words made her uneasy. Maybe she could use this to her advantage. "If being Italian doesn't make you different, what does?" Her stomach clenched as she anticipated the answer. What exactly did she expect the other woman to say?

"Oooh, a game. I love games." Monica's cherry lips split into a wide grin, revealing upper canines with slightly sharp points, like fangs. Ugh. Bet that was an ick factor with boyfriends.

She didn't understand how a simple question became a game but if games were the only way to get information out of Monica, she'd give it a try. "So how does this work?"

"You ask questions and I say hot, warm, cool or cold depending on whether you are close to guessing what makes us different."

Hot and cold, she could handle this. "Fine. Let's start. Are you mafia?"

Monica's nearly transparent eyes widened as she choked out a laugh. "What? Are you kidding?" Several guffaws followed as Savannah pursed her lips in annoyance. "I can't believe…you would ask…such a ridiculous question."

"A simple hot or cold would do." It wasn't that funny.

"Okay, okay." Monica fanned herself and took a deep breath. "Waaay cold."

"I got the point. Let's move on."

"Aw, Savannah, you're not having any fun." Monica's full lips turned down at the sides and she placed her hands on her hips. Her dress stretched perfectly over her tall, lithe form. The pale blue enhanced the creaminess of her skin.

"I'm fine. Let's keep going. How about this one. Are you part of any covert group or operation?"

Head tilted, Monica tapped a long red nail against her chin. "Hmm, a tough one. I guess I'd have to say warm."

How could that be warm? It was a yes or no question, meaning hot or cold. Just as she was about to object, Luke approached. Damn it, right when she was getting somewhere with this ridiculous game.

"You behaving yourself, Monica?"

"We discussed what makes Italians so different from Americans," Savannah said, suddenly eager to keep their game a secret.

Luke's eyes narrowed then he smiled. "I would say there are quite a few differences."

Monica stepped closer and rolled her eyes exaggeratedly. "Nobody asked you." Tossing her hair back, she drew a line along Savannah's shoulder. "You're moving slow, Luke. One would think you've lost your edge. Such lovely skin."

It took everything within her not to pull away from the other female's touch. *Slow, edge*? What was she talking about? "I'm right here. If you need to say something to me, you can." For some reason, Monica's taunting of Luke grated on her nerves.

"I think I'll leave that to Luke." Licking her lips, she bit down with one canine. The unusually sharp tooth punctured her lower lip and blood dribbled down her chin.

"What are you doing?" Savannah gasped and took a step back. "You're bleeding."

Monica's pink tongue scooped up the drops. "So I am, ouch."

"Enough." Luke cupped his hand around Savannah's waist, his touch comforting and possessive in the subtlest of ways. "She is not interested in any of your invitations."

"I'm jealous," Monica said, wiping blood off her chin. "She is going to be beautiful to watch." Turning, she slipped away and disappeared through the crowd.

Luke rubbed his hands along Savannah's arms, and she realized she'd gone cold. As he guided her out of the club toward the car, she scratched her forehead, wondering what the hell had happened. "What did Monica mean by beautiful to watch? Watch what?" And why had she bitten her own lip?

"Do not concern yourself with her. She is what you Americans call a drama queen. Lives to stir up trouble."

She sighed. Deja vu. Once again, they were fleeing into the night and he evaded her questions. "I didn't mean for us to go. If you're not ready, we can stay. I just don't want to be around Monica any more. She's a bit frightening. Both her and Lorenzo." Honestly, she didn't much care for the entire crowd.

"You already mentioned you did not like Lorenzo." He slipped into the driver's side and started the car. "He is harmless."

She didn't believe Lorenzo harmless for a second. "I don't like the way he watches me." He made her skin crawl. "Why do you go there? They are so different. I mean you're a bit formal at times. Still, you seem fairly normal. Different from those at Blood Bar."

"Thank you," he replied.

Of course he'd be polite. Was he being sarcastic? "I didn't mean the comment as an insult to you."

"I did not take it as such." Luke's brows drew together as he drove.

"Luke?"

"It is complicated."

Of course. "Try me."

"It is more of a societal thing, doing what is expected of me."

Savannah turned toward the window and rested her head back against the leather seat. Strange, they seemed to come from two different worlds and yet she understood perfectly what he meant. The two years she'd spent with Ben had been full of expectations. Cocktail parties, dinner meetings, charity events. Even now, she spent her days working to meet demands of bill collectors. "You mean, versus doing what you want." She bit her lip. "If only life were so simple."

He cleared his throat. "If only," he said.

She glanced at him, met his gaze momentarily then turned away. The silence between them settled into something comfortable and bittersweet. After a few days of clashing, they'd finally found a common ground. Rich and poor, they played to life's demands and others' wants. Too bad, this common ground consisted of the biggest disappointment in Savannah's life and the one thing she strived to leave behind.

* * * *

Savannah pivoted on the balls of her feet and pushed her bag further up on her shoulder. Weaving around passersby, she concentrated on covering ground. The sun dimmed in the late afternoon sky. Luke would be awake at any moment if he wasn't already. How had she gotten so lost? Served her right for sneaking around. Still, she was a grown woman and free to do what she wanted.

Her heels burned. Even with flats, the blisters on her feet grew irritated from walking. This was Luke's fault. If he wasn't such a night owl, she probably wouldn't have been so anxious to see the sun. No one traveled to Rome to be cooped up inside, no matter how luxuriously decorated an apartment was.

Tucking her arms close, she walked faster. The city sights had given her a much-needed break, but now exhaustion from a restless night and day had caught up to her. She couldn't get over Monica's words from last night or Lorenzo's intrusive stares. What did Monica mean when she'd agreed they were part of some covert group? Luke said he wasn't an agent but maybe he referred to being a British agent. And of course, the chase from the other night. Luke had known someone chased them, but who? And why?

So many questions made her head pound. She was an aspiring chef, not Nancy Drew. She'd traveled here because she needed to pay bills, not solve some bizarre mystery.

Making her way down a narrow cobblestone street, she paused and leaned along a wall. She didn't understand why he insisted on going to Blood Bar if each time he came home depressed and moped around in his room. Societal obligations couldn't be too demanding if he spent so much time at home.

She pushed off the wall and made her way to the next corner, hugging herself as a chill wracked her. Graffiti covered walls and littered streets were not on her list of tourist spots. "Shit, my wonderful luck."

Somehow she had walked straight into a less appealing part of Rome. Bending, she dug through her bag and removed a crinkled map. She must have made a wrong turn somewhere.

"Lost, beauty?" A stocky man with ruddy hands snapped her map and bag from her grasp. "Maybe we can help."

His taller and thinner companion grinned. "Little ladies shouldn't be out alone. Especially as the sun sets.

Where had they come from? "Leave me alone." She lunged for the bag but he held it high. "What do you want?" From their accents it was obvious they weren't Italian but neither did they look like tourists.

"Oh, oh. Are you ever a beauty," the stockier male said.

Legs shaky, she lifted her chin and faced the two men. "Give me back my bag."

"I say no." The stocky man's lips spread wide, revealing crooked, stained teeth. "Here." He handed her bag to the tall, thin man next to him. "See if she has anything of value there."

Tall and Thin accepted the large leather pouch. "What are you going to do?"

"Taste the wares, of course."

Please, no. She stepped back, waiting for her opportunity to make a run for it. She'd be damned if she'd accept this fate after fighting so hard to get a second chance at life. "I don't have much money but you can help yourself to whatever's in my bag."

The stocky man laughed. "Don't worry, we will. After."

Oh God. The fluttering in her stomach grew panicked. Why had she wandered around alone?

"You always get to have fun. I want to join you." The tall, thin man tossed her bag to the side.

"Fine, you take one side," Stocky said. "We'll search for valuables later, but I go first."

They spoke of her as if she were cattle to be handled. Enough. It was now or never. Turning, she took off at a run but didn't get more than twenty feet, when a thick arm wrapped around her waist.

"No, you don't." Alcohol laden breath caressed her cheek. "I thought you were an intelligent woman, but it appears I made a mistake." The stocky man spun her around, grabbed her shirt.

She slapped his hand away. "Leave me alone."

Tall and Thin moved closer, crowding her. He entangled one of her arms and used his weight to swing and slam her against a brick wall. He was stronger than he appeared. "That's how it's done," he spat out.

Air rushed from her body, and she coughed in an attempt to catch her breath

"Yeah, yeah." The stocky male smoothed a thick hand down her neck and chest. "Ah, there's a nice girl."

A numb pain traveled up her back and down one leg. Dazed, she turned to the side, trying to push away from him as bile rose in her throat. "Don't." She hated her voice, which sounded far-away, weak.

Stocky neared, his yellow teeth repulsive, his breath so rank she feared she'd vomit.

"Such a sweet sound," he said to his taller companion. "She's moaning for us. Appears the woman likes it dirty. Grab her other arm again."

"No." A shot of adrenaline washed through her, spurting a second wind. She thrashed within their vise-like grips, tentacles of fear strangling her where their hands didn't. They continued to explore her, pulling open her cardigan and kneading her breasts through the cotton of her collared shirt. Material tore, buttons flew.

"No. Help!" She jerked, more violent now.

The thin man snorted. "No one to hear you."

Their stroking stopped as they stared at her torso, eyes dark. Without looking down, she knew what held their attention.

Stocky smiled wider. "You're flawed, not so perfect." His eyes gleamed with pleasure. "Even better. Now I don't have to worry about messing up your pretty skin." He gripped one laced covered breast and squeezed until she sobbed. "Mmm. We're going to have a lot of fun with you. We can take turns." He licked his chapped lips.

With a sinking feeling in her chest, she pushed both attackers once more.

"Uh oh, she's feisty." The tall, thin man slipped behind her and held her arms back. His arousal pressed into her rear. "There you go. I'll hold her still. She's yours. Watch her legs."

She bucked, and they laughed at her pitiful attempts.

No use, they were too strong. Unshed tears blurred her vision and for the second time in two years, she wished she had died the night of the accident.

Chapter 10

Dream as if you'll live forever, live as if you'll die today.
—James Dean

Bloody woman. Luke raced through Rome's backstreets, sticking to shadows where possible. Cement and stone walls covered with graffiti flashed in his periphery. The skin along the side of his forehead and on the tops of his hands blistered and burned. Fuck, he should have worn gloves. Nevertheless, he had not been thinking of protecting himself when he'd realized Savannah had gone. Logic had told him she should be fine. These days, women were quite adventurous and many went almost everywhere without a chaperone. Still, he could not shake the feeling something was wrong.

As the sun dipped behind buildings, he hastened his pace, following her scent up and down streets. She had obviously gotten lost or decided to wander in circles.

Screams echoed between walls, and he paused. Savannah. With lightning speed, he covered the length of the street and turned a corner. Down a narrow lane, two males held her to a wall. One tore her clothes while the other restrained her.

As both men pushed aside her undergarments and groped her pale flesh, he curled his hands into fists. It took everything inside him not to rush the men and snap their fragile human necks. "Harm another hair on the lady's head and you both will wish you had never been born," left him in an animalistic growl.

The tall, thinner man jumped away from Savannah, his expression panicked as he searched out their witness. His heavyset companion ran a hand over his round face then narrowed his gaze in Luke's direction. "We'll give you a turn if you keep your mouth shut."

Sunset left Luke draped in shadows, giving him an advantage. Not that he needed one. They knew not what they dealt with. "What makes you think I want a turn?"

The heavyset male laughed nervously. "You'd have to be crazy not to." His chapped lips broke into a wide grin, displaying crooked teeth. Eyes wary, he took a step back. "Why don't you come out of the shadows and see for yourself. She's a looker."

Savannah was definitely a temptation. He had been fighting demons since seeing her nearly nude form last night. "Stunning."

Savannah pressed herself along a wall, her midnight hair in disarray. The blood trickling down her cut lip rocked him to his core, even as saliva pooled in his mouth. He wanted to taste her and his hunger sickened him.

To cover what her shredded clothes did not, she crossed her arms over her chest, keeping her eyes averted. Her feelings of shame flooded him.

Look at me, pet, he whispered into her mind, hoping she would heed him. She raised her eyelids. Her tear-filled gaze met his and her lips trembled as if she wanted to say something. Instead, she turned away.

"I told you," the heavyset man said. "You can give her a turn after us." The two men laughed, creases around their eyes and mouths easing with relief.

The desire to snatch the men and sink his fangs into their weathered skin made him shake but pure terror radiated around her, holding him back. "I do not share."

The laughter ceased, and the thinner of the two men scowled. "We found her first."

Was this to be reduced to child-like bickering? Enough. The sudden pallor of Savannah's face concerned him. Closing the distance between them, he locked his hand around the thin man's throat and raised him a foot off the ground. "Do you think I care?"

Eyes bulging, the man heaved for breath, kicking in futile attempts to loosen Luke's grip.

"Fuck off." The heavyset male's brow creased in anger as he pushed toward him. "Who do you think you...are?" Nostrils flared, he paused mid step. Bingo. Luke relished the moment the man realized he stood on the losing side. His gaze flickered back and forth between Luke's singed forehead and hands. "Who are you? What do you want?" He took a step back.

Luke departed the shadows. He imagined he looked a terror. Remnants of sunset would highlight the reddish tint of his eyes. He turned slightly so his back faced Savannah. "I want you both to leave before I bestow on you a death more painful than any you can imagine." He threw the thin man within his grasp several feet then inched forward.

Picking himself up, the man stumbled away and tugged on his larger companion. "Let's go." It did not take long for his companion to see reason. After a few puzzled stares, the two took off running.

They'd bought hours—maybe days—before he found them again and exacted his punishment. As the echoes of their retreating footsteps faded, he bowed his head and breathed in deeply, trying to calm the fury that streamed through him. He turned.

Savannah stood huddled against a building's brick wall.

"Are you hurt?" His voice sounded gruff, and he cleared his throat.

She shook her head but shaking wracked her body. Whether she admitted it or not, she was seconds away from a breakdown.

"Ah, pet." He rubbed the back of his neck, bent his head. "Rome is not always like this. There are kind people here and some parts of this city are so beautiful, they seize the breath within you." He fisted his hand, the sudden need to convince her of life's goodness like a rock crushing his chest. Perhaps the forlorn expression on her face bothered him. Or maybe he did not want her hope to fade. He did not want her to be like him. "I promise you, love, there is still good in this world."

Jade green eyes widened, she tilted her head, sniffling. "And you, Luke. Are you good?"

He coughed and let loose an uneasy laugh. She would reach to his core—past any pretense. He might as well have been standing nude before her. "I do not know anymore." He looked away, unable to deal with the innocence in her gaze.

She picked up her bag then pulled her arms tighter around herself, making a poor attempt to fix the scraps left of her shirt and cardigan. "I'm sorry I left. I wanted to see Rome."

Her movements and words left him revisiting the image of men tearing at her clothes. She could not blame herself. If he weren't an animal confined to night, it would be different, but to think about being human served no purpose. "Christ, Savannah, what if I had not reached you in time?"

"I know." She turned away.

"Forgive me. I speak in anger. Do not blame yourself. This is their fault." And his. He took off his blazer and turtleneck then handed the latter to her. "Night cools. Put this on." He huffed. She'd made him into a mother hen.

She accepted the clothing and turned around to slip it on. Her scars glowed bright beneath the dim light of dusk. His gut clenched. What exactly had she been through? Even more so, why did it matter?

"How did you find me?" she asked.

"What does it matter?" His insides trembled at the realization he might not have gotten there to save her, to prevent those men from going further. "As is, I might not have made it in time."

She bit her bottom lip as if she wanted to object. "You made it here, that's what matters."

He could not face her, did not want to acknowledge the tear tracks on her face.

"Luke?"

Hands on his hips, he paced. "What, Savannah?" She jerked at his tone, and he cursed his inability to control his emotions. "Is there something wrong?" he asked, his tone gentler.

"What happened to your hands and forehead?"

She concerned herself with him? He wanted to be honest with her but she would never understand. "Do not worry about me. I am more worried with how you are doing. What can I do to make you feel better?"

"Can you carry me...like the night after Blood Bar?"

He stilled. Was she serious? Did she actually want him to touch her after what those men attempted to do?

She stood, chin lowered and face averted. His turtleneck dwarfed her small frame, making her appear more delicate.

"Are you sure?" He moved forward, slowly and purposefully, hesitant in case she changed her mind.

Her full bottom lip quivered, drawing his attention to drops of blood at one corner. She exhaled softly. "Please, I— Don't make me ask again."

"Shh." With one arm wrapped around her back, he scooped her up, cradled her to his chest. She weighed nothing. "I have you, pet. No one will hurt you now."

"Thank you." She rubbed her cheek against him. "I don't think you're as bad as you believe yourself to be." Her whisper caressed his throat.

He bent his head and brushed his lips along her hairline. "I wish you were right."

* * * *

Savannah lied to herself. Technically it wasn't a lie, simply a choice not to speak the truth aloud. Her attackers had realized it too. Their eyes had widened with fear as they'd watched Luke. He was different. Faster, stronger. His scent drifted to her nose as she buried her face against his chest.

Right now, she didn't care. Angel or demon, god or minion, he was her savior. He carried her through the city back to his apartment building, refusing to let her walk.

"Please," she said. "You can't take the stairs. Eight flights of stairs is too much. Put me down, we'll take the elevator."

"Not a chance. You asked me to carry you, did you not?"

"I didn't mean for you to walk up eight flights. I'm fine. I didn't hurt my legs."

Luke sighed. "Look, I know you do not like the elevator. Let me carry you."

She didn't protest any further. Couldn't, when his bottomless gaze held her captive. He carried her up through the stairwell then down the hall to his front door. He shifted her in his hands to open the lock, fingers shaking as he fumbled with the keys. The lines between his brows grew pronounced. She'd never seen him this agitated.

"Please, Luke. Tell me what's wrong."

"Damn key." Slipping his keychain into a pocket, he shoved the door back. As it swung wide, he walked to the sofa and set her down.

"Your door. You broke it." Perhaps concerning herself over his walk upstairs was unnecessary, considering he'd done that and damaged his door without breaking a sweat.

"I can fix the lock tomorrow." He seemed to move rigidly and with restraint, as he folded several cubes of ice in a moist cloth. "Here, put this on your mouth, wipe away any blood."

She did as asked and drew in a breath at the cold sting of ice on her cut lip. "It's not bleeding anymore."

"Good." He wouldn't meet her gaze as he leaned back along the counter, gripping the edge of the black and gold granite top. The ridges of his knuckles paled. Gone was his cool, calm demeanor. "Forgive me."

Forgive him, for what? She lifted her head. "You keep apologizing to me and I still have no idea what I'm supposed to forgive you for."

"I should have been there sooner."

"None of this is your fault." She stood and walked toward him. "If anything, it was my own fault. I don't want to think what would have happened if you hadn't arrived."

Luke pushed off the counter and turned his back to her. "I will be inside my room if you need me."

God, she didn't want him to leave. Not when everything was still so fresh. The stocky man's hands on her, his sour smell. She slapped at her arms as if it would make the feeling of repulsion disappear. She could have been raped, or worse. "I didn't think. Maybe I deserved what I got."

He faced her. "No. Christ." His words wafted out as no more than a whisper. "If I could turn back time, change what happened, I would." He squeezed his eyes shut, his chest and shoulders trembling.

"Do it," she said, lifting her chin. She had to be crazy but desire swelled within her. He grounded her, his arms a barrier from the world and all its evil.

"What?" Luke's midnight gaze shot up and met hers. "What are you saying?"

"I'm saying I want you to erase the feel of them." She stepped toward him, suddenly confident and uncaring whether her actions were logical. She wanted to feel him, to touch him.

"You are not ready." He bowed his head. "You are reacting after what happened."

"Please." She couldn't handle another man telling her what she could or couldn't do. The confidence ebbed, and she took a deep breath. "P-please, do this for me? Touch me, hold me."

With a sigh, he ran a hand along his temple. "Shit. Either way, I damn myself."

Her back hit the wall and his mouth crushed hers as his body surrounded her, pushing forward. He leaned with strong forearms along the wall on either side of her head then moved closer, kissed her more deeply.

He was right. She should have been shocked or frightened or angry at him for dominating her so completely after what she'd been through. And yet she couldn't be any of those. His touch made her feel light, exhilarated. A pitchy whimper left her as her limbs melted beneath him. "Luke."

"Pet, you are so sweet." He kissed her jaw. "So good." He pushed away from her slowly, his expression pained. "Not right. Damn it. I cannot do this."

Perhaps the sudden harshness in his tone or the coldness of his words had made her freeze, but she hadn't been right for Ben either. Lost in limbo, she couldn't turn away from the passion still rippling through her or the cold cruelty in Luke's gaze.

What had she done? "Luke?"

"Please go, Savannah." He turned away and pressed a hand along the counter. "Pardon my forwardness. It shall not happen again."

"Stop this. Stop this now. I'm tired of apologies and your ridiculous way of speaking. Why are you playing games? What is it you want from me?"

"Go." He said more forcefully this time.

"No, I won't, I..." Oh, God. What was she doing? He wasn't her lover and this wasn't a lovers' quarrel. He was her boss and he'd just told her to leave. *Never beg another man again.*

Nodding past a lump in her throat, she turned and ran to her room. She closed the door and leaned against it. No big deal, it was only a job, right? Fired, and only a few days as a companion. She lifted her hand and rubbed the center of her chest. But, God. A raw sob broke from deep within her. When had losing a job hurt so much?

Chapter 11

Life: It is about the gift not the package it comes in.
—*Dennis P. Costea Jr.*

The scent of death intermingled with exhaust fumes. The gush of blood through Luke's lips slowed to a trickle, a signal the body he held had been bled dry. Blood went stale within a matter of seconds. He cradled the male's neck and pulled away, closing his eyes as a wave of ecstasy rushed through him. He laid the tall, thin male next to his dead companion. Their glassy eyes, cold as the cobblestones beneath them, stared at the night sky blanketing the city. The moon shone bright, even over the lights of Rome.

Luke pulled a handkerchief from his pocket and wiped the sides of his mouth. Crimson stained the pale yellow cotton. Tossing it on top of the shorter man's barrel-like torso, he stood. Savannah's attackers were dead.

He should have felt a greater sense of justice in their deaths and yet drinking them dry did nothing to alleviate the hollow ache in his stomach. A baser need within him hungered for more torture and destruction. Only the terror in their expressions as he'd exited the shadows gave him a small measure of satisfaction. Anger and waning control had made the attack messy, according to vampire standards. Both men wore puckered gashes along the side of their necks where his fangs had ripped through their skin. Neither man had made it difficult, their bodies paralyzed before they'd realized what struck them.

Luke left the bodies lying in the alleyway and returned to his apartment. Leaving them so visible was not a wise decision, but if he touched them again, he'd rip them to pieces. To do so would only confirm him a monster.

Savannah had not left her room, and he sighed with relief. Despite the satisfaction of his kills, his thoughts remained disturbed and unpredictable. She was not like others. Everything about her drove him crazy and yet he felt for her.

Reaching into the freezer, he removed a bottle of Grey Goose and poured himself a tumbler full of the clear liquid. He sat on a living room sofa and downed his drink, relishing the sting of ice-cold vodka as it numbed his lips, tongue and throat. He tipped the bottle and filled his glass again. Drowning himself in alcohol for the unforeseeable future held great appeal. After all, he hadn't been tanked in decades.

"Cheers." He lifted the glass in toast to the darkness. The comfort night brought was so enjoyable. Gone with his humanity were blurred images and the sentiment of being lost. Vampire eyes gave the night life...a whole new rhythm and familiarity. Walls seemed to breathe as they hugged his living room and kitchen. The surface of the coffee table gleamed, its curves encrusted in detailed designs. Like vampires themselves, these material luxuries were beautiful but without life.

Reclining, he rested his head on the sofa and pressed a remote control to open the blinds. Moonlight streamed in behind him, highlighting the rest of the living room furniture and the white marble tiles of the kitchen floor. The rag Savannah had used on her cut mouth lay on the granite island across the room. The faint scent of her blood tempted him. How had life gotten this complicated? Merely a kiss, some touching.

He did not need Broderick to confirm she was too good for him, although he would be having a serious talk about his investigations. No way was she the lady portrayed in Broderick's file. Jumpy, high-strung, a sensitive wreck—definitely traits of a victim. And she was the most beautiful woman he had ever known.

He took a sip from his glass and froze as a door creaked down the hall. Savannah. He breathed the clean scent of her as she got closer. She had showered. His head swam and he sank back onto the couch. *Coward.*

Long, pale legs crossed several feet before him. A jagged scar ran the length of one thigh, slipping right beneath the hem of her silk shorts. Where had she found such seductive miniature shorts? Those certainly were not amongst the articles of clothing he'd purchased.

She wore a matching silk camisole, the dark waves of her hair loose down her back. Oblivious to his presence, she turned on a dim light near the sink, walked straight to the refrigerator and pulled out an apple. Next, from a drawer, a thick wooden cutting board and knife. Face flushed, she brushed her hair back and twisted it over one shoulder.

Sitting amongst the shadows, he waited for her to realize he was there. Then the moment she became aware of him flooded his senses. He regretted knowing he stole her calm. Her pulse heightened and the sweet scent of blood inundated the air as the knife she cut with slipped and sliced through her skin.

She snapped her emerald gaze up to his. "Luke."

His sluggish mind did not heed logic or caution. Vaulting off the sofa, he strode toward her. Too fast. *Slow down, you are scaring her.*

Mouth open, she backed away. "What are you doing awake? In here?"

"I could ask you the same thing." His words slurred slightly. One more bottle and he would surely be the veritable idiot he felt. "A bit early, is it not?"

"I couldn't sleep." Her gaze moved over him, pausing on the expanse of his chest showing beneath his open jacket. He had yet to put a shirt on after rescuing her earlier. "Are you drunk?"

"Bloody hell, woman, do not sound so incredulous. Unfortunately, I am not quite pissed. I should be there soon enough."

"Have you been drinking here this entire time?"

Her tone reminded him of Victoria's when he'd spent an extra hour hanging out with mates at gaming hells. He scowled. Christ, why the hell was he thinking about Victoria? "I have not. And if I had been, it would not be any of your business."

She wrapped a white napkin around her thumb. Red seeped through.

"You are bleeding." Again. He unleashed a stream of air, a force of habit rather than a need to breathe. Even with two recent kills sating his urge, she pushed him to the edge.

"So." She stepped back. "I can take care of myself."

This past night had proved her words a lie but he resisted pointing out the obvious. The blood stains spread, eating the white of her makeshift napkin bandage. He swallowed. "There is a first aid kit inside the cupboard to your left. I keep it on hand for mo—emergencies." Christ, he had nearly said mortals. He shook his head at his carelessness.

She reached up with her good hand, opened the cupboard and took out a white box. "Thank you, again. You can go back to your drinking now. I'll use one of these Band-Aids." She waved the sticky strip. "It'll make me good as new. You needn't worry. As I said before, I can take care of myself."

She was angry. "Sarcasm?" He moved forward. "Because I am not quite sure you can take care of yourself?"

Savannah frowned as the Band-Aid slipped along her finger. "I've done fine on my own, until yesterday."

"For Christ sakes. Please be careful. You cannot even put on a Band-Aid." Luke wrapped his hand around her wrist.

"Hey, stop." She tugged on it but he did not let go.

"Wash it off." He opened the kitchen sink faucet and thrust her thumb in the running water. Blood and water swirled down the drain. "See." He met her gaze. "Not so bad now, right? I swear, you behave like Victoria. Always without a care. I told her many times to be careful but she never..." He let go of her wrist, stunned that he'd spoken openly of his late wife. "Wipe your thumb dry. The bandage should not slip."

"What were you going to say?" She stepped toward him. "She never what?"

Fuck. "Nevermind." He turned, strode to a nearby shelf and grabbed an empty tumbler. Blast his ridiculous mouth. Taking another bottle of vodka from the freezer, he filled his glass. At this rate, he did not really need a glass but it seemed barbaric to do otherwise. "Want any?" He offered her the bottle without facing her.

"No thanks. I'm not a vodka fan."

She did not like vodka. At least he understood why she'd nursed her drink the other night. "Why did you have me order Grey Goose at Blood Bar the other night if you do not like vodka?"

"Force of habit," she said. "Ben used to buy it for me."

Luke snorted. He would think any memories of Ben would be motivation to refuse the drink.

"Your turn to answer my question," Savannah said. "Who are you? Who is Victoria?"

He released a long sigh and crossed the room to sit on a sofa. "Victoria was my wife."

"Was?" She neared and sat cross-legged in a chair next to him.

"She passed many years ago." More than two hundred years, and the words to describe the night of his late wife's death stuck on his tongue, Victoria's screams for help were still so vivid. "I prefer not to discuss this."

"Okay." She bit her bottom lip as if in thought. Her breasts weighed heavily against the thin, silky camisole.

He wanted her. The knowledge broke him as he thought about Victoria. "It is late."

"What was she like?"

"Savannah." His tone held a note of warning. And yet, he yearned to confide in her. Damn drink made him delusional.

"Please, Luke. I'm not tired."

Sipping, he stared at the ash-strewn fireplace. He could barely recall Victoria's face and her voice had faded over time but he remembered loving her smile. "She was happy and beautiful, like a sunny day in Bath. When she would laugh or smile, her whole face would light up." His lips curved at the memory and he was surprised to see a similar expression on Savannah's face. Why had he never noticed a dimple to the left of her mouth?

"Are you telling me she never got angry at you?"

Luke laughed. "Do not be daft. Of course she did. Quite a good portion of the time, in fact." He sometimes wondered how she'd ever put up with him, or his mother.

"Not a surprise," she said without a hint of sarcasm. Still, her eyes twinkled as she pursed her lips slightly. She teased him, and it felt surprisingly light within his chest.

"Victoria hated it when I would go wandering with my mates and detested imposed dances and society parties."

Savannah rolled her eyes. "Who wouldn't? Women's evening wear is rarely comfortable. A nip here, a tuck there, a pinch everywhere. Not to mention, high society can be so boring, at least it was for me."

"Yes. She often expressed frustration with the propriety of our, ahem..." Christ, what was he doing? He could not discuss late eighteenth-century society with her. She would think him mad.

"Propriety of what? Your social class?"

He tilted his head, hiding his relief at having caught himself before he'd revealed too much. "Yes, one could refer to it as such." He leaned forward to stand. "Enough talk for tonight."

"Why? I want to hear more." She smiled wide, her dimple peeking through again. "Your wife sounds wonderful. Or sounded."

Luke paused, his thoughts muddled over the strangeness of their conversation. "She was."

"I think she and I would have gotten along." Savannah's words were almost a whisper. A sense of loss and confusion washed over him.

"What's wrong?" She frowned. "Have I said something offensive?"

"No." Through the daze, Luke knew she spoke the truth. Victoria would have enjoyed Savannah's passion and sense of humor. Savannah behaved more a rebel than Victoria ever had and yet he imagined they would have made great friends.

"I didn't mean anything by it."

"No, please." Luke stood and rubbed a hand over his face. He grew tired—no, exhausted. And unfortunately, more sober than he'd hoped to be. "You have done nothing wrong."

"Why do you look so upset?" she asked.

"I have not talked about Victoria in a long time."

"Okay." She scooted to the edge of her chair. "Maybe you needed to talk about it, get it off your chest."

Such human naivety. Perhaps she had a point, but where did these moments of closeness leave them? She remained his victim and until he spoke with Broderick about getting her back on a plane to Boston, nothing had changed. Even still, he was not sure returning her was an option. Head bowed, he said, "Thank you for this discussion, but I find myself tired and suddenly very sober. If you will excuse me, I bid you goodnight."

Chapter 12

Passion, it lies in all of us, sleeping...waiting...and though unwanted...
unbidden...it will stir...open its jaws and howl... It hurts sometimes more
than we can bear. If we could live without passion maybe we'd know
some kind of peace...but we would be hollow...
—Joss Whedon

Lorenzo sat back as the stunning blonde before him lifted her leg and slid off his lap. An amazing release. Made even more so by recent good news, a crowded bar and watchful eyes. *"Mille grazie, signorina."* He buttoned his pants and zipped the fly closed. Based on his contact's phone call earlier, he had even more to bargain with. Apparently Luke's latest gem of a victim was definitely more gem than victim. Lorenzo had suspected something different since the beginning.

White fangs flashed as the blonde smiled. "My pleasure." She pulled down her snug leather skirt, winked and walked away.

"I see you haven't changed a bit." Rafaelo Costa neared his table. Vampires and humans alike averted their stares from the well-known Ancient, his presence almost overbearing.

"Rafe, just in time." Lorenzo's nerves stirred as he stood and nodded with respect. "I've arranged for a more private location in the back."

"It's a wonder you didn't think to take care of your business there too." He raised one dark brow.

"I have a reputation to uphold." And he simply liked to fuck, but that excuse wouldn't please the Ancient.

"So you do." Rafe pushed aside a curtain and slid into a black leather booth. "I must admit your call surprised me, especially after what transpired between you and Drago. Why did you contact me?"

"I want to make a deal with the Ancients."

Rafe's steel gray eyes narrowed. "Is this a joke? If you've wasted my time..." He rose.

"No." Shit. This wasn't working out how he had hoped. "I know the Ancients are watching Luke."

"Drago's concern, not mine."

"He sees Luke as a threat. Only two hundred years old, and his strength rivals those of our kind who are three times his age."

"I don't know if I'd agree with such a far-fetched assessment and quite frankly, I'm not sure what Drago sees these days." Rafe sat down, brows drawn together. "Mr. Evans is of no interest to me so if you're looking to make a pact, you've contacted the wrong Ancient."

"You know I cannot contact Drago. You said as much yourself."

"Not my problem."

Lorenzo sat back, released a long exhalation. He would have to tell Rafe what he knew. "What about the woman, his latest victim? Does she interest you?"

"Beautiful women are a dime a dozen. Why don't you tell me what you want?"

"I want my life back. I want any kind of bounty on my head to disappear. And I want free reign over any activities I choose to partake in."

Rafe pulled aside the curtain surrounding their booth. "It doesn't seem to me you're suffering much."

"I'm a marked man. It's no way to live. I can't go a day without your minions down my back."

"Hire more security."

The urge to grab Rafe's collar and shake him senseless surged but the rash move would only get him killed. Instead he lowered his voice. "You're not listening."

"No, you're not. No one crosses Drago. And considering you fucked his sister and almost got her killed, I'd say you're a thousand steps back from everyone else. If you want to walk free, you'll have to negotiate terms with him."

"I've tried. You're his right hand man. You have to help me."

The table between them trembled. "I don't have to do anything."

"I could make it worth your time." He lifted a decanter and poured the Ancient a glass of whiskey.

Rafe smiled then his expression grew serious. "Cut the bullshit. I could care less about you being a hunted man and so far you've offered me no reason why I should help you. Actually, you've only given me a desire to up the bounty on your head or finish the job myself."

"Have you heard of the Blessed?" Lorenzo calmly slipped out a cigarette. "I know you have your underground blood circuit, therefore, you must know of them."

"What do you know about the Blessed?" Rafe leaned back in the booth, eyes steely, mouth a straight line.

"I know enough to know they interest you."

"I don't play games."

"I know their blood is sacred and powerful," said Lorenzo.

"Doesn't do me any good." Rafe stood as if to leave.

"Fine. I know the human must have a near death experience and be blessed before returning to earth. I know they have to stop breathing for a certain period of time." He reached across the table and grabbed Rafe's arm. "Please, I'll tell you what I know about Savannah Michaels."

Rafe looked down at the hand in warning and Lorenzo pulled it back. The Ancient sat. "Who is Savannah Michaels and why should I care to know more about her?"

"Luke's latest victim. Aren't you watching him?"

"I told you, I don't involve myself in Drago's games." He leaned forward, pinpointing Lorenzo with his eerie silver eyes. "Is she a Blessed?"

"I have reason to believe she is. My contact says a car hit her nearly two years ago. Savannah stopped breathing for several minutes."

"And who is this contact of yours?"

"I am sworn to secrecy, but what if I could get you proof?" How far should he offer to go? No risk equaled no reward. "A blood sample? Or what if I brought her to you so you could see for yourself?"

"I'm not sure your buddy Evans would agree."

"Don't concern yourself with Evans."

Rafe rubbed a hand over his jaw. "Last I heard, you and Luke were pretty chummy."

"He isn't a friend so much as a nuisance, a temporary one." Especially as Luke refused to partner with him.

"Fine," Rafe said. "But I'm not making any guarantees. Bring me something of interest and I'll get you a conversation with Drago."

"I don't need your help to get a conversation with Drago."

"You do if you want to walk away alive. You're fortunate his sister Cybele is not vengeful."

Lorenzo rose, set down his empty glass. "I'll contact you when I have the woman."

Rafe removed a black card from his pocket and slid it across the table. "Direct them here. It's a blood auction. I'd like some privacy now. I'll exit through the back when I'm done." He lit a cigar. "One more thing. If you don't go through with this deal and make it worth my time, the price on your head will go up."

Lorenzo nodded and closed the door behind him, leaving Rafe in Blood Bar's back office. He couldn't stand how the Ancient walked around so high and mighty. Not for long, though. Soon enough, everyone would answer to him.

* * * *

Savannah swung her hips and hummed as she chopped red peppers. It was not yet dawn, but her vivid dreams and rumbling stomach had kept her from sleeping. Images from one of her dreams replayed of a Boston society party scene. Only instead of Ben, Luke accompanied her. Her skin had warmed beneath his soft caresses and kisses.

She shivered and exhaled a shaky breath. A dream, but her response had felt real.

Across the room, a rumpled blanket lay on an empty couch. She pictured Luke as he'd been last night, bared to the waist beneath his jacket. An empty vodka bottle sat on the wooden coffee table.

Cutting board in hand, she turned and swept the finely chopped vegetables into a pan with melted butter. Onions and peppers sizzled, and her stomach rumbled. "Shh, you'll wake the whole house up."

"And if the whole house is already awake?"

She jumped, and the knife and board clattered to the floor. "Luke." She turned. "Stop sneaking up on me. And what are you doing here? You're never awake at this time." She reached to the stove and turned off the burner.

He shrugged. "Trouble sleeping."

"I'm sorry." She bit her bottom lip and pulled the pan off the burner then picked up the knife and cutting board. "I woke up starving."

"Why would you apologize? Hunger is natural." He turned and picked up the empty vodka bottle off the coffee table.

"I meant I'm sorry you couldn't sleep, and about last night. I didn't mean to push you."

"Do not apologize for the past. You had nothing to do with Victoria's death."

Savannah released the breath she held. Perhaps their talk last night would give them a chance to start over. She twisted her lips. "I wanted to know more about you. Monica said—"

"Monica is a tease in more ways than one. Probably better if you do not associate with her."

So much for getting to know him, but no way would she deal with cold, bossy Luke again. "Maybe you should have told me my boundaries before you dragged me to bars and forced me to hang out with your creepy friends. What is it about you, anyway?" She stepped closer. "What's with your sleeping habits? Not to mention, I never see you eat. You go to clubs you don't like and spend time with strange girls who have fangs and men who give me the willies. You don't even seem to like these people and yet you walk within their social circle. Why?" She lifted her hand and exhaled a long breath to calm herself. "And don't give me your excuse about obligations because I know that is bullshit. You're not the type of man to let anyone tell you what to do."

"And how would you know what type of man I am?" Luke asked, stepping closer.

She swallowed and lifted her chin. She hated how he wound her up then left her weak-kneed. "I just know." A silly answer.

He rolled his shoulders, stretching his back. "Have you considered, maybe you are not meant to determine what makes me different?"

"What do you mean?"

"Exactly what I said." Opening a cabinet beneath the counter, he tossed the empty vodka bottle in a trash bin. "Some answers are better left unknown." He turned and leaned back on the countertop. His expression challenged despite the apparent resignation in his eyes. "Go on, I know there are thoughts you are holding back."

She stepped within a few inches of him and lifted a hand to the side of his head. The temptation to take him up on his invitation was too hard to resist and yet his sudden accommodating attitude made her wary. "Your burn from yesterday is gone."

"I heal quickly."

"Who are you, Luke? Give me a straight answer."

"You would not believe me if I told you."

She caressed his lips with her fingers, hesitant to push further. Probe more, and she mightn't like what he had to say.

"What are you doing?" He frowned.

"I don't know." And she didn't, or maybe she didn't want to think about it. She stretched her neck, inexplicably drawn to him.

He parted his lips, enticing her to taste them.

She couldn't think, nor did she want to. And so she kissed his mouth and nibbled along his jaw, teasing and taunting.

He placed a hand against her shoulder. "You are playing with fire."

"Burn me."

His eyes widened as his nostrils flared slightly. And then she spun, moving with him as one. Her shoulders were crushed against the kitchen cabinets. His chest melded with hers as he kissed her with what seemed like a lifetime of pent up passion and hunger. Their tongues danced and he nipped her mouth, teasing, inviting her in. Holy hell.

"Luke." She pulled back, stealing a breath and attempting to steady herself. He'd moved so fast.

He touched his forehead to hers. "You do not know what you ask. I am not right for you."

She shook her head. At this moment she didn't care who he was or what secrets he guarded. She didn't want to hear what was right for her or not. "Kiss me," she said.

Cupping her rear, Luke lifted and set her on the granite countertop. "You drive me insane."

She opened her legs and clenched him around his narrow hips, pulling him closer. Sliding her hands down his smooth neck, she dug her nails into his shoulders, whimpering as she parted her legs wider. She could feel him, thick and hard against her core. A thrill shot through her.

Luke slid a hand beneath her thin camisole and lifted it over her head. The built in bra within it tugged her breasts upward, releasing them with a bounce. One brow arched, he roved over her with his intense gaze. "You are going to be the death of me, woman." He leaned forward, laved one nipple with his tongue. Fire seared along her skin, raising goose bumps on the surface of her flesh.

Pushing her hands against the flat granite surface below, she thrust her breasts up to him, dropped her head back and moaned. Never had anyone made her feel this sexy or erotic. She bared her scars without feeling ashamed.

He kissed each with such reverence, her breath caught inside her chest. "These have given you strength."

His words, so close to the truth, brought tears to her eyes. Bending her head to avoid his gaze, she ran her hands down his chest. "Remove your clothes."

For an infinite second, Luke hesitated, appearing as if he wanted to say something. Instead, he stepped back, pulled off his black jacket, pants, socks and shoes. His olive toned skin shone smooth and firm under the glow of recessed lights. A flawless statue come to life.

"And your briefs," she said, worrying her bottom lip with her teeth.

"You first."

She slid off the counter then removed her silk shorts. She wore no underwear beneath.

He released a hiss of air.

"Now you." She swallowed, dropping her gaze. Heat suffused her cheeks as she reached to touch him. She didn't want to compare but could not deny Luke put Ben to shame. Would he even fit? Vibrations strummed through every honed line of his intensely masculine body as he watched her, hunger evident in his expression. No turning back now.

Slipping her hand around his thickness, she glided up then down his length.

He moaned, letting his head fall back.

She rose up on tiptoes and kissed the exposed flesh of his throat. "I need you."

Luke met her gaze, held her shoulders. "Are you sure?"

She nodded. Even aroused, he held a certain formality.

Pulling her forward, he kissed her as if starved for the taste of her, the feel of her. Digging through his hair with her fingers, she kept in rhythm with his mouth, yielded to his touch. He cupped the underside of her thighs and lifted her so she cradled him between her legs.

"So wet," he said. Wrapping his arms around her, he shoved her against the wall, cushioned her back with his forearms.

Her hips bucked as if of their own will, the movements hurried and forceful. She rode along his length, enveloping him in her juices. "In me. Now." Her breaths came out in whimpers.

He pulled away from nipping the tips of her breasts and ripped open a small silver package. Carefully, he smoothed a condom over his head and down his length then with one drive upward, sheathed himself within her. "Bloody hell. You are so warm. Fuck, Savannah."

Savannah cried out as he filled her, stretching the walls of her channel to accommodate all of him.

Tensed, he stilled, giving her a chance to adjust. "You okay?"

"Yes." She bit down on the inside of her cheek as she ground herself against him. His movements seared her as he rocked his hips back and forth, thrusting each time with more force. He braced his hands along the wall behind her.

"Luke." Her panting grew hurried, and she squeezed her eyes shut, rolled her hips faster, harder.

"God, Savannah, I can feel you." He pounded harder, almost to the point of pain.

She felt a cry rip from her throat and her moist core tightened around him, milking a climax from him.

Luke moaned, pulling her against him as he squeezed her body.

As the waves of ecstasy rippling through her dimmed and quiet contentment stole over her, she lay against his chest.

He caressed her hair, and the coolness of his body tempered the heat within her. The silence comforted her, made her smile, but soon seeds of doubt breached the surface of her thoughts. Tonight they'd crossed a line, leading to the most incredible of experiences. But would tonight's pleasure become tomorrow's pain?

Chapter 13

*Trickery and treachery are the practices of fools that have not the wits
enough to be honest.*
—Benjamin Franklin

"Luke." Savannah smoothed a hand over several suede pillows and
the sheet. It was dim in the room, but he could discern her creased brows
and narrowed eyes as she realized she lay alone. He had held her asleep
within his arms until his hunger grew unbearable. Even after feeding,
he'd planned to sneak back onto the couch with her but could not bring
himself to approach her sleeping form. Instead, he stood a short distance
away, fixated on her small movements and sounds.

She shifted on the couch and pulled a thin blanket up over her shoulders.
Mid afternoon sunlight streamed into the living room like transparent
spears through the blinds.

Still hesitant to leave the cloak of shadows, he stepped forward. He
should go back to his room. An affair would only lead them down a
dangerous path. Nevertheless, he had given her fair warning she was too
good for him. And sex was sex, was it not? *Liar.*

Her stomach rumbled, and she brushed a hand over her ribs and down
her abdomen. Sadness and a mix of frustration filtered through him from
her, but he knew nothing of her thoughts. Did she think of him as more
than a meal ticket? *Idiot.* Did it matter?

Shaking her head, she rubbed her arms as if to block a chill. Luke could
tell when she lifted her chin and smoothed back the blanket, thoughts
of him were pushed aside. A woman accustomed to dealing with hurt,
she was resourceful in her self-preservation. She reached for the portable
phone on a nearby side table. Who would she call?

"Max."

The sound of joy in her voice triggered a pang of hurt mid chest. An
unusual sentiment and one not easily understood. He recalled reading of

a Max in Broderick's file. Not an ex. Her boss, a bar owner. The clock above the stove read two twenty-nine PM. A six hour difference between Rome and Boston meant this Max would be gearing up for the nighttime pub crowd.

"Savannah?" Max asked, his deep Irish brogue echoing through the line. "How the hell are you?"

"Hmm, I could go for a pound of your wings right now. Or a pint of Guinness and a plate of potato skins," she gushed into the phone line, her tone almost flirtatious. Luke had yet to experience this side of her, and it captivated him. There was a freedom to her tone as she relaxed into the corner of the sofa.

"Sounds like you're not getting enough to eat over there." Max's voice held a hint of concern.

Savannah laughed. "Oh, Max. Man, do I miss you. But don't worry, everything is fine. I'm simply a bit homesick."

"Now ya got me worried, love. Is everything okay? If you're missing me, your *employer*, something's not right about this picture."

Love. These days, terms of endearment were used loosely. Even he called her pet and love. Of course he did not mean anything by the terms. Or so he preferred to think.

Twisting her fingers in the sheet, Savannah shivered and her smile faltered. "Max, you're more than an employer to me and you know it."

"Aye, and you to me."

She cleared her throat. "Italy is beautiful, stunning. Still, I miss the pub, the night crowd. I bet Tricia and Pete are there already, am I right?"

Luke frowned. Strange, as she did not strike him as a night person—at least not in going to Blood Bar.

"Of course," Max replied. "And Jason, Kelly, Colin and numerous others. But we'll be here when you get back, begging you to regale us with tales of delicious meals and dates with Roman gods. I'd personally prefer to hear about the goddesses. I've always been a fool for big, chocolate-brown eyes."

She laughed again, only this time it sounded forced. "If you only knew. Goddesses and gods there may be, but gods certainly aren't dating me. My new employer might have the looks down in the god department but he is far from datable. It seems Romans can be highly overrated. Not to mention, he hangs with a strange crowd."

Should he be glad she thought him handsome or insulted she thought him a poor date? Despite his misgivings, he could not fault her logic.

"He's not trying any funny business with you? Because if he so much as harms a hair on your head, I swear—"

"No, Max." She blushed as she glanced down. The silky camisole had slipped to the side, revealing one rosy nipple. Luke's gut stirred. "No funny business," she said, tugging her camisole into place. She bit her lip.

Max laughed. "All right. Try to enjoy yourself there. Learn some new recipes. You didn't spend these last couple years working your arse off for nothing. I'll have plenty of work for you to do when you return."

"Goodbye, Max." Savannah ended the call and set down the handset, leaned her head back. Had she meant what she'd said? Why did she lie about them spending the night together? Maybe last night meant nothing to her.

Luke fisted his hands. He would have to ask Broderick to investigate Max further.

Her stomach rumbled, and she swept the cover aside. "Shh, grumpy. I'll get you something. Be quiet." Pushing herself to a standing position, she stumbled into the kitchen. She had yet to sense him.

Her long, toned legs moving as she walked to the fridge and took out a carton of eggs, several slices of cheese and an apple hypnotized him. Munching on the apple seemed to steady her appetite while she whipped the eggs and cheese. Neat and efficient, she sauteed the red peppers and onions she'd put in the pan earlier. She was at home in the kitchen, her mood lifting even as she cooked. She ate with the same precision and tidiness she used in preparing her food, as if her meal should be savored.

Never could he remember ever eating with such passion. Neither Victoria nor his mother had enjoyed the kitchen and although his housekeeper, Mrs. Thompson, frequently allowed him to sneak freshly baked scones and jam, he ate in a hurry and never gave taste much thought.

While washing up, Savannah hummed, scrubbing the omelet pan with long, firm strokes. Her thoughts seemed to be elsewhere as she continued to rub the already clean pan. He took a step toward her, pausing as she squeezed the sponge and pulled her arm from the shallow sink water. "Damn it."

The pungent scent of blood flooded the air. Saliva pooled on his tongue and he backed against the wall. He had just fed. Cravings should not be so strong, especially since he'd recently killed.

Streaks of red dripped down the underside of her sud-soaked forearm, tinting bubbles in the soapy water below a pinkish hue. Pushing past his hunger, he stood behind her. "Where are you hurt?" he rasped.

"Fuck." Savannah jumped and turned around. "You scared me." Her wary gaze pinned him. "How long have you been standing there?"

"Not long," he lied. "Is the cut bad?"

"I'm fine, really."

Who was she trying to convince, him or herself? He edged closer. "I heard talking."

"I made a phone call," she said.

"That cut definitely appears to have a sting to it." He nodded at her arm.

She released a long breath, as if weighing her options. "Truth is, it burns like hell but I want to be a chef. No way I'll ever make it with my latest penchant for injuries. They only seem to happen when you sneak up on me, though." Her brows drew together. "I think you may be hazardous for me."

If she only knew how close she was to the truth. "You cut yourself without any help from me." He rubbed his forehead.

Eyes narrowed, she said, "Hello? Only a joke. Don't go serious on me."

"Let me see the wound." He grasped her arm then grabbed a nearby towel. It was a long but clean wound. He held the cloth against it, using one corner to wipe off stray drops of blood. Closing his eyes, he felt muscles along his jaw pulse. Every moment spent close to her, he walked a fine line. Beneath the strong scent of life-giving fluid that ran through her veins, he detected the faint aroma of orange blossoms and locked onto it as if it were a lifeline.

"It's practically a surface cut," she said. "Luke, are you okay? You look...I don't know...sick."

"What?" His hand stilled in wiping. Her voice rang out as if from afar.

"Are you okay?" she asked and placed her hand over his, her short, ruby red nails drawing his attention.

"Blood." Had he lost complete control? The pulse at her neck beat a seductive rhythm beneath her skin. He ached to caress the long ivory expanse between the side of her jaw and the top of her shoulder. "I can smell it."

"You can?" She sniffed the air and wrinkled her nose. "I can't. I smell eggs and onions. You must have an exceptionally sensitive sense of smell."

"I do." He met her gaze, felt her trepidation—or was it his own? "This wound is a bit deeper than the surface but you are going to be fine. I am going to put on a bandage. Is that okay?"

"Sure." She tilted her head, studying him as he wet a clean towel and held it to her forearm. "Have you always had such a keen sense of smell?"

The question did not surprise him. Of course she was curious. He should be cursing his stupidity and yet his admission gave him a sense of relief. He tired of living in a world full of deception. Grew weary of trying to fit into the mold of vampire or human when he did not feel he fully belonged to either.

Savannah shifted in place, her nervous energy almost tangible. "I can see well. I've always had twenty fifteen vision."

He rubbed his forehead. His mind was too clouded to think about right or wrong. What he should and what not to say. Did it even matter? "My sense of smell has improved with age. Hold this to your cut for a moment. I shall get the first aid kit." He placed her hand against the damp towel then swallowed a sigh of relief at the distance he created between them. From a cabinet on the other side of the kitchen, he removed a first aid kit. He bought the kit years ago and yet could not recall any of his former companions using it quite as much as Savannah.

"How unusual." She came to stand behind him, her arousal like an invisible fog coaxing him.

"Savannah." He half turned and tensed beside her. "No."

"No, what? You didn't say no last night." Her voice sounded husky in the gray light of dawn. Casting her gaze downward, she pulled the towel off her arm. Burgundy liquid pooled from the slice, dripping onto the floor.

"You are hurt." A knot caught in his throat as he cut a piece of gauze then turned, gripped her arm. "You are still bleeding. We need to stop the blood." The vein at the base of her wrist thrummed upward as if straining toward his mouth.

"Luke, please. Stop worrying about my cut. It doesn't hurt."

"Savannah, I cannot."

She frowned, trailed a finger over his hand, which cradled her elbow. "I don't understand."

He breathed in deep and looked away as her touch taunted him. How had he let her get to him? Her scent, her voice?

Wetness splattered against his skin and he swore fire engulfed the underside of his arm. A stinging pain ate through his mind's haze, doubling him over. The acrid scent of burning flesh infiltrated every pore.

"Bloody hell." He hissed and yanked his hand from her arm as several drops of her blood trickled down his forearm and over his wrist. Everywhere red touched, the skin blackened and burned. Supporting his arm, he ran over to the sink. The rush of water washed away the blood, exposing new flesh and damaged muscle where his skin had melted away.

Savannah backed away, her face a mask of terror. "I-I'm so sorry, I don't know how... I couldn't have done... I don't know what happened."

Fury gripped him, and afraid of what he might do, he held himself immobile. Who was she? Had she done this on purpose? He shook his head and grabbed a kitchen towel, carefully wrapping his forearm. When he glanced up, he could see disbelief through the glassy glaze that covered her eyes. "Maybe I should be asking what the hell you are."

* * * *

Body-wracking sobs made Savannah's steps clumsy as she rushed down the hall toward freedom. The door to leave was behind her but she couldn't heed logic. Besides, she'd tried that already and it had only gotten her into more trouble. Must she learn all life's mistakes through experience? She shivered, recalling her attackers' hands on her. She wanted away from them, from Luke and from the idea others might truly have a reason to avoid her. Did Ben's shunning of her suddenly have justification?

No, she wouldn't accept it. And yet she'd seen the proof herself. Luke's arm couldn't be explained. Plain and simple, her blood ate through his skin.

"No." Salty tears clung to her cheeks and dipped between her lips. Exhaling a shuddery breath, she brushed the back of her hand across her face.

The hallway dead-ended with a winding staircase and she climbed it.

What the hell! Life's experiences had turned her into a fairytale-hunting pansy instead of a reality-facing warrior. Anger carried her up the rest of the steps in a hurry and she burst through the exit to the roof with the momentum of a freight train at full speed. Cool air hit her face and yanked her out of her spiraling thoughts. The view stunned her, forced the breath from her lungs and made her swollen eyes widen. She stood staring. "Incredible," she whispered.

Small maples shaded forked pathways as flowers of every color and shape wove around the paths like perfect accessories. Sweet and musky fragrances wafted past in symphonic harmony. This was how Alice must have felt when she stepped beyond the tiny door into the white rabbit's topsy-turvy wonderland. Unlike Alice, though, she wanted to lose herself here, never to be found again.

With deep, long breaths, she calmed her thoughts and scanned the area. Garden? Who was Luke kidding? He'd built a veritable forest on the roof of his building. Sniffling, she bent and inspected a flower's delicate, lavender petal then fingered a small white sign in front of several stems. Neat, black letters spelled *Epilobium angustifolium*. So much detail, so much thought. Did he even take time to enjoy it?

She walked a bit further and sank onto a soft patch of grass below a tree. Exhaustion tugged at her. The mid-afternoon sun peered through leaves above and a cool breeze whirled around her. Though she trembled, she wasn't quite ready to leave this newly discovered sanctuary. What kind of man created something so beautiful? The same kind of man who touched her with so much passion and carried her through the city. The one who'd fought to protect her then left her alone. The one whom she'd burned with her blood and who most likely thought her a freak now.

Groaning, Savannah buried her head against the tops of her knees and rocked to the wind's sway. So many physical scars had healed and yet emotional ones still held her. She choked back one last sob and squeezed her eyes shut, hoping when she awoke, the nightmare would have ended.

Chapter 14

Do not bite at the bait of pleasure, till you know there is no hook beneath it.
—Thomas Jefferson

Luke sat outside Cafe Sant'Eustachio and downed an espresso. The bitter, sugar-infused drink coated his throat and gave his system a jolt. Although admittedly, he did not need caffeine. His kind hardly slept and his nerves had been on edge all day. The chaotic shuffle of evening tourists throughout the piazza did nothing to soothe his anxiety. Most finished up their tours of the Pantheon and now searched for a hot meal.

He leaned back in the wrought iron chair and cradled his injured arm. Perhaps he'd reacted harshly with Savannah, but what could she have expected? It could have been much worse—for both of them. Her blood had burned him straight through skin and muscle. He brushed a hand over his wrapped wrist and forearm then winced at the soreness and stinging. It hurt like hell but comforted him. He must have a sadistic bone within him to enjoy the pain. In a strange sort of way, it made him feel human.

"Unusual choice of meeting place." Lorenzo walked across the small piazza toward his table and pulled out a chair. "Is there a reason you dragged my ass to this caffeine-lovers' paradise when I could have started the night in an alcohol-induced stupor at Blood Bar?"

"You do Blood Bar every night. Do you not grow tired of the crowd?"

"You forget I'm a marked vampire. Like a rat locked inside a damn cage," he bit out, "I'm limited as to where I can play."

"You play fine, considering."

Lorenzo snarled. "What do you know of it? I'm sick of being a prisoner. Spent half my human life inside a four by six and I refuse do it again."

He had a point. Luke knew nothing of Lorenzo's past, nor had he ever cared enough to ask. It did not take a genius to realize Lorenzo was not a good individual—most vampires were not. Still, today was the first time

Luke wondered if Lorenzo had reason to be so unhappy. "Did you spend time in prison?"

"A closet, as a child, but save your pity for someone who cares."

"I have no pity for you," Luke said. "I would be a fool to pity another vampire." Besides, as a mortal, he too lived in life's cage. A gilded cage, but one nonetheless. "And my interests today extend beyond tragedies of our pasts. I asked you to come here because I need your advice."

"My advice? Now you have my attention." Lorenzo dipped one blond brow mockingly, reclined in his chair and removed a cigarette from a silver box. "Does this have something to do with the woman?"

He had no reason to doubt Lorenzo. The other vampire had always cared for his best interests, befriending him when he had first become immortal. "It does."

"I'm listening." Lorenzo leaned forward and ran a hand through his blond hair.

"Have you ever heard of different kinds of blood?"

"What do you mean?"

Luke rolled up the right sleeve of his collared shirt. A white dressing covered his forearm. Two red lines bled through the underside. "I mean an extremely different kind of blood."

"Was it your blood I scented?" Lorenzo's lips tightened into a thin line, his gaze suddenly alert. "Take off the bandage," he whispered.

With one tug, Luke tore and removed the binding. Two lines burned by Savannah's blood still bled, scabbing in some areas. The skin around the cuts shone, pale.

Lorenzo sniffed the air. "Two distinct blood scents. Vampires don't scab. How long ago did this happen?"

"This morning. Something is wrong." He pulled more gauze out of a pocket and wrapped his arm before rolling his sleeve down to cover it. "Savannah's blood did this. One minute I cleaned her cut and the next, my skin withered beneath intense heat. Felt like I had stood beneath midday sun. Almost burned straight through to the bone."

"Incredible." Lorenzo swallowed and smiled, his expression brightened. "Vampire killer."

"I am hardly dead and you need not appear so gleeful. This is some pretty drastic stuff."

"You don't even know the half of it." Lorenzo leaned closer. "I don't know how much more proof you need. The Ancients must know about her. It has to be them pursuing you."

Luke fisted a hand in his hair. Christ, if Lorenzo spoke the truth, he was in for far more trouble than he imagined. A vibration on his hip distracted him. Broderick called and he needed to talk to him, but now was not the time. He needed privacy. He turned back to Lorenzo. "Have you heard of anything like this before?"

"I only know one person who may know about this type of blood. Fuck, this ups the ante for sure." Lorenzo's expression took on a faraway look as he stood and paced.

"What do you mean, ups the ante?"

"What?" He paused, cleared his throat. "I mean as far as the Ancients' motivation. Is she still in the dark about our existence?"

"Yes." Across the piazza, two children chased each other around a pole, laughing as their mother tried to calm them. His phone vibrated again. Broderick's name flashed across the screen. He declined the call. Between Lorenzo's rambling and his own racing mind, he could not keep his thoughts straight. A man leaned against a building wall reading a newspaper, and yet Luke would have sworn he glanced their way every so often. Lorenzo's hypothesizing made him paranoid.

"Fuck, you slept with her, didn't you?" Lorenzo blew a long stream of smoke. "You told her what we are."

"If I slept with her, that is my business. I have not told her anything, but I will not deny she suspects I am unusual." Although after what happened this morning, she could not argue much in respect to his strangeness. She too was quite a mystery.

"Unusual. Quite the understatement of the century." Lorenzo laughed. "Was she a good fuck?"

Liquid heat shot through his veins at Lorenzo's jest. "You overstep your boundary."

"I'll assume it was good." Lorenzo smiled. "What now?"

"Now I am here talking to you. You mentioned someone who will know about this blood. Who were you referring to?"

Lorenzo's smile disappeared. "I can't talk about my contact here." He inclined closer. "Give me some time and I'll contact you."

"And until then?"

The man reading the newspaper now stared at them openly then folded the paper and walked away.

"Your only option is to lay low." Lorenzo turned. "What is it you keep looking at?"

"Nothing. I thought I saw someone."

Lorenzo rubbed the back of his neck. "I'll be in touch quickly, but sit tight and don't do anything."

"Like what?" Luke crossed his arms. "I cannot exactly feed off her."

"No, but if the Ancients know she is a vampire killer, you can't put her on a plane and send her back to Boston for safekeeping, either."

Luke did not want to admit it but he was right. "I know."

Lorenzo extinguished what remained of his cigarette and stood. "You know where to reach me if you need help." He turned and left.

* * * *

"I'm coming." Savannah slipped a robe on over wet skin and ran to the door. Who rang so insistently and why wasn't Luke answering? "Hold on a sec." Reaching the door, she twisted the lock and pulled it open a crack. "Yes, can I help you?"

A man stood there, gray-blue eyes widened as he combed over her with his gaze, pausing where she held her robe together with one hand. He cocked dark brows and smiled, leaned against the doorframe. "Son of a bitch. Man, am I glad to see you."

Holding the door steady with her foot, she quickly tucked one flap of her robe beneath the other and double knotted the belt. "Excuse me?" She was pretty sure she'd have remembered meeting him. Despite his endearing smile, the air around him buzzed with a sort of barely restrained strength. He stood almost as tall as Luke, which put him at maybe six foot one. Broad shoulders. He could definitely take her, although it wasn't as if she was thinking about challenging him. "I don't believe we've met."

"I don't think I will excuse you." He winked as if to soften his bold words. "And you're right. We haven't met, at least not in person. Are you going to let me in or stand there checking me out? Is Luke home?"

Heat rushed to the surface of her skin. Cheeky ass, but at least he knew Luke, or so he claimed. "I'm not sure."

"About what? Letting me in or Luke being home?"

Both, but she wasn't going to tell him that. "Letting you in. Want to tell me what this is about?"

"I need to talk to Luke. I'm a friend."

"You're going to have to come back."

The smile and humor disappeared from his face. "I don't think so."

She sucked in a breath, her stomach quivering from a sudden bout of anxiety.

"Shit, Savannah. Don't look at me like I'm a freak. I'm not going to do anything to you, but it's important I get ahold of Luke. I called him twice today and he hasn't answered my calls."

He knew her name. How the hell did he know her name? She bit her lip, considering her next move. Where was Luke? "How do I know you aren't lying?"

"You don't." He leaned one hand against the door frame and hung his head then met her gaze. "Look, you've been through a lot these past couple years. An accident, physical therapy. This whole thing with Luke is some deep shit. I can help. I swear you can trust me."

"How do you know so much about me?"

The man sighed and straightened. "Let me in and I'll tell you what I know."

Savannah held the door steady and blinked. He obviously knew Luke and for some reason, a lot about her. She could slam the door and get nowhere or take a risk and maybe learn more about Luke. A risk wasn't likely, as she wasn't up for another one of life's cruel lessons. "Tell me how you know me then I'll let you inside."

"I'm an investigator. I did your background check before Luke took you on as a companion."

Background check? She ducked her head and stared at the floor, giving herself time to digest his words. It made sense and considering Luke's conservative nature, she shouldn't be surprised. And yet she was. He hadn't mentioned a detective. Biting her bottom lip, she moved away and let the door swing wide. "You try anything and so help me God, I will come back from the dead to make your life a miserable hell, *capisce*?"

He raised his hands in surrender and grinned. "Understood." He walked into the kitchen and pulled out a mug from the cabinet then poured himself some milk, making it clear he had been in Luke's home before. "How long has he been gone?"

Savannah shrugged and sat on one of the living room chairs. "Not sure." She hadn't seen him since she'd burned his skin some hours ago, but probably best to leave details unsaid. If she played friendly, perhaps she'd glean some information about Luke. "So did you discover anything interesting in your investigation of me?"

His gray blue eyes tracked her as she stood and filled a glass with water before sitting on the sofa again.

"You would know better than I, wouldn't you?" he asked. She remained silent as he sat diagonally across from her. "Actually, digging into your past felt like trying to solve a Rubik's Cube. Every time I thought I headed down the right path, I'd hit another dead end."

Time to roll her dice and see what she could get. "Are you like Luke?"

That had gotten his attention. Both hands around his mug, he sat back. "What do you know about Luke?"

"Enough. It wasn't difficult, you know. He's pretty secretive. At first, I thought him some kind of special agent but Monica at Blood Bar set me straight. You know her, don't you? She's the pretty blonde with fangs."

"Wow." He shook his head, and while the guy was pale to begin with, his skin blanched even further. He was buying her story. Now, if he'd just give an inch. He sipped the last of his milk, watching her. "Has he fed from you yet?" His gaze flicked to her neck, and she straightened her shoulders.

What could he possibly mean by fed? The mere thought was ludicrous and yet she'd been witness to everything. He never ate normal meals, slept all day, his skin had blistered the afternoon he'd found her in the alley. Of course, sunlight.

No way.

"Savannah?" Broderick pushed for an answer, but her mind remained too fogged to give him one. How much was myth and how much was truth? The crap about wooden stakes, garlic and crucifixes. Too insane, yet the main question resonating was not how vampires even existed, but whether she felt something true or had it been contrived as a critical piece of some expertly planned seduction?

"Shit." He smoothed a hand through his hair and knotted it into a fist. "You didn't know, did you?"

She pursed her lips slightly in an attempt to control any trembling. She'd asked for this, wanted the truth. And yet, she hated the weakness which shook her insides as a result. Crossing her arms, she lifted her chin. "I want a yes or no answer here. Was I meant to live past four weeks?"

* * * *

Luke climbed the stairs to his apartment, taking the menial task to digest everything Lorenzo said. Christ, what was he to do with Savannah? He had not seen her since the morning, but so much had changed in such a short time. Once again, Lorenzo had been proved right. Her seemingly potent blood made a trip back to Boston a suicide mission. He had been careless. His desire to eradicate greed had become an obsession, and it might cost an innocent woman her life. He rubbed his eyes. He could not allow Savannah to pay for his wrongs.

As he neared his door, the scent of another caught him off guard, and he tensed. Not fully vampire yet not completely human either. Broderick, the man he wanted to see. But why would Savannah open the door to a complete stranger?

Luke smoothed his hand over his throbbing arm and slipped a key into the lock. The fact his PI showed up in person versus calling him meant he probably knew about Savannah's blood. Perhaps he'd come to explain why he'd sent him a victim whose blood could burn him to death.

"Luke." Broderick stood diagonal to where Savannah sat on a sofa chair. She wore a white terry cloth robe that nearly matched the pallor of her skin. Her eyes grew wide and her lips trembled. He did not need to be Sherlock Holmes to understand something had happened.

He took off his lightweight coat and laid it on a table as he entered the living room. "Now, does this not look cozy?"

Broderick hung his head then met his gaze. "We need to talk."

"I quite agree," Luke said.

"She told me she knew."

"You know better. You should have known better from the start." Luke inhaled a deep breath. Even as an immortal he had never been able to completely shake the habit of breathing, but nothing eased the immense pressure building in his chest. Uncapping a decanter, he tilted the intricately detailed crystal and poured a glass of whiskey with as much composure as he could muster.

Broderick looked at Savannah then back at him. "I know I fucked up but I've a lot going on. It doesn't excuse it though. For that I'm sorry."

"No, it does not." Turned away from Broderick, he ran a hand through his hair. He had not planned for Savannah to find out about him this way. He sensed her stand behind him. Her breaths were short and the sweet scent of her sweat mingled with that of the whiskey he sipped. "I will not hurt you." He faced her. "I give you my word."

Gaze fixed on him, she took a step back. "I knew you were different."

"After what happened this morning, I believe we can say we are both different."

Broderick frowned. "What happened this morning?"

Savannah bit out a sarcastic laugh. "I wasn't planning on killing you. I'd say your different is a bit extreme, wouldn't you? You're a freaking vampire. A blood-sucking monster—"

"Savannah." Broderick moved toward her.

"No." Luke drank the last of his whiskey and set his glass on a marble side table. "She is right. Still, you should find solace in the fact that I cannot drink from you without risking death."

"Shut up, Luke. She isn't right." Broderick looked at her. "You aren't."

Tears glistened in her eyes, and she shook her head. "How could you let me come to care for you?"

Luke tightened his hands into fists. "I tried to end it before it started. You did not want to hear I am not right for you." The words pained him but they were necessary.

She nodded and wiped at her tears. "What now? Are you going to kill me? Is that why you brought me here?"

"Perhaps I originally intended to, yes." His chest seized. "I did not know you."

"So it's okay?" She took another step back. "I won't make it easy. I promise you."

"You need not fear me."

"You expect me to believe such a blatant lie after everything you told me?"

"If I wanted you dead, you would not have a chance to make it difficult. I admit I brought you to Rome as a victim, but I made a mistake."

Sniffling, she lifted her chin. "I want to leave. I'd like to go back to Boston."

Luke glanced at Broderick, who now leaned against the kitchen island with his head bowed. "It is not a simple situation," Luke said. "You know I am a vampire. You saw what your blood did to my arm this morning."

"Yes." For the first time since he'd entered, her expression turned contrite. She averted her face. "It wasn't on purpose. I don't know what happened."

"Nor I."

Broderick lifted his head, met his gaze.

"That is why you are here," Luke said. "You know something about her blood."

Broderick rubbed the back of his neck. "I think we should discuss this privately." He nodded at Savannah. "She's received enough shocks for one night."

"Don't even try to protect me." She crossed her arms.

"When were you going to tell me the truth about her?" Luke asked.

"I didn't know." Broderick lifted his hands. "I swear. I'm still not sure about everything. I only have hypotheses."

"It is your job to know. I pay you to know."

"I told you I had other concerns." Broderick sighed. "This may take a bit."

"I have time," said Luke.

"You mentioned her blood and your arm." The investigator glanced at Savannah then back at him. "What did you mean?"

Rolling his sleeve up, Luke walked forward and lifted his bandage. Blood seeped from the jagged cuts on his arm.

"Shit," Broderick muttered under his breath. "This is bad."

"I didn't mean to." Savannah rubbed her face. "And I truly did feel miserable about it until I discovered you wanted to kill me."

"This is my fault." Broderick bent his head then looked at her. "Your ex did a damn good job of covering up what happened in your accident. When you answered the ad and I investigated you, you fit the bill perfectly. A snooty gold digger who got burned by an up-and-coming lawyer."

"I see," she said.

But Luke could sense she did not. He could feel her sadness and ached to pull her into his arms. She would never accept a monster. He turned to Broderick. "We have had a trail for the past few days. Do you think the Ancients know about her?"

"Who are the Ancients?" Savannah asked.

"They are law in vampire society," Broderick replied. "You can think of them as the rulers of our world, if you like. Whatever they say goes. If they want something, it's theirs."

"Wait a minute. Are you telling me someone's after us because of my blood? Ridiculous."

Luke cocked a brow. "Is it? What do you think vampires drink? Or did Broderick's history lesson omit minor details about our oh-so-desirable traits?"

She narrowed her emerald gaze. "Still doesn't make any sense. If my blood burns vampires, they wouldn't want to drink it. It might kill them."

Luke sighed. "Exactly, which makes you either a powerful weapon or a dangerous adversary. Vampires do not play games, Savannah. And it does not take a rocket scientist to figure out the possibilities with blood that kills."

A knock interrupted their conversation and Luke turned toward the door. The scent of their caller was human, which surprised him as he rarely had visitors, let alone human ones. "This conversation is not finished. I will be just a moment," he said, walking through to the foyer.

Their caller was plain of face and dress. Veins in his neck pulsed and a couple drops of blood stained his collar. Someone recently had fed from him. He was a blood slave. The male dipped a hand into his jacket pocket, removing a small black card. "I received a message to give you this." He held up the card. "It's for tonight."

Luke accepted the card. One side had two moons, a white one and a red one. The white moon bled several drops of red. He turned it over and read an address. "The Palantine Hill ruins?"

The man nodded. "Yes, sir. The entrance to the underground tunnels is through the ruins. You won't be the only ones there. Follow the crowd through an entrance on Via Fori Imperiali. Arrive around nine tonight."

"What is this for?"

"A blood auction. I am sure you have heard of them. Both your and the woman's presence are requested."

"Who made such a request?" Luke asked.

"I could not say. I was not provided this information." The human's heartbeat remained even, his eyes trained on Luke. He spoke the truth. Was this Lorenzo's way of reaching him?

"Fine. I presume dress is formal?"

"Of course." The man smiled. "Tonight's theme is a masquerade."

"Goodnight." Luke shut the door.

"What did he want?" Savannah stood behind him as he turned around. Her chin lifted in her stubborn way. He could sense her emotional turmoil. Her expression was one of bravado and yet the pulse in her neck beat rapidly. She bit her lip when it trembled beyond her control.

"Our presence is requested tonight."

"I'm not going anywhere."

"I am afraid we do not have a choice."

She bent her head, averted her eyes. "I don't want to be a part of this anymore. I want to go back home," she said in a quiet voice.

"Home no longer exists for you." He moved closer then turned away because it was easier to remain stern when he did not have to face the fear in her eyes. *Coward.* "Do you understand me? There is no going back. Not if you want any chance at a real life."

"I understand you. Doesn't mean I like it."

Chapter 15

If death meant just leaving the stage long enough to change costume and come back as a new character... Would you slow down? Or speed up?
—*Chuck Palahniuk*

No going back. Could she ever really understand? She wasn't sure. The sob building in her chest left no room for air, making her gasp in anguish. A web of tear tracks covered her cheeks, and she buried her face against the soft cotton of her pillows. What had she gotten herself into?

Twisting the ivory silk of her comforter in her hands, she closed her eyes and released soft, controlled breaths. Things could be worse. Right? She might have found herself raped and bloodied on a cobblestone street in Rome. Or worse. She might have bled to death, alone and cold on one Boston winter night.

"Savannah, are you awake?"

Luke. He haunted her even with her eyes closed.

"You are not dressed."

She opened her eyes, tugging the comforter to her chest. Luke stood in the doorway to her room. She hadn't heard him open the door. "I told you I don't want to go anywhere." And the fact he wanted to continue this pretense of her as his companion drove her nuts. "And I know you understood me because your English is beyond excellent."

He entered her room and set a velvet box on her dresser. Another piece of jewelry, to be sure. "And I thought you understood you do not have a choice." For a moment, his eyes seemed to flash burgundy, but when he faced her, they were as dark and fathomless as ever.

Prior to this afternoon, she would have chalked the sight up to some kind of optical illusion. Now, she wasn't so sure. She rubbed her forehead, suddenly lightheaded. Perhaps she had gone off the deep end. No doubt a result of answering the companion ad of a bipolar vampire whom she feared she'd begun to fall for during the past few days. As if that wasn't bad enough, her blood burned him and instead of running like an intelligent woman would, she'd somehow let him convince her she needed his help to protect her from vampire royalty.

"Refresh my memory," she said. "Why do I need to be here?"

"Do not play games with me, Savannah. I never wanted it to get so complicated."

"Lucky me, otherwise I'd be dinner." A prospect she'd rather not dwell on.

A frustrated growl came from him, and his exasperation clearly showed by the muscle pulsing along his jaw. "I will not tell you again, Savannah. Get dressed."

A rebellious retort seemed to curl up on the tip of her tongue as if the words themselves retained more sense than she. Luke's expression hadn't changed—same intrusive stare, same straightened lips. And yet she sensed he'd reached the end of his rope.

"Fine." She stood and took a step toward him. "Do you have a dress color preference this time? Or maybe there is a hairstyle you would find more becoming?"

He closed his eyes a moment then met her gaze. "Since you mention it, the deep lavender dress would suit the event nicely and loose curls will do."

"Damn it." She pushed at his chest. "You won't give an inch will you? Why must we go to this...wherever it is we are going? Answer me. Over the last few days, I've been attacked, screwed my employer, learned you're a vampire and to top it off, you accused me of trying to kill you when in actuality your kind is trying to kill me, use me or whatever. It's been overwhelming to say the least. The last thing I need is you dragging me around and dressing me up like a doll." She wavered, suddenly exhausted with the pendulum of her emotions.

"Sit down, Savannah."

She sat, too tired to argue.

He strode forward, squatted in front of her. "You truly think so ill of this? You believe what we experienced together was a roll through the hay, so to speak?"

"That's all you got from everything I said?" She leaned forward over her thighs. "Vampire, human, it doesn't matter. A man is a man."

"I am sorry I did not admit what I am until now, but considering the circumstances of our meeting, I am sure you can understand my logic. I am no longer a human male and you cannot categorize me as such." He tilted her chin until she met his gaze. "What is it you want from me?"

Life, love and happiness? She could have pinched herself for such wishy-washy thoughts. "I want to know what happens now."

"We go to the masquerade auction and we learn what we can."

"What kind of auction is this, if we must enter through ruins?"

Luke stood. "So you were listening."

"Only to part of what the man said."

"It is a blood auction." He glanced away, breaking the connection with her stare.

Her stomach rolled and she thought she'd be sick. Why had she not expected this? "Of course." She swallowed a wave of nausea. "You have to eat. What was I thinking? I hadn't even considered." Or rather, she'd avoided it.

"I'm not going to drink blood, Savannah." One side of his sensual lips lifted in a knowing smirk. "The auction is for rare blood types. What your blood did to me today, I've never experienced. I don't know any other vampire who has. At the auction, there may be others like you."

"But there'll be other vampires there." It would be like entering shark-infested waters.

"And? You went to Blood Bar multiple times, not to mention the first auction I took you to. Who do you think goes to these events?"

"I went before I realized what you are."

His hands clenched at his sides as he straightened into a stance she'd seen before. Head erect, shoulders back. She wasn't going to change his mind.

"I am not leaving you here," he said.

"What about everything you told me? What if they try something with me?"

He shook his head. "It is a masquerade. They won't know who you are."

"Still vampires can probably sniff out the fact I'm human, right?"

"Clearly. Vampires have highly sensitive senses." He frowned as if she'd asked a silly question.

"Don't look at me like I'm an idiot. You've only proven my point. If they can sense I'm a human, what's to stop them from sinking their fangs into me?"

"You shall go as my blood slave. Unlike humans, we rarely covet possessions of others without permission."

"Wait a minute." She crossed her arms. "Are you telling me I'll be your *possession*, as in a *thing*?"

Luke's mouth curved up slightly on one side. "It is the safest way."

* * * *

"Are you sure you know what you're doing?" Broderick asked. "If it were possible, I'd say this latest stint with Savannah is giving you alcoholic tendencies. What are you on, glass four in the last thirty minutes?"

Fortunately, Broderick had missed his indulgence in Grey Goose last night. "*If* it were possible, I would have to agree." Luke downed the glass of whiskey and leaned his head against the sofa's cushions. "One more thing. After this is done, you are fired."

"Good." Broderick crossed his arms across his chest. "Saves me the trouble of quitting."

"Glad we are on the same page."

Broderick nodded. "So what now?"

"You heard the human messenger," Luke said. "I am taking her to the auction. Would you have me do something else?"

"How about not going?"

If only it were that easy. "None of this is going to stop unless I put an end to it."

"Or the Ancients will put an end to you."

A real possibility but one he would risk. "I will not change my mind."

"So she matters." Broderick stuck a toothpick between his lips and rolled it along with his teeth and tongue.

Luke lifted his head. "Yes, she does."

"I know it doesn't matter as I screwed this up royally, but the ex hid everything pretty well. He has to have some kind of insider connections. I'm talking botched police reports, missing hospital records. On paper, Savannah is a borderline psychopath who made an attempt on her own life by running into the street. A high-strung woman who targeted wealthy men—never mind Whitman didn't have a cent when dating her. None of it makes sense when you dig deep. And before you give me hell, save it. I know I messed up."

No doubt he did know; dark circles marred Broderick's eyes. "You never told me she was a borderline psychopath on paper. In fact, your file explained nothing about an accident."

"I know. I'm not trying to excuse my errors but pages and pages of her medical history were missing. None of it makes sense and I have a feeling I haven't even scratched the surface." Broderick let out a long breath. "What's more is, I haven't heard from Dominique in a couple months."

What was Broderick going on about? Luke stood and paced. "What does your friend have to do with any of this?"

"Nothing, but last I spoke with her she was on assignment in Europe. She usually wouldn't go so long without at least giving me an update." He drove a hand through his hair. "I'm concerned something has happened."

"You should have told me from the beginning you had other things on your mind. Christ, we could have avoided this entire bloody mess."

"Hey now," Broderick said. "This so-called mess started way before Savannah so if we're going to be calling each other out, we might start with the fact you've been too far gone for a long time."

Luke whirled and faced him. "Bollocks. Are we going to begin this game over again? Too far gone for what? Damn you. If you did this as some sort of sick lesson, I swear—"

"Fuck no. It's not a lesson. Although admittedly, yeah, maybe I'm taking a bit of pleasure in the fact you've got to step back from this."

"That is not your—"

"I'm not done," said Broderick. "You're like a ticking time bomb. For the past few months you've been a drone on this greed nonsense. Victoria is gone and has been gone for over two hundred years. To say it's time to move on wouldn't be sufficient. I'm not saying you should forget her, but she would want you to live your life as best you can." His shoulders rose and fell with a restless exertion. Face flushed, he frowned, massaged his temples.

Luke closed his eyes. Two hundred years of vengeance weighed heavily on his shoulders. "Fine. What now? You must have finally done the job I paid you to do originally. Otherwise, you would not be here."

Broderick nodded. "What do you want to know? Shit, there is so much to say I don't even know where to start."

"Everything. Who is she? Was any of the information you gave me true?"

"Yes, a lot of it. She has a history of dating rich men. Her longest relationship besides Ben was with a wealthy art collector. Bit of a strange man, if you ask me. From what I gathered, he thought of Savannah as part of his collection rather than a living, breathing human being. I'm surprised their relationship lasted the few months it did."

No wonder she despised being a trophy. "That explains why she did not like me telling her what to wear."

"Wait," Broderick said, brow furrowed. "You told her what to wear?"

"She asked. And she possesses the same annoying trait of sarcasm you have."

"Probably keeps her sane, especially when dealing with you."

"You can keep side commentary to yourself." Despite Broderick's explanations, why a woman like Savannah would answer a random companion ad was a mystery. She had no problem mingling within society's more exclusive circles. Seemed to feed off wealthy men. And yet, she struck him as neither pretentious nor egoistic. If anything, she behaved in the complete opposite manner. Could it be an act? Or perhaps her accident changed her. "What about the accident? You have yet to mention it."

"Have you asked her about it?"

"I am asking you," said Luke.

"I'm still making sense of it. Her two years in physical therapy were painted as an overdue trip to the psych ward. Forget identity theft. Her ex has replaced her identity completely. But get this." He pulled an iPhone from an inside jacket pocket. "I got two eyewitness accounts stating Mr. Benjamin Whitman was actually quite cozy with his so-called psychotic wife-to-be on the night of the accident. Not what you'd expect to hear, considering he didn't come to visit her once at the hospital."

"The guy sounds like a bastard."

"I'd say you're being kind. I pulled some strings to get this but he sent her flowers via some floral website. Take a look at what his card read." Broderick flipped through a few photos on his iPhone then zoomed in.

Dear Savannah,

Look, there's no easy way to say this... You're in it for the long haul. From what I hear, doctors are estimating a year plus in intense physical therapy. I'm not sure we can handle that. You know, the job and everything... Anyway, I think we should take a break for now.

"Signed the thing *love, Ben. Love*, my ass. I bet he wouldn't know the emotion if it came back and bit him in the neck," Broderick said.

Luke growled. "Do not tempt me." He handed the phone back to Broderick. "If I ever see him, I will drain the prick dry. Although at this moment, I cannot say I am any better. I may have made her a prime target for the Ancients."

"I'm sorry I got her in this mess too." Broderick bowed his head. "And I hate to tell you this but it gets worse."

"What are you talking about?"

Broderick huffed. "Have you ever heard of the Blessed?"

Luke leaned back. He had no idea where this would lead but Broderick's paler than normal complexion did nothing to provide him any comfort. "No. Are they some kind of order?"

"Not really. They're human, just special. Sometimes humans die, stop breathing, caput." Broderick slashed his hands like knives for emphasis. "Some come back."

"You mean near-death experiences."

"Yeah, exactly. Legend says there are those who die long enough to reach heaven. Not everybody does."

Luke nodded, rubbing his chin. "You mean, assuming the Bible is right and it is either eternal happiness or a lake of fire, we are talking those headed for eternal happiness?"

"Actually, I referred to the length of time one must be considered dead, not whether or not they go to heaven—although that's sort of a given." He shrugged. "Anyway, it turns out the magic number is three hundred and thirty-three seconds. Get it? Number three, there's three of them, trinity, et cetera."

"I understand." How often did this sort of thing happen? "Cutting the noose a bit close, is it not? On average, a human brain can only survive up to six minutes without oxygen once the heart stops."

"So I've heard."

"So what goes on with these Blessed? They reach heaven and what happens?"

Broderick shrugged. "No one seems to know. All my answers seemed to get skewed. One guy said they came back with good powers, another mentioned they can perform miracles of healing, which is usually considered good. Still, the answers were vague except for this one lady. Um, a…Lady Claire. She's some psychic in Queens who owns a tiny dark arts book store. She told me blood from a Blessed is sacred and was used in ancient times to destroy evil."

"Does she know this for a fact? Has she ever met one of these Blessed?"

Broderick shook his head. "No, I asked her." He stuck a hand inside his jacket and pulled out a folded piece of paper, yellowish and stained like it belonged to an old book. "But she did tell me to give my friend this."

Luke took the thin paper and opened it up. The illustration was detailed with colored ink. Something one would see in an older history text. A battle took place on the page, coming to life through the pained expressions of several fallen knights. Vampires, if he were to go by their flawless skin and the exaggerated length of their canines. A young male stood over them, one arm sliced open as it dripped blood on the damned creatures. His other hand clutched a sword. "I assume this boy is a Blessed."

Broderick nodded. "Read the caption."

"*Immortalis nex*. Latin for immortal death. You think this is Savannah? You believe she is here to kill immortals?"

"Doesn't matter what I think or even whether she is capable of this." He pointed to the page. "If the Ancients believe she is a Blessed, they will hunt for her." Broderick stood. "Take her to the auction tonight. See what you can learn, but be careful. I've a few phone calls to make."

Chapter 16

Nothing in life is to be feared. It is only to be understood.
—*Marie Curie*

To Luke's pleasure and surprise, Savannah complied with the deep lavender dress and loose curls. Light lavender crystals covered the scars across her clavicle. The color complimented the soft glow of her skin and as expected, drew stares from those around them. Admittedly, more stares than he cared for. The silver mask she wore hid three quarters of her face, lending a mysterious sensuality to her.

"What is this place?" Savannah turned and scanned the underground chamber. "I mean, I can see we started in some type of ruins but I would never have guessed there was so much beneath them. Not to mention, we probably shouldn't be here."

"You need not worry. I promise not to turn you over to the city authorities."

"I didn't think you would." She twisted her lips as her brows drew together. "I can't imagine your kind answers to *mere* human authorities."

Another sarcastic barb. Savannah had been making them since they left his apartment. It could be worse. At least she no longer refused to do everything he requested. A small victory, but a victory nonetheless. He could not hope to convince her it repulsed him to be inside his predator's body or that he drove himself mad with prolonged periods of fasting. She saw him as a monster, but he could hardly expect otherwise. "I would never call humans mere, but you are right in thinking my kind answers to no one."

Savannah crossed her arms over her chest, walking slightly ahead of him. "So what is this place, anyway?"

She avoided probing further about vampires, which made him heave a sigh. If she preferred small talk, he would be happy to acquiesce. "Many believe Palantine Hill to be the origin of Rome. Mostly it was known as a place for the wealthy to live due to its proximity to power and splendid views. In regards to the underground tunnels, I could not say if those were built prior to the establishment of Rafe's blood market or not. Rome has been rebuilt many times and there are vast ruins beneath it."

She came to a stop beside him. "They're looking at us."

"I am sorry, my dear, but you are wrong." He hesitated then placed a hand along the small of her back. She shivered beneath his touch and yet her skin warmed. "They are not staring at us, they are staring at you. You are stunning."

Her skin flushed pink and she lifted a shoulder. "Flattery toward your *lowly* blood slave will not gain you forgiveness."

He'd expected as much, but still it stung. "I would not ask or presume that to be the case. I speak the truth without hidden agenda." He lifted her hand and tucked it into the crook of his arm. He would be patient, waiting for her acceptance. For some inexplicable reason, it mattered to him. "Tonight, I request you do your utmost to withstand me. Your role requires affection between us as my kind treats our blood slaves with reverence."

"Why call them slaves?"

"Ego. We are vain creatures." He swept a hand out for her to walk ahead of him. "Take a seat in the second row."

She sat, bent low to his ear. "What exactly are we going to watch?"

"As in any auction, an auctioneer will describe items and auction them off to the highest bidder. The only difference is the subject matter."

"The only difference, really?" she asked.

"I believe so. There may be some demonstrations."

She frowned. "What do you mean, you believe? You haven't been to one of these before?"

"No, Savannah. Contrary to your assumptions, I am quite different from the blood-sucking monster you have me pegged as." Or so he would like to believe.

She laughed, and the rhythm of it danced through him, yet he sensed bitterness rolling through her. "No, I assume nothing about you. I believe I've learned my lesson in making assumptions." She let her gaze trail down his length and back up to his face. "I seem to be a magnet for impossible relationships."

He leaned forward, trailed a finger along the side of her face. "Is that why you ache to run? Even now, I sense tremors moving through you. Is it fear or desire that frightens you?"

Outlined by her silver mask, her startling eyes were piercing. She breathed in deep and exhaled a shaky sigh. "Maybe both. I knew you were different since I first laid eyes on you. I never imagined how different."

"And yet you stayed."

She nodded. "Yes, I did. You can call it whatever you want—ignorance, greed, desperation. I call it living. I made a promise to myself to keep fighting and if it included answering an ad to make money and pay off my debts, so be it. Doesn't mean I belong in your world."

This, he could agree on. "Somehow I will release you from your confines here. I swear it."

Hope shown within her eyes even as her lashes dropped, breaking their connection.

"Luke, nice of you to join us." Rafaelo Costa approached, pausing to fix his silver stare on Savannah. "And who is your lovely guest?"

As if he did not know. Annoyed at having their conversation interrupted, Luke stood and lifted Savannah by her hand. "Rafe, meet Savannah. Savannah, Rafe."

"A pleasure." Rafe lifted Savannah's hand, gently kissed the smooth skin on top then faced him. "You've been keeping secrets."

The muscles throughout Luke's back bunched. Of the three Ancients, Rafe kept most to himself, which only made Luke wary. Still, most vampires would find it beneath them to confront another in public. He smiled. "Some treasures are best kept as secrets lest they lose their value."

"Touche." Rafe tilted his head, rubbed Savannah's hand with his thumb, which he hadn't yet released. "Enjoy the auction, my dear." He bowed and left.

Savannah sat and massaged her fingers. "Why did he hold my hand for so long?"

"He is an Ancient with many abilities. Through touch, he can read minds, thoughts and memories." Luke took his seat beside her.

"So he read my mind?"

At this point, the Ancient probably knew everything about her. "I would bet he knows more about you than you do about yourself."

She shuddered. "Are all of you capable of such power?"

"No, we are unique—like humans. We each have different talents, but most do not develop until we have attained a certain age."

"And how old is Rafe?"

Luke shook his head. "No one knows. I would estimate him to at least have a couple millennia under his belt. Do not worry," he said, and placed a hand on her thigh. "I will protect you." Or he would die trying.

Savannah nodded but her posture remained stiff.

Lights dimmed around them except for one bright light above a stage with an altar on it. The audience sat in a half circle around the rounded platform.

"Now what?" She leaned back in her chair, legs crossed.

"We watch, listen and wait."

* * * *

Savannah couldn't have imagined blood contained so many unorthodox properties. And these vampires auctioned it off like self-proclaimed merchants cashing in their ticket to wealth. They offered up everything from bloods which supposedly tasted sweeter, helped indigestion, and maintained longer arousal to blood that served as an aphrodisiac or increased physical strength. Hilarious claims, under any other circumstances.

She hadn't yet heard about any kind of blood burning through skin and muscle. She clenched her hands as she recalled the image of Luke's sizzling skin.

"You are cold." Luke bent close, rubbed her back. "It is almost over."

"I'm fine," she lied, pulling away from his touch. Her terse tone wouldn't help anything. His affection was only an act. She knew that but couldn't help her reactions. She hated the thought she wanted more from him. How could she desire him? Not only had he lied to her from the start, he wasn't even human.

Interrupting her thoughts, Luke cupped the back of her neck with one hand, drew her close and kissed her. His lips, firm yet soft, teased and scolded in the same instance. His tongue hinted at many pleasures awaiting her. When he pulled away, she ached to follow with her mouth, to press her mouth to his, but some small shred of sanity intervened, stopping her from making an even greater fool of herself.

He didn't say anything further. He didn't have to. With his midnight stare, he warned her not to fight him.

As the auction finished, attendees stood and left. Eager to follow the crowd and avoid being alone with Luke, she rose.

"Did you not find what you were looking for?" Rafe approached.

Savannah tried hard not to shy away. Something about the male seemed overpowering and the black velvet mask covering one side of his face only added to his mysteriousness.

"I am not sure what you are referring to," Luke said, appearing calm despite the tension she sensed emanating from him.

Rafe stared, his gaze unnerving, as it seemed to burn through them and see too much. He was insanely handsome with dark hair and silver-gray eyes, but his watchfulness and overwhelming presence frightened her. Luke had introduced him as an Ancient. How many humans had he killed in his lifetime? She shivered at the thought.

Luke's hand braced the small of her back, his touch electric, intimate.

"Come with me." Rafe signaled they follow him down a stone corridor. Torches lit the walls, reminding her of some Indiana Jones flick. Luke pushed her along, and she bit her tongue to keep from asking questions. She wasn't used to so much restraint but the quieter she was, the safer she'd be. From what she'd observed of other blood slaves, they followed a *seen and not heard* motto.

"In there." Rafe paused before a dark entrance, his lips curved into a sly smile as he met her gaze. "Don't worry, it's not all dark. And Luke won't leave you alone. You'll see a light once you go around the tunnel's curve." He turned to leave.

"What about you?" Luke asked.

"Don't concern yourself with me. I will see you soon." He walked away.

Hesitating to step where she couldn't see, she inched forward. Rafe knew she feared being alone. Had he seen the night she was hit amongst her memories? Did he know Ben had abandoned her? She hugged her bare arms and took a step into darkness.

Luke moved ahead. "Stay close." He pulled her to his side, his hand trailing over her left hip. An undeniable spark moved up her side.

She cleared her throat and breathed easy at the feel of his touch. He knew also. He might not admit it, but somehow sensed her fear. Somehow such a realization left her feeling more vulnerable than Rafe's probing into her mind. "How can you see anything? It's pitch black here." She followed with careful, slow steps, gripping his bicep.

"Our eyes are different than yours. We can see better at night."

Another reminder of their differences and yet his presence provided some measure of safety in the darkness. She pressed her finger harder against the flesh of his arm, pulling him closer. "I don't have a good feeling about this. Do you have any idea what awaits us at the end of this tunnel?" The thud of her heart pounded a faster, erratic rhythm.

"No," he said. "But Rafe wants something. He would not have let us go, either way. At least now I have some time to decide what I need to do next."

Savannah released a lengthy sigh. His admission he didn't know what was going on did nothing to soothe her unease. Her only comfort was, whatever waited for them in this dank, black passageway couldn't be worse than what she'd been through over the past couple years.

Chapter 17

Promises are like the full moon, if they are not kept at once they diminish day by day.
—German Proverb

Luke gently patted Savannah's thigh as she shifted in her seat. "They'll be starting soon enough."

"That's what I'm worried about. This isn't exactly the most inviting of places."

He tried to see it from her point of view. A circular space with a platform in the middle. Black velvet curtains fell from the ceiling, hiding all but a foot around the perimeter of the platform. Lit sconces protruded from the stone walls every few feet and between them, arched entryways led to dark tunnels—similar to the one they'd entered through. The space certainly wasn't cozy. If anything, it felt dark and secretive. "You're right, in that it doesn't make one feel welcome, but I'm sure it serves its purpose as far as secrecy."

"I guess. I still think there has to be a better way to get here," she said. "If not, they should build safer passages. It's completely illogical to wander through the dark when it's obvious these vampires have means to design a bright, comfortable hallway."

"Bright, comfortable hallways hardly provide secrecy," he said. "Rome is an immense network underground. But don't worry, we shall not stay much longer." He understood her discomfort, but beyond Rafe's indirect order, Luke had his reasons for staying. As Lorenzo suggested, he needed to know what he dealt with in regards to Savannah's blood.

She rubbed the flesh along her upper arms. "These auctions are monstrous. I don't understand how you could bring me here."

Several guests turned their heads and stared at them. He chuckled, pretending she'd told the cleverest of jokes. "Keep your voice down, dear. Despite the unusual tone of this auction, I would not call it monstrous.

We are quite civilized beings." He could not explain the sudden need to defend his kind. Most times he would have agreed with her.

"Civilized? You use our blood for home remedies and erotic drugs. Almost every vampire here is accompanied by at least one blood slave. What about that is civilized?"

"For God's sake, Savannah," he ground out, temper flaring at her attack. "The list of humanity's wrongs is beyond comparison. Need I mention the Holocaust, the Crusades, slavery? Even today, women and children are trafficked through countries to use as prostitutes. Human sweat, sickness and toil cranks out luxury toaster ovens for a merciless class of wealth. And if any rise up to rebel they become martyrs to a so-called cause. What cause? Do not lecture me on being civilized when your kind is far from it."

"I understand."

"Do you?" he asked, his tone harsher than intended.

"Yes," she whispered. "I hadn't thought about what we've done as a race."

Her sorrowful expression made him feel quite the cad. "Forgive me. My intention was neither to chastise you nor to have you believe we are saints. We have our vices and we are damned creatures for a reason, but like humans, not all of us choose to be such."

She frowned, appearing far from convinced.

"I want to help you, Savannah." He cupped her cheek, forcing her to meet his gaze then dropped his hand. After what she'd experienced, asking her to trust him pushed limits. "I know my words currently have no meaning, but I will show you, somehow." He gently squeezed her hand.

The curtains lifted, revealing two nude women on a raised stage.

"What is going on? Why are they chained up?" Savannah pushed forward in her seat, biting her bottom lip.

His grip kept her from standing. "No, they are willing participants."

"Willing? Why?" she asked.

"My assumption would be due to the pay received for their services."

"No amount could be enough," she whispered beneath her breath.

Luke turned away so she could not see his grim expression. How ironic her words were since he now understood what type of woman she was.

"Is something wrong?"

"Not at all." He cleared his throat, sensed her unease and did not fault her. The sight before them would be disturbing to anyone unaccustomed to society's darker tastes. One of the women was a vampire, who due to her strength lay shackled to an altar. The other, a human, hung held by chains spilling from the ceiling, a life-sized puppet meant to test their vices. Females displayed like props in a macabre play.

"Thank you, ladies and gentlemen, for joining us tonight." A tall, dark-haired male strolled opposite the small group and climbed the stairs of the raised stage. "I am Armand and will be your host. In this more intimate setting, you've been invited to witness the abilities of some of our more rare blood samples. These too will be up for auction, however, for privacy's sake, I ask you to hold your bids for everything until afterward. Bids will be made anonymously." He turned and signaled the bound females. "A special thanks to our guests for their participation tonight. Carmina is the human blood slave you see hanging in chains and Lena is our vampire. And now, let us begin."

As before, lights dimmed. Only a bright spotlight shone down, highlighting the nude women.

"We shall start with a highly potent aphrodisiac." Armand dipped a slim dropper into a glass vial. With only a few drops administered orally, the vampire, Lena, writhed in place. Within minutes, her movements grew hurried, her hips undulated as she whimpered.

"What's wrong?" Savannah asked.

"I am not sure she would think anything is wrong. I imagine she is nearing a climactic state. An orgasm."

Even beneath muted lighting, he could discern the flush that tinged the tops of Savannah's cheeks.

"I see," she said.

Armand ran a hand through the air over Lena's body. "Right now, Lena is in a near-tortured state, as she is restrained and unable to release herself. The mere whisper of my hand over her tickles her skin, but if I were to touch her here..." He caressed one of her protruding nipples with his palm and she arched up, crying out with her release. "You see, with one brush of my skin against hers, she is mine to command."

Savannah trembled alongside Luke.

"You feel her." He sensed Savannah's heightened breaths, her arousal. And behind them, shame.

She turned away from the stage. "No."

"It is natural to feel aroused."

"Don't be absurd."

Although the desire to elicit further feelings from her tempted him, he let the subject go. Images of their night together came to him, of Savannah's daring, her thighs embracing his hips as she coaxed a climax from him. Hardness against softness. He closed his eyes briefly then turned and watched the stage.

Armand still spoke. "This same amount of blood administered to a human would remain in effect for hours," he said as his gaze swept the crowd, lingering on Savannah a moment longer than Luke liked. "Since we do not have an abundance of time, I regret we can't show you such a lengthy test." He smiled as the crowd chuckled. "However, I will now demonstrate the healing properties of our next sample. Watch carefully Carmina's reaction."

Armand took out a knife then dragged the blade up the human's stomach, plunging it deep through her ribs. Carmina screamed. Her face cringed and paled as her breathing labored. Savannah's hand came to rest on Luke's thigh. "I think I'm going to be sick."

He wrapped an arm around her shoulders, tugging her against his chest. "Everything will be okay."

"I have mortally wounded her, puncturing a lung. Without help, she will die." Armand removed a vial from inside his coat and opening the cap, poured several drops onto Carmina's open wound. A bright light covered her body and color returned to her face. Within a minute, she lifted her head and tugged on the chains.

"So you see, a few drops of blood and this human is stronger than before I harmed her person."

The audience clapped and whispered with appreciation. Armand demonstrated several other samples with flourish but none interested Luke as much as the one with healing properties. He fingered the bandage on his arm, annoyed to find such a small movement pained him. His injury was indeed serious and although he preferred not to think about it, he could not help but wonder whether this blood could cure a vampire. And if it did, what would Rafe request in exchange? He glanced at Savannah's still profile. Despite his predicament and lacking resolution, he refused to hand her over.

As the auction ended, the room grew brighter. Vampires and their blood slaves rose from their seats, approaching Armand with questions regarding blood samples and the bidding process.

"Did you enjoy this auction more?" Rafe stood a few feet away from them. A smile played on his lips.

"Quite interesting." Luke turned toward Savannah, noticed the pallor of her face below the edge of her mask. "But I believe we shall be calling it a night." He held out his hand to her, and she slipped hers within it.

"Do you mean to tell me nothing interested you?" Rafe asked.

Enough of riddle-like, mysterious questions. The vampire was hardly a type to avoid confrontation so his sly manner did not become him. "What is it you want?"

"I know of your wounds. I could smell them when you arrived." He tsk-tsked. "The scent of rotting vampire flesh is unnatural. So unnatural, most would not recognize it. I've only come across it a few times before but I would never forget the smell."

Savannah stiffened beside him. Luke squeezed her hand in reassurance. "How do I know the blood you have will even work?"

Rafe shrugged. "You don't. Neither do I."

Not much of a sales pitch, if the Ancient desired some kind of exchange. "I believe our time here has come to an end." Luke took a step, tugging Savannah with him.

Rafe moved aside. "You don't have many options."

"And? You are not requiring funds, so what is the purpose of your ramblings?"

"Careful, Evans. I don't tolerate rudeness." Rafe's gaze raked over Savannah then he reached and tipped up her mask. "Exquisite." He closed his eyes and sniffed the air. "And her blood smells sweet. I can see why she has been so hard for you to resist."

"I'll ask you once more. What is it you want?"

"An exchange," Rafe answered. "A vial of her blood for a vial of the curative blood."

"No." Savannah backed away.

"She's outspoken, isn't she?" He turned to her. "You weren't always so open though, were you? I'd say the change is better for you."

God help him. Rafe's question reminded him that with a mere touch, the Ancient had seen enough of Savannah's past to know who she'd been and who she'd become. Luke would give the world to truly know her, to be completely sure he'd made the right decision in helping her. Instead he was put to the test, learning to trust again when he'd thought the capability beyond him. "She has made a decision. I will not exchange her blood."

"Fine." The Ancient waved a hand nonchalantly. "But your wound will only grow more painful and infection will spread with time."

"I thank his lordship for the counsel." Luke bowed in respect and took Savannah's hand. "Good night."

"No. Wait." She rushed forward.

"Leave it alone," he said.

Instead of listening to him, she approached Rafe. "Do you mean his wound will get worse instead of healing?"

"Of course. To his body, your blood is venom. It will slowly destroy him."

"If I were to give you a vial of my blood, do you promise me Luke would be cured?" she asked, her emerald eyes pleading.

"I meant what I said earlier," Rafe said. "I have no idea as to the blood's effects on a vampire."

"But there is a chance, right?" She looked back and forth between him and Rafe. "I'll do it."

"No," Luke said.

Rafe cupped Savannah's chin. He held her gaze for several moments. "A vial of your blood for a vial of the healing blood. You have my word."

Luke gripped Savannah's wrist. "I said no."

She yanked her arm back and spoke to Rafe. "You have yourself a deal."

Chapter 18

Gratitude is when memory is stored in the heart and not in the mind
—Lionel Hampton

"What in bloody hell do you think you are doing?" Luke's eyes burned fiery red.

"What do you think? You don't expect me to leave you with rotting flesh? If it spreads, you could die." She shook her head. "Again." Savannah lifted her chin, her mouth twisted in its familiar stubborn frown. "As strange as it feels to say such an absurdity, I'm not going to let it happen."

"It is not your concern."

"Well, according to you, nothing is my concern, but I can't—I won't leave you hurt when I can do something about it." She averted her gaze.

Why did it matter? Was it a feeling of responsibility, the decent thing to do? The Savannah he'd come to know would take this on as an act of kindness, but he was not inclined to receive charity. Although her blood burned him, he'd initiated everything by publishing a companion ad. "I do not need you as a protector."

"Men." She threw up her arms. "Obviously it doesn't matter what species you belong to. Why won't you ever let us help you?"

Rafe slipped a hand in his pocket and removed a vial. "I'll give you two some space."

"No, wait." Savannah pushed forward, swept up her silky shawl and exposed the pale underside of her wrist. "Here."

"Savannah." Luke grabbed her arm. He could not let her go through with this. She understood neither Rafe nor the vampire world. The Ancient saw her memories. He knew what her blood was capable of. Giving him a vial of her blood would only secure her capture. She would never make it back to Boston—let alone out of Rome—alive.

"My lord." Armand approached Rafe then lowered his voice. "It appears we have a problem."

Luke could sense panic in Armand. The vampire was nervous. "What kind of problem?" he asked.

"We are being attacked. We don't yet know what they want." Armand's gaze strayed to Savannah then back to Rafe. "They are mostly vampires and a few humans."

Luke's temper flared as he considered the fact he may have walked Savannah into a trap. Had this been planned? "What is the meaning of this?"

Rafe's fangs lengthened and his eyes glowed a deep red. The color of blood. "I don't know but I intend to find out. I imagine I'm not the sole contender for her blood." He nodded in Savannah's direction then turned toward Armand. "Take a couple guards and secure the perimeter."

"Yes, sir." Armand hurried from the room.

Screams sounded from outside the walls of the room. Luke could not pinpoint their origin, due to their echo.

"You both need to come with me," Rafe said.

Luke tensed, ready to face off with the Ancient if necessary. He edged forward in front of Savannah. "I think not. How do we know your intention is not to harm her?"

"Harm her?" Rafe frowned. "If I wanted either of you dead, I would have done it long ago."

"Someone has been hunting us," Luke said.

"Not I." He sighed. "It isn't Drago either. He finds your travel companion ads a nuisance and a possible media issue if your games got out of hand, but he currently has larger interests. And Cybele would never send someone to hunt you, as she relishes the hunt too much to do so." Rafe's fangs disappeared and the pomegranate color of his eyes faded to an icy gray as he gazed at Savannah. "Right now, neither of them know about you or your…attributes. If they did, you wouldn't be standing here. And yet, you haven't the slightest clue what you are."

Though her fear filled his senses, she lifted her chin and placed her hand on his arm. "What am I? Why don't you tell me since you seem to know everything about me?"

"Your mind doesn't want to accept what you are yet, which is why you can't remember what happened. What I know could be unimportant to you. I've only scented your kind of blood once before. It happened over two decades ago but I remember it as if it were this morning."

"I want to know more," she said.

"Now is not the time," Luke wrapped an arm around her as shouts rang out. Their attackers neared and a wave of aggression flooded the room. "They're too close." He couldn't risk Savannah getting hurt in any crossfire.

"He's right." Rafe started toward an exit. "We'll need to find you a safe escape route."

Luke paused and scanned the room. Someone else had joined them. The steely odor of their body hung heavy in the air. "Wait." He held up a hand.

Savannah's eyes widened. Her chest lifted and fell with her shaky breaths. "Do you think they'd come here for me?"

"Bloody hell." Luke did not know whether he'd seen the barrel of the revolver first or had felt the bullets' vibrations. His only thought as he pushed Savannah aside was her safety.

As he collided with her, sandwiching her between him and Rafe, she gasped. The three of them hit the ground and rolled for cover. Luke's injured arm took the brunt of the impact, and he sucked in a sharp breath as pain pulsated through his torso. Rafe's men poured into and out of the room, pursuing shooters. The sounds of footsteps and shouts faded. Savannah's heartbeat thundered in the quiet. She lifted her head. "Is it over?"

He wanted to remain on the ground with her in some sort of semi-embrace, but he had to move quickly. "I doubt it." If anything, the danger was just beginning.

Someone hissed. Several feet away from them, Armand lay on the ground, jerking with tremors.

"Oh God." Savannah pushed herself up onto her hands and knees then sat back on her heels. "Is he going to make it?"

"Not likely," he said and rushed over to the injured vampire.

"But how? I don't understand. You're vampires." Brows knit, she held the back of her right hand to her mouth. "I don't feel good."

"You need air." Rafe came to his knees then stood. "They used silver. In large quantities, it can rot our bodies but we might save him yet." He met Luke's gaze. "You reacted quickly. Your powers grow strong for one so young." *Take her and go. You're free, for now. Move.*

Rafe's expression held no gratitude, but the words whispered through Luke's mind were enough to assure him the Ancient would not be a threat tonight. "Which is the fastest exit?"

"You two can leave through there." He pointed to one of the arched entryways. "And exit via one of the back tunnels. I'll make sure you are left alone."

Luke did not pause to question anything, but took Savannah's hand and led her through the entryway and down a dark, narrow passageway.

"Are you sure we'll be safe here?" Her voice shook.

"We have no choice." He did not want to consider why Rafe let them go or whether there would be consequences. Instead, he squeezed Savannah's hand in an attempt to comfort her. "Stay close."

Water dripping down stone walls and the clacking of her heels echoed between the walls. Her breaths were light but quick. "Thank you."

"For what?"

"For saving my life once again."

He smiled at the reluctance in her voice and the irony of the situation. Tonight had turned into a holy mess and yet he had never felt so right. "I would never have let anything happen to you."

She nodded, and he could hear her hesitation when she said, "He didn't say thank you."

A laugh bubbled up within him. "Who? You could not possibly mean Rafe?"

"Why not?"

"He is an Ancient." Luke turned, only to catch her frown. She did not understand, Rafe's status alone made him exempt from explanations. "In your society, do the rich explain away their mistakes?"

She laughed. "What mistakes."

"Exactly." He nodded. "Letting us go without insisting on a sample of your blood was his show of gratitude. Not to mention, it would take more than a few rounds of silver bullets to bring him to his knees."

"I guess. What did he mean by you reacting quickly and your powers?"

"I felt the intruders' emotions, their presence." If he had not reacted with speed, he did not want to imagine what could have happened. "It is unusual for our kind to have such abilities at what we would term a young age. Kind of like a newborn who can crawl."

"I see." She paused, pulling at her bottom lip with her front teeth. "Can I ask you another question and get an honest answer?"

"I will do my best."

"Who do you think would take such a risk and attack us when we're with an Ancient? If they're as powerful as you've described, wouldn't that be suicide?"

He had not caught more than a glimpse of the shooters' faces but one male looked vaguely familiar, reminiscent of someone he'd seen at Blood Bar. "I am hesitant to say, as I know the Ancients have made many enemies. Still, one shooter looked familiar. I do not know him but Lorenzo might."

"Shit." Savannah tripped, crashing into his back. Her hands floundered as she tried to catch her balance.

"I have you." Luke turned and steadied her with a hand to her waist. Heat from her skin seeped through the material of her dress into his palm. Her skin tingled beneath his touch.

"I'm sorry, I can't see," she said.

"Let me be your eyes. Walk ahead. I promise to keep you safe." He guided her forward, wondering whether the next few weeks would make a liar out of him.

Chapter 19

The guilty one is not he who commits the sin, but the one who causes the darkness.
—Victor Hugo

A wave of shudders moved through Savannah as she tiptoed on a bed of crushed stones, Luke's hand steering her through the blackness ahead. A cool breeze whistled past, and deep bass pulsated around them. "Music?"

"We must be walking beneath a club," he said. "I felt a rush of air. An exit should be near."

A tremor of disappointment lanced through her that this moment's intimacy would soon end. Ridiculous, she had such thoughts. They were walking through a dank, dark tunnel and only hours ago, she'd found out Luke had been planning to kill her. And yet, he hadn't so much as attempted it in the many days they'd passed together. Not to say there hadn't been opportunities...

"What is it?" He turned her around, ran a hand over her face, neck and shoulder. "You are shaking. Are you all right?"

No. Yes. She shook her head, not trusting her ability to speak or the complex feelings built up inside her.

"Savannah?"

She searched out his face in the dark, unable to see him but sensing his nearness. "Why didn't you kill me?" She wanted to know. She didn't care about the fact she stood with a vampire in the dark. What mattered was hearing some sort of answer, some sort of reason to convince her all she'd felt between them hadn't been a hoax.

"I do not kill innocents, not if I can help it."

"I'm far from innocent." She bent her head. "I enjoyed some of it. I liked wealth." She'd enjoyed the limelight with Ben. The expensive dinners, impromptu trips and beautiful clothes he'd bought her. The extras—superficial as they were—had only made his denial hurt more.

Worse than the pain of crushed bones and a year and a half of therapy. She caressed her left hand where his ring had once lain. *A beautiful emerald like her eyes*, he'd said. Lies.

"No sadness." Luke brushed her jaw line and she leaned into his touch, closed her eyes. "You do not understand how beautiful you truly are."

How she wanted to believe him. She coughed a nervous laugh as he eased forward, one hand still wrapped around her waist while with the other, he tucked her hair behind her ear. He moved to kiss her and the darkness around them only made this knowledge more thrilling. *Back away.*

"Savannah." He crushed his lips, moist and soft, over hers.

Butterflies fluttered deep within her core. This was wrong and could only lead to more pain. But how could she deny what felt right and good? Her mouth opened to him, inviting him in. Then she floated, flying through nothingness and yet filled with everything. Her hands moved behind her, found a grip along the wet wall. It didn't matter she couldn't see. As long as she could feel his lips, his hands. He nipped her jaw, and another breeze whistled around them, coaxing the tips of her breasts into hardened points as they pressed through the thin material of her dress. Clasping the zipper pressed against her back, she tugged it down, freeing herself enough to slide the fluttery sleeves off her shoulders. She cupped the mounds of her breasts, enjoyed the weight of them in her hands. "Kiss me here."

As he laved the flesh of one nub, rolling it into fiery ecstasy, a gasp escaped her. He shoved her dress up her thighs, and she wrapped her legs around him, pulled him closer then he gripped her rear with one hand, rubbed the lips covering her wet core with the other. She moaned, relishing his touch.

"Ah, there we go." He slipped his index and middle fingers between her folds. Tingles traveled through her, making her knees weak. Holy Hell. She pressed her body upward and leaned her head back, letting tension ease from her body. Strands of her hair clung to her lips. Her eyelids grew heavy.

"So wet, so beautiful." He pumped in and out of her, his smooth palm grinding against her clit. The chill of his skin heightened her senses, leaving goose bumps along her limbs.

"Luke." Her body hummed beneath his touch. She saw herself, strapped to an altar like the vampire Lena had been, and didn't feel shame, only ecstasy. Behind closed eyelids, she played out the fantasy. Back arched above the stone, she rolled her hips faster and faster. She tossed her head from side to side, and he hovered over her. His canines scraped the skin of her neck and chest as he kissed her hungrily. *More.*

Urgency pushed her. Wrapping her arms around him, she tried to show him her need but instead he stilled. *No!* she wanted to scream.

He wrapped a hand over her mouth and held it there. "No," he groaned, lowered her to the ground, pulled her zipper up. Her fantasy dissipated and the small space between them felt vast. "We must go. Someone approaches." He gripped her hand and tugged her forward.

Icy fingers of fear crept up her neck. "Who is it?"

"I do not know. I sense a vampire...maybe a human or both, but they are too far for me to identify. Walk forward, I am right behind you."

She did as he asked, not because it was her preference but because she trusted him and she grew exhausted of fighting her attraction. An impossible attraction. They were too different. And yet for some reason she wasn't ready to let go. Another acknowledgement she wasn't anxious to investigate.

* * * *

"Damn it to hell, where have you both been?" Broderick paced the foyer of Luke's apartment as he and Savannah entered.

"Pardon me?" Luke asked. What had put Broderick's panties in such a bind?

"Oh, cut the polite British bull. I placed feelers out tonight and got word from my contacts there was an attack at the auction." He pointed a finger at him. "You should have called."

"It was not foremost on my mind." Luke removed his coat and hung it on a coat rack before he entered the living room. Broderick followed. "There was some trouble tonight," Luke said. "As you can see, we remain unscathed." He poured a couple glasses of whiskey.

"You still got me worked up for nothing. I went down there searching for you both. Besides." He flung a finger toward Savannah. "She looks stunned. You at least owe me an explanation."

She looked glassy-eyed and her cheeks were flushed, lips plump from his hard kisses. He swallowed at the memory, turning to hide any arousal that might make itself evident in his face or person. Stunned would not be how he would describe Savannah. Still, he indulged Broderick and poured a third glass of whiskey. He held it out to her. "Here, this will make you sleep." Something he would be hard pressed to find.

She approached and took the glass without a word, then sat on his sofa.

"I apologize for inconveniencing you, Broderick, but Rafe detained us before allowing us escape through an underground tunnel." He rubbed his neck and averted his gaze. "The exit demanded some navigation and we took back streets to avoid catching unwanted attention."

Broderick's gaze flicked between him and Savannah. "I see. It was no inconvenience." He grabbed his glass. "So what did good old Rafe have to say? Did he auction off any kind of cure for your arm?"

"Oh no." Savannah stood. "We forgot about your arm."

"I did not forget," Luke said. "Blasted thing hurts like the devil." He rolled up the sleeve of his collared shirt and unwound the blood-soaked gauze covering his wounds. "We dealt with more pressing matters."

Savannah glanced at the gashes in his forearm and sat back down. "This is my fault. If I had known..."

She faded fast. "Give us a moment," he said to Broderick then slipped his good arm around her and lifted her off the sofa, supporting her as she walked. She complied without protest and laid her head against his chest. So small, next to him. As he guided her down the hall to her room, he kissed her temple, resisting an urge to kiss her lips, as he might not be able to stop himself from going further.

"You can leave me here," she said.

He paused outside her door and let her warmth part from his body. "Are you sure you do not need help getting ready for bed?"

Face flushed, she smoothed a hand over her dress. "No. I don't think that's a good idea right now."

Right. What was he thinking? He should be thinking about how to extract her from the mess of his world, not dragging her deeper into it. He looked down, smiled. "Believe it or not, I only considered your state of mind. Nevertheless, you are right."

"It's more a matter of getting sleep after everything tonight and...you know...we have a guest."

He nodded. "I better go talk to Broderick and calm his anxiety. Come get me if you need anything."

"Yeah, I will." She stepped back as he headed down the hall. "Luke." He turned.

"We need to contact Rafe about the blood for your arm."

How could he ever have thought this woman selfish? "Do not worry yourself about me. Sleep well." He continued down the hall toward the living room.

"Sleeping like a rock?" Broderick glanced up as Luke entered the living room.

"I hope so. I did not stay to make sure."

Broderick grinned. "Bet you're giving that decision second thoughts."

Luke snatched up his glass of whiskey and sipped. "Rubbish."

"Aw, come on, man. You can't chalk this up to saving the innocent. Since when did you become a superhero? You care. Admit it."

"She is a good woman. I already told you she matters." Christ, he could not afford to care.

"Yeah, and I'm sure it's her *good* side keeping you up at night." Luke opened his mouth to object but Broderick shook his head and continued. "Save it. I'll give you time to adjust because you've tried to forget you have feelings for over two hundred years. I'm going to catch some shuteye, if you don't mind."

"Fine." Luke contemplated saying more but decided against it. He was exhausting any excuses when it came to Savannah, even to himself.

Broderick took several steps then turned. "I gotta tell you, man, I don't have a good feeling about this."

"You never have a good feeling about anything."

"Has served me fine so far."

"I beg to differ, considering our current circumstances. Besides, there is a lot about Savannah we do not know. Have you uncovered anything further from your phone calls earlier this evening?"

"Nobody's heard about a blood able to kill vampires. I should have expected as much. Something like this demands a high price. Her blood is basically the equivalent of liquid power." Broderick scratched his temple. "I think it's time you go into hiding. What about my cabin?"

"The one southwest of Cortina d'Amopezzo?"

"Yeah. You and Savannah should head there. Might be good for you while we track down who is hunting her."

"I know what your idea of good is and you can forget it," Luke said. "Nothing is going to happen between us."

"And why not? Because she's not Victoria?"

"No. Yes... Maybe." He was not sure he could handle losing someone close to him again.

Broderick sighed. "It's been over two hundred years. Don't you think a couple centuries is time enough to grieve?"

That argument, he refused to tackle again. "We will go because I need to get her away from this mess and time away will help us plan." He strode across the living room and set his glass on the granite island in the center of the kitchen. "Make arrangements to leave in a couple days. I need to talk to Lorenzo."

Chapter 20

By that sin fell the angels.
—William Shakespeare

Luke's insides twisted as he entered Blood Bar. The night was the same as any other. Still, he could not fathom living constantly amidst sin as Lorenzo did. The distractions had never bothered Luke before—bored him perhaps—but this time, he wanted answers. He grew agitated as the other vampire doled out orders and dragged on cigarettes as if an immortal lifetime could not provide him with enough nicotine.

The after-hours crowd abounded, dancing and stealing into shadowed corners. Vampires and humans, intoxicated from choice drinks and drugs. A dark-haired woman nibbled Lorenzo's jaw as he threw his head back and released a cloud of smoke. She sat nude from the waist up and at first glance resembled Savannah but as he edged closer, she turned. Her hair appeared more of a brown than black and her breasts, though high, would barely fit in his hands. Her lips curved into an inviting smile as she flirted with her dark eyes from beneath long lashes.

He longed for Savannah's seductive emerald gaze, and eyes closed, pictured her above him. Her full, heavy breasts sinking into his chest, her ebony hair draped like a curtain around them. She would suckle his bottom lip then move over his jaw and chest to his stomach.

"Are you going to join us, Evans, or do you prefer to stand there lusting?" Lorenzo interrupted his imaginings. The vampire's knowing gaze lit with laughter as he slid a hand down and cupped the brunette's rear. "I can assure you the real thing is much better."

"We need to talk," Luke said.

He turned and gave the woman in his arms a deep kiss, then pulled away. "Give me half an hour, go get yourself a drink, but don't cover up. I want to admire you from here."

She smiled and slid off his lap but not before turning to wink at Luke.

"Sit down." Lorenzo motioned to a chair beside him. "What can I do for you?"

"I saw a familiar face last night. I have seen him here at Blood Bar. He may be a halfling."

"I heard of the attack. Whoever you saw, he wasn't one of my men but I'm gathering what info I can."

Why would Lorenzo bother getting involved? What did he have to gain? When about to ask those questions aloud, Lorenzo leaned closer and said, "Rafe gave me the blood."

"Makes no sense. Why did he not give it to us last night?"

Lorenzo scanned the bar. He stood. "We need more privacy. Follow me."

"I cannot stay long. We are leaving town."

Lorenzo raised a dark blond brow. "We, as in you and your latest meal?"

"Her name is Savannah."

"I haven't forgotten. I will make this quick." He started toward the back of the bar. "Where will you both be heading?"

They passed several groups of humans dressed as vampires, their outfits the signature black associated with his kind. Unease made his gut clench. The shooter from the auction was not amongst the crowds. Still, Lorenzo gave off a nervous energy that put him on edge. "I have not yet decided but I want her out of Rome."

"This will help you."

He followed him into a back room, where Lorenzo opened a refrigerated safe standing against one wall. Removing a vial, he held out the blood. "Blood to cure your arm. I'm supposed to exchange it for a sample of Savannah's."

Of course. He should have known better than to trust it was over with Rafe. "As you can see, she is not here."

Lorenzo's mouth curled as he uncapped the vial. "Would be a pity to let this perfectly good blood go to waste, don't you think?"

"Rafe will kill you."

"Let me handle him."

"No." What the hell was Lorenzo playing at? "How do I know he did not switch the blood with another type?"

"Good question." Pulling a dagger from the belt at his waist, Lorenzo left the room and returned with the brunette from earlier. He dragged her forward by her arm, held it up and sliced with the dagger across her wrist.

"What are you doing?" Anticipating Lorenzo's next move, Luke stepped forward, tensed.

"No." Features constricted in pain, the woman tried to yank her arm back. "Stop." Blood pooled at the cut's surface as her skin stretched, exposing muscle.

"Let's see, shall we?" Before Luke could stop him, Lorenzo poured several drops of blood from the vial into her cut. She screamed and fell to her knees, cradling her injured arm. Lorenzo bent and hauled her up from the floor by the back of her neck. "Show us your arm."

She shook her head, lips trembling.

"Now." He seized her wrist, pulled her arm straight.

The pale skin on her forearm glowed, pulling closed as blood clotted then formed a long scab. "What is happening to me?" The scab transformed into a pink scar which slowly faded to an ivory skin tone. She turned her arm over. "Amazing. It looks as if you never cut me."

Lorenzo nodded at the door. "You may leave. I'll call you when you're needed."

The woman hurried away without a glance back.

"You may have scared away your pleasure for tonight," Luke said.

"There's more where she came from." He held out the vial. "Ready to give it a try?"

Luke took off his jacket, rolled up his sleeve then removed his bloody bandage. The cut beneath had spread and festered as if his skin and body belonged to a human. The infection would only worsen with each passing day. "Does not seem I have a choice." He lifted his forearm and let the remaining blood from the vial drip into his wounds.

Heat seared up his arm, engulfing him in a bright glow. The sting of the cuts seemed minimal at first, like pouring alcohol onto open flesh. But the burn grew intense as if the blood were some kind of elixir eating through him. Luke bit down, puncturing his tongue with a fang to keep from yelling. "Bloody hell," he rasped, gripping his injured arm by the elbow. Sweat beaded along his hairline.

Creases knit Lorenzo's forehead as he glanced between the vial and the arm. "Why is it taking so long?"

"How the fuck would I know?" Luke panted rapid breaths in an attempt to drive away the consuming heat. His festered skin stretched and mended, closing completely in some places. To him it seemed an eternity before the pain calmed and the glow dissipated. "Shit." Soaked with sweat, his shirt clinging to his chest, he collapsed in a nearby chair.

Lorenzo approached slowly, his eyes comically wide. "It didn't heal."

To tell him he'd stated the obvious appeared a waste of time and energy, both of which he lacked. Instead, Luke grunted. The wounds had closed slightly and the infection disappeared, but blood still seeped from the claw-like marks. "I did not have much hope."

Trembling on unsteady legs, he stood and pulled down his sleeve, straightened his shoulders, which cost him strength. He turned away, hiding a grimace as he adjusted to the throbbing of his forearm.

"There is no cure against her." Lorenzo lowered himself into a chair. His gaze clouded as if his thoughts were elsewhere. "What now?"

"I keep searching." What else could he do to protect Savannah? He could not even imagine the consequences of her blood in the wrong hands. He moved to leave then stopped. "One more thing. If you find any other so-called cures, do me a favor."

Lorenzo glanced upward, meeting his gaze.

"Make sure you test it on some other vampire before you try it on me," Luke said.

* * * *

Lorenzo sensed Luke leave his office even as he shook off a dazed feeling. Few things stunned him, but even with seven hundred years to get used to immortality, the reality of possibly dying was a shocker. A few drops of Savannah's blood could destroy him. The knowledge frightened as much as it turned him on.

"You let him go, sir." Giovanni entered the office, his face a mask of confusion. "Where is the woman? I thought you wanted to use him to get her. I should go after him."

Woman? She was a goddess fit to be his queen. A vampire killer with no known cure for her blood. "Calm down. I didn't let anyone go. I made him trust me more. You're only a halfling. You may have the advantage of walking during daylight but Luke is a pureblood. He will not be an easy kill. Although with her, I might be able to finish such a job quite quickly."

"Sir?"

"Never mind." Feeble minds.

"Have you changed your mind?"

"No." If anything he wanted her more, but he had loose ends to tie up. Once Rafe realized Lorenzo's men stole the vial of blood, he would be none too happy. "I will never change my mind about her, do you hear me?" She was his ticket to freedom. Power.

"Do you want me to kidnap her?"

"Don't be foolish."

"What should we do?" Impatience laced Giovanni's tone.

"Stay calm and shut up. For now, keep an eye on them. I need to know where they head off to in the next few days and what their plans are."

"And afterward?"

"Leave it to me." He lost patience with Giovanni's questions. Though eager to show his worth, the halfling was young and behaved recklessly. "I'll give you instructions when the time comes." He pulled his shirt tail from his pants and began to unbutton his shirt. "For now, bring me a woman."

Giovanni nodded. "Do you have a preference?"

An ebony-haired waif caught his eye. She didn't have Savannah's curves but her face was decent. Not green eyes, more of a dark blue, but he could almost pretend. Easing himself lower in his seat, he caressed his sac. "Her. The lone one beside the bar."

"Nice choice. Do you want her drugged?"

Running his tongue along one fang, he smiled. "No, buy her a drink and bring her to my office. I'll take it from there."

Chapter 21

Lying is done with words and also with silence.
—Adrienne Rich

Savannah paced the wooden plank floor, rubbing her arms. They'd spent an entire day driving only to end up in an icy cabin in the middle of the Italian countryside. If anything, she would have guessed the thick cream and navy curtains hanging over the windows were trapping cold air within the cabin instead of keeping it out. "This place appears cozy. It's deceiving." She grabbed a throw off a living room couch and wrapped it around herself. "I'm freezing."

Luke tossed another log into the fireplace, fueling the growing fire. "Come closer, you will feel warmth here."

She approached and took a seat on a thick rug a few feet from the hearth. "Will Broderick be here soon?"

"He had a few things to take care of but should make it tonight."

Several hours alone with him. Either way, it wouldn't make a difference. He'd barely touched her since after the blood auction. He'd gone from passionate to distant and pensive overnight. She pulled her bottom lip between her teeth and chewed gently.

"Are you getting warmer?" Luke asked.

She nodded, resting her chin on her knees.

"You hungry?"

Actually, she was starving but she didn't trust herself to accept his kindness. What if she was the one blowing every action out of proportion and getting giddy? Maybe she had never interested him. "I'm fine. Can you tell me why we are here again? I get this is Broderick's cabin, but I'm not sure why we left so suddenly." She winced as her stomach rumbled.

"I told you why. It is for your protection. We need to discover who is chasing you. And considering your growling stomach, it would seem your body disagrees with you being *fine*." He entered the kitchen. "We do not have much in regards to provisions, only what we picked up from the town market. Broderick should bring more tonight. Do bread, cheese and apples work?"

Delicious. "Fine." She didn't know what more to say as he removed a loaf of bread from a brown paper bag and cut several slices. He appeared at home preparing food. Ironic, since he no longer ate and probably hadn't for years. Ugh, did she even want to think about his age? She cleared her throat and turned back to the hearth. Flames crackled, comforting in the awkward silence.

"Where are you?" he asked. "Your mind seems elsewhere."

Hers? He was the one on a single-minded mission to evade whoever or whatever chased them. Being on the run suffocated her. It was like a moving cage and unfortunately, a recurring theme in her life. Trapped within bad relationships, inside hospitals, in a body that bore the scars of her hardships. Immured by debt. "Nowhere."

"Savannah?"

"It's nothing. I was thinking about the past few days."

"I am sorry. This trip came faster than anticipated. We will make sure we get you warmer clothes."

He couldn't avoid her. "And why did it come faster? Why are we here? I don't see a need for this secrecy, having Broderick buy our train tickets and rent our car. I thought Rafe let us go."

Lips lifted in a half smile, he sat beside her, placed a bowl of apples and a cutting board with bread and cheese between them. "Sounds like you have quite a bit on your mind."

"Don't play, I'm serious." And scared. She met his gaze.

"As am I. I will not let anything happen to you." He pulled off his sweater then unbuttoned and rolled up his red-stained sleeve.

"Your arm." She brushed her fingers along the three slices on his forearm. Blood seeped slowly. "It looks better, somewhat. The wounds appear fresh. Did you go back to Rafe?"

"No. According to Lorenzo, Rafe gave him the healing blood in expectation I would return to Blood Bar. He wanted to exchange it for yours."

Luke appeared bothered but she couldn't determine what caused it. "You don't seem convinced."

"I do not see why Rafe would use Lorenzo. Why not come to me? It does not make sense."

"Why didn't it heal you?" she asked. And what did that mean?

"Seems Rafe's sample was not quite what I hoped for."

"Are you sure it was the actual sample?" she replied, frowning. She'd never trusted Lorenzo and that he'd use a false sample wouldn't shock her a bit.

Luke shrugged. "I could not say. Although, he did demonstrate its properties on a human woman. Still, I am not sure what to believe these days."

"You should have told me." She sat up straight, suddenly finding it hard to breathe. "Oh God. Please don't tell me this is why we left so abruptly. Are they are chasing us?" She touched his good arm. "We have to go back. Rafe will kill you if you took the sample without exchanging my blood."

"No. I do not believe Rafe had anything to do with this. If he desperately wanted your blood, he would never have let us go the night of the auction."

Which was a logical conclusion, but if Rafe or the other Ancients weren't chasing them, then who? "Either way, this won't stop until we go back." In a quieter voice she said, "I should know, I've been running my whole life."

"This time, running is your only option. We are not humans, we are vampires, powerful, immortal. Damn it, Savannah. You are not going to reason with them. You are going to find yourself chained in some basement being used as an experiment. Am I painting a vivid enough picture for you?" His eyes burned a deep burgundy as he leaned over her.

Savannah swallowed, frightened but unwilling to show weakness. She must not have done a good enough job, as Luke bowed his head and turned away.

"Forgive my anger," he said. "It is not my intention to frighten you. I... worry for your safety."

He wouldn't look at her, and his face remained hidden amongst shadows. Obviously, it bothered him to admit any concern. She wanted to comfort him but wasn't sure what to say. "I'm not afraid of death."

"Shh." He turned to her, placed a finger against her lips. It felt cool against her warmth. "Do not say that."

"It's the truth." Her lips tingled as they grazed his skin.

"Do not be naive. They would not kill you, Savannah. You are too valuable."

She swallowed over a knot in her throat. Of course. She was a fool to think otherwise. She would be imprisoned but kept alive because she was of use to them. Not treated as a person, but as an object for destruction and torture. Always an object. What would happen when they no longer needed her? "Why not send me away? I become more and more involved the longer I stay here."

Luke neared, cupped her face. "It is not so simple."

He made sense, but running was what she always did. As he massaged her lower lip with his thumb, she shivered. Her eyelids grew heavy, drooped, eclipsing the fire's light. "Luke, stop." Her voice came out raspy. "You're distracting me." And heaven help her, she didn't want him to stop. When his mouth replaced his finger, couldn't bring herself to protest. Soft and moist, his lips melded with hers.

He smelled clean and masculine. She wrapped her arms around his neck, pulled him closer and inhaled to catch her breath. His body felt hard against the softness of hers, and he dwarfed her, making her feel small, feminine. But this was wrong, wasn't it? "Please." She pushed against his chest and broke their kiss. "I'm not another romp in the sack."

He pulled away and stood with his back to her. "I never said as much. Still, you know I cannot offer you more."

Did she come across as so desperate? "I never asked for more."

"You did not have to ask aloud." Luke turned and met her gaze. "I can see it in your eyes. As much as I wish it, I am not fairytale material."

She broke his stare, her gaze falling to his mouth. Fangs weren't visible beneath the edge of his upper lip, nor had she felt them when he'd kissed her. Did she want the impossible? "Maybe I'm not looking for the fairytale." Didn't that make her insignificant?

Everything was jumbled inside her. She didn't have time to decipher her emotions before he wrapped a cold hand around her neck and pressed her against the wall. Despite his firm but gentle grip and the fireplace mere inches away, an icy tremor shook her.

"Do not push me," he growled. "Your desire clouds my mind." He leaned close. "You cannot change who and what I am."

"I'm not trying to change you," she said, biting her lip as she turned away.

"Really? Do you want to sink your teeth into fresh warm flesh, dip your tongue into even warmer blood? Would you like to know what blood tastes like?"

"I've tasted it before." Her limbs stirred with desire even as her stomach flipped in disgust. The thought of feeding from another person repulsed her.

"I am not talking about a cut lip." He pulled up her chin, forced her to stare directly into his dark eyes, which deepened to plum. He smiled, lifting his lips to reveal two sharp-tipped fangs.

Her heart tripped, threatened to pound from her chest. How could one tangy liquid be sufficient to sustain life—and an immortal one at that?

"How can I put this so you will understand?" He leaned his head back. "Strawberries and cream."

What the hell was he talking about? "You're h-hungry?"

Making a blatant display of interest, he swept her face and body with his gaze. "At my apartment, you indulged in strawberries and whipped cream. Why? Because they are delicious, right? You are my strawberries and whipped cream."

A wave of nausea washed over her. She probably wouldn't ever look at berries and cream the same way again. "You don't have to be so direct. I get the point."

"Do you?" He leaned closer. Even now as she struggled to digest the meaning of his words, his scent taunted her. "Still interested in me? In knowing my blood and having me know yours?"

"Stop it." She shoved against his chest, trying to slide along the wall. He was too strong. "What, it makes a difference now because you aren't planning to kill me afterward?"

"Yes, it does," he replied.

Tears clouded her vision. She wouldn't even bother asking him why it made a difference. There was no point, and she didn't want to hear excuses. He was evil for publishing an ad and enticing her only to teach her a lesson. And she hated her desire to take an easy way out, as that had gotten her in this situation. But most of all, she despised herself because, despite everything, she cared for him, maybe even loved him.

"Go to hell." Hands fisted, she pushed against him. He stood firm, like a rock, until she went limp in his grasp. Tilting her head up, she met his stone cold gaze. "You're a monster."

The red of his eyes blended to a dark brown and his fangs retracted. Loosening his grip, he stepped back. "At last, something we can agree upon," he said then turned on his heel and exited the room.

* * * *

Savannah awoke, startled by someone saying her name and a rustling noise. "Hello?" Her head pounded from crying herself to sleep.

"Are you okay? You were mumbling in your sleep." A cool hand hooked under her arm, pulled her to a sitting position. Broderick hunched over her, his gray blue eyes reflective in the moonlight streaming through the living room windows. "Damn it," he muttered under his breath. "He's being an ass, am I right?"

"I'm fine," she lied, shivering, and turned toward the fire. Only a few embers remained.

"Let me take care of that for you." Broderick removed a few logs from a pile beside the fireplace and tossed them into the hearth. Lighting several pieces of newspaper, he spread them over the logs. "There, that should get the fire going faster."

"Thank you."

He removed a throw from a sofa and draped it over her then sat on a nearby ottoman. The gesture was so thoughtful, she wanted to cry. Why couldn't she fall for nice guys? "You're not like Luke, are you? I mean, a vampire."

"I'm a halfling. My mother was human, my father a vampire. I have features from both races. For example, a vampire's strength and speed but a human's need for more sleep and food. And I can walk in daylight."

She rubbed the middle of her forehead, trying to soothe the ache away. "I didn't even realize such races could mix." Hell, she hadn't even believed vampires existed up until days ago.

"It's not as common, as we must be born and cannot be created through the drawing of blood." He paused. "Do you want to tell me what has you looking so forlorn?"

She shook her head. "It's nothing. I'm homesick."

He reached beneath her chin, turned her to face him. "He's not as bad as he makes himself out to be."

Could have fooled her. "What was she like, his wife?"

"Truth be told, I never met Victoria. She died a hundred and fifty years before Luke and I met."

"What?" He must have loved her a lot to still be holding onto her memory.

"Don't worry," Broderick replied. "Luke's not too old. Two hundred or so is fairly young for a vampire."

Young? Luke had lived during the Industrial Revolution in Britain. "No wonder he is always so proper. Society called for it then."

"Maybe. Luke was nobility and he didn't readily embrace his change," Broderick said. "He still doesn't."

"What else do you know?" she asked.

He dropped his hand, stood and stirred the logs in the fireplace with the poker. "I only know what he has told me," he said as he lowered himself to the floor beside her. "Have you tried talking to him?"

"Are you kidding?" She laughed. "I can't even get him to carry on a normal conversation yet alone something personal and intimate. He's like a beast—only his outside appearance is deceivingly appealing."

Broderick's lips twisted into a wry grin. "He can be a bit prickly at times, but beneath the needles, he's a good guy."

"Lucky for anyone who gets to meet the sweet and caring side of him." Had any other women gotten beneath Luke's rough shield. Monica? The thought of the beautiful vampire annoyed her. "I need a drink or something." She rose to her knees only to find Broderick's hand clasped around her upper arm. "What?"

"I know you've met that side of him. Don't brush it off too hastily. He cares about you."

If Broderick spoke the truth, Luke had a strange way of showing it. And yet, nothing about meeting him had been what she would term normal. Hell, he was a vampire. His earlier comments alone were enough to scare her off. She sat down, exhausted from her swinging emotions. "Even if he does care, what potential do we have for a happy ending?" She met his gaze. "Luke is right. This is no fairytale. Even if he did turn me, I wouldn't be like you, would I?"

"No," Broderick said. "You would be like Luke, a pure vampire."

"I couldn't do without sunrises and normal food. I've always dreamed of being a chef in my own place." She bit her lip. "It's why I answered the ad."

"I'm sorry." He tucked several stray strands of hair behind her ear. "I should have dug more on you. I should have pushed Luke harder."

"I think we've all made mistakes we wish we could change."

"My, my, enough of these cozy scenes and I shall think you have other intentions, Broderick."

At the sound of Luke's voice, she jerked. He leaned against the wall next to the hallway, his expression thunderous, his arms crossed.

"I'll take my cue." Broderick sighed and stood up. "The fridge is now fully stocked so help yourselves." He attempted to go into the hallway only to be blocked by Luke. "Don't even think about taking out your issues on me, Evans. I'm not in the mood for your bullshit now and despite being a halfling, you know I'll give you a run for your money."

Luke's eyes flashed burgundy before he stepped back, letting Broderick pass. A nervous stirring whirled in the pit of Savannah's stomach. She brushed the heated skin of her arm with a hand. As Luke approached, she wished she could construct an invisible barrier to put up between them. She wasn't ready for more tears.

"What kind of restaurant would you open?" he asked.

"What?" She inhaled deeply and released the breath slowly, trying to calm her surprise. "Why do you care?"

He sat on a sofa opposite her. "I want to know what dream was so important you would answer my ad and travel four thousand miles to achieve it."

She cleared her throat. How much had he overheard? "I see it as a Tuscan-styled restaurant. Cozy, lots of wood and plaster." She paused and looked around. Creamy plaster and wooden walls stood as backdrops to suede, sage-colored sofas and a dark leather recliner. The rug she sat on seemed to be made of some kind of thick animal fur. A stone fireplace crackled several feet from them, chasing away any cool air seeping through a big bay window on the other side of the room. "Different colors, but cozy-looking like this cabin."

"What kind of food would you serve?"

"The food will be American with an occasional international flare." She frowned, suddenly annoyed she wanted to tell him more. "I haven't decided anything else." *Liar*. She'd spent years conjuring up every detail of the restaurant, but why speak about a dream unlikely to happen?

"It sounds like a good plan so far." His voice almost sounded wistful.

"What about you?" she asked.

"I do not have dreams." He turned toward the window. Snowflakes hit the fogged glass as wind whistled through the night. Dark and cold, the scene outside seemed to mirror the emotions playing across his face.

For some reason she couldn't explain, she didn't want to give up on him. "What about when you were human? Did you have plans and hopes then?"

A crease formed between his brows, marring the perfection of his face. "I am not sure I remember much before I was turned."

"Or maybe you don't want to remember." She continued boldly, "I want to know how you became a vampire. And, I want to know about Victoria."

Chapter 22

The moment you have in your heart this extraordinary thing called love and feel the depth, the delight, the ecstasy of it, you will discover that for you the world is transformed.
—Jiddu Krishnamurti

"I was turned a couple hundred years ago." Luke leaned back on the sofa. The fire in the hearth danced before him, autumn orange flames jumping up, licking the stone sides. "I had recently married Victoria, after a short courtship. Not uncommon during those days. She was perfect." He smiled in remembrance of his visits to her family home in London.

"Nobody's perfect," Savannah said.

"I realize the truth of those words now." He shrugged. "I was young and naive. She seemed perfect to me then. Beautiful, innocent and fresh. Of course, I can think back now and see we did not know each other well, but in those days, people did not court for years. I loved her in my way and I know she returned the sentiment."

Savannah shifted to her side on the rug and supported her head with one hand, and he could not help but admire the soft curve of her hip. "You still love her," she said.

"Yes. Although my love for her has changed with time, I believe some part of me will always love her." Or the happiness she represented in his mind. "But that is neither here nor there. You asked how I became a vampire. It happened over two hundred years ago and Victoria and I were on our holiday—what you now refer to as a honeymoon—in Rome. We strolled late one night, but I did not fear easily. I enjoyed a young man's stupidity."

"Huh, I'm not sure you're talking only about young men."

"Such a bitter statement." He clenched a fist, hating life's cruelty.

"I only speak from experience," she replied, head bowed.

"I know, and you must forgive me. I have committed wrongs and if given a chance, I would change many of them. But I cannot turn back time."

She nodded. "What happened?"

"When the attack started, I thought I had everything under control. They wanted our money and there were only two of them. I quickly left them indisposed. But when I finished, there were more of them and they held Victoria."

As Savannah sat up and pulled her knees close to her chest, her anxiety encircled him, squeezing. He breathed in deep in a futile attempt to overcome the potent sentiment.

"Two men held her to the wall as another two taunted me. I think I must have gone mad, as the rest is a blur." Or so he wanted to believe. He still recalled the flash of light as one fired a pistol. The burn as a bullet sliced through his shoulder and the scent of gun powder infiltrating the air along with a cloud of smoke.

"Were you hurt?" Her voice sounded far away.

"They fired several rounds, grabbed anything of value and ran."

"You were shot." As if she expected him to still show some sign of injury, she combed his form with her gaze. "And Victoria?"

Beneath the echoes of the men's shouts and laughter, he barely heard what Savannah had said. He could still feel the bullet's sting and the cold cobblestones beneath him as he crawled to his wife's limp body. The impression of her pale, icy skin would be imprinted on him forever.

"Luke?"

"She was dead." He shut his eyes, described what he remembered as clearly as if it happened yesterday. "I moved over to help even though I knew I could not change fate. Like some beautiful porcelain doll, she lay still and cold. Her eyes remained open, lifeless. A growing puddle of blood stained her gray dress."

"I'm sorry," Savannah said.

"As am I. And yet, I cannot help but wonder if she was the lucky one." He met her gaze.

Her emerald eyes looked huge in her pale countenance, and she squeezed the blanket on her lap.

"Do not look so surprised. Two hundred years later, I can concede my kind has some advantages, but I would never have chosen to become what I am."

"Why did you become a vampire?"

"Please, Savannah." He stood and paced, suddenly too anxious to sit. "Are you so naive? Do you not think I begged as they came to my wife and I like vultures to a small feast? My only consolation was they refused to touch her. Stale blood is like venom to my kind."

"Did it hurt?"

Luke ran a hand through his hair. The pain might have been excruciating but after losing Victoria, he'd felt nothing. Numbness had dominated him. "There are those who say transition is the worst possible pain a human can feel. I honestly must say, I could not feel a thing. My mind had left me."

"Sometimes helplessness is the worst pain." She curved her lips in a sad sort of smile. "Time in the hospital, an ambulance ride, physical therapy—that was the easy part for me."

Muscles taut with the anticipation he would finally hear her story, he sat.

"My turn to share a bit about my past. You know Ben and I were engaged but you don't know what it was like living with him. I too was foolish. Seems to be a trait common to women also. Deep down inside I knew he treated me awfully. I became a trophy and played my part with pride. Who wouldn't enjoy glamour at first?" She bit her lip and turned away. "I behaved an idiot, but to my credit, I thought it was real. That they were my friends, and Ben loved me." She laughed, the sound bitter. He wanted to comfort her but doubt left him immobile. "How ridiculous it sounds now, huh?"

"Not ridiculous. Innocent." He ached to catch the tears threatening to fall from her eyes.

She took a deep breath and released it slowly. "That night, the night I got hit, I remember lying there. I woke up and couldn't feel my legs, or my arms, but I lay awake. I could see and hear. At times I wish I had gone deaf and blind. Only for the moment Ben denied knowing me." A sob wracked her as she bent her head. "I lay there dying, helpless, a few feet away from him and Ben said he didn't know me. He would have left me to die on a cold, hard street. And to think I was ready to spend my life with him."

Bloody bastard. Unable to help himself, he wrapped her trembling form in his arms. "I am sorry." This indeed was a pain beyond any he could imagine. Victoria had never refused his affections. "If you want me to, I will find him and make him my lunch."

She laughed through her tears and huddled into the crook of his shoulder. "No, but thank you. I mostly feel sorry for him now. If you asked me a year or so ago, I probably would have said yes." She twisted her lips into a sad smile.

Luke nodded because it seemed the right thing to do. Savannah was more gracious than he would ever be. For over two hundred years, he'd pitied those so consumed by greed they could not truly appreciate good in life.

How truly ironic. His obsession with vengeance did not leave him that far removed from those he pitied.

"I want to ask you a question." She paused as if searching for the right words. "The men who attacked you and Victoria, you killed them, didn't you?"

He'd assumed she would ask him this sooner or later, although he had hoped it would be later. "Yes," he replied. "I will not lie. I must tell you I relished it in the moment. Regret for what I became followed later."

"There's no reason for you to regret what happened. It was not your fault."

"Coming from the woman who finds me repulsive?" He studied her face, searching for something he could not name. The hollow space at the base of her neck pulsed rapidly between the lapels of her open shirt collar.

"I don't find you repulsive. I just... I don't know." She sighed.

Unwilling to wait for her to find words, he leaned in, slipped his hand beneath her collar, cupped the back of her neck and pressed his lips to hers. A groan stirred in his chest as she sank into him.

* * * *

Savannah's muscles stiffened when it dawned on her she kissed him back, and she pulled away. Luke's touch gentled, but his body thrummed with restrained power as he hovered above her. His gaze deepened to midnight as he studied her, focused on her lips then met her stare.

She lifted her chin. Her breaths deafened in the silence. "We start this, we finish it." Her pulse skipped into turbo speed as she waited for a reply.

He brushed strands of hair back from her face, caressing the line of her jaw. "Are you sure?"

"I won't lie to you either. I'm nervous, but I'm a grown woman. Let me deal with my emotions."

"You are not answering my question."

"Yes, I'm sure," she whispered and let her eyelids fall closed as he slipped an arm around her waist and hoisted her to a kneeling position.

"Enchanting," he murmured as he brushed his mouth along her cheekbone, cradling her to him as if she weighed nothing. "Look at me, Savannah."

Guiding her into the middle of the lush rug, he laid her down. With one tug, he pulled his sweater over his head and tossed it aside. The fire's shadows leaped across the ridges of his abs and chest, highlighting his strength. Her stomach flexed in anticipation. "Light from the flames suits you." She reached up and traced them across his skin.

"Now you." Luke shoved the hem of her collared shirt over her stomach and ribs. Beneath the dim lighting, a blush stole over her skin. "So soft." With his thumbs, he caressed her ribcage and the underside of her breasts as he inched her shirt up higher. Her instinct was to cover herself, but he caught her wrists. "Do not hide from me. Take off your shirt."

She did as asked then lifted her pelvis. One by one, he undid the buttons of her jeans, eased them over her hips and down her thighs. Despite the fire, the air cooled her skin. "What about you?" She fidgeted under his stare.

"Do you realize how special you are?" he asked.

Did she? Could she? Without thinking, she brought her hand up and fingered a long scar over her collarbone.

"The outside is stunning, but not what I am referring to. I mean you, Savannah Michaels. All of you," he said, brushing kisses along her jaw and over the curve of her neck. He lingered on the rise of her breasts, and beneath his lips, her heart raced. She didn't understand why her stomach fluttered even as her feet and hands dug into the rug. She wanted this. Her body grew heated, her breathing uneven.

He removed his pants and briefs then covered her with his body, engulfing her frame with his size. He suckled one pink nipple, rolling his tongue around the tip.

Savannah moaned, arching beneath him as she pushed against his mouth. He represented pure strength. Muscles in his stomach and arms flexed as he held himself above her.

"What about Broderick?" she asked, suddenly remembering they weren't alone. The realization sent a thrill coursing through her.

"If he wants to live, he will not depart his room." Between her thighs, he held her core, cupping it as he slid two thick fingers into her. "Moist," he whispered, gently pumping in and out.

The sensation of being spread and filled nearly pushed her over the edge. Following his rhythm, she undulated her hips, bringing him deeper with every roll of her pelvis. *More* she thought, her impatience growing as his pumps slowed.

Luke let out a soft, deep laugh. "Patience, my pet. Relax." He eased from her, kissed her ribs and stomach. "It will be worth the wait."

She inhaled, then released a slow exhalation, concentrating on calming her pulsing insides. His kisses fluttered over her stomach and inner thighs, and her muscles tensed in anticipation. When his tongue flicked her clit, she whimpered and her back bowed upward. "Please, hurry."

Hands supporting the curve of her spine, he pulled her closer, suckled, flicked and prodded. The caress of his lips rivaled heaven.

Her hips and torso writhed beyond control. "Luke, please."

As he pulled away and slid up her body, the friction from their skin touching tantalized her. Kissing her passionately, he wedged her legs apart with a knee. "Open for me, love."

He couldn't move fast enough as he slipped on a condom. She'd come apart, waiting. Then he hovered over her entrance and thrust forward.

She lifted her pelvis and met his drive forward, enjoying his thickness as he slid further, spread her with every inch. Wrapping her legs around his waist, she drew him flush against her.

"Amazing." Luke flexed his hips, pulling back then propelling forward again.

Sweat droplets pooled at her hairline as she moved with him. With each thrust, she concentrated to keep up with his rhythm as he moved faster and harder. Small ripples unfolded from her core and her back arched upward. "I'm going to come."

"Yes, love."

Gasps left her as she moaned. Waves of pleasure shook her even as her muscles tightened and released. Luke climaxed afterward, his groan low and guttural as he drove deep within her.

Their breathing calmed and yet she couldn't pull away. But he didn't either and for now, everything was right.

Chapter 23

A little sincerity is a dangerous thing, and a great deal of it is absolutely fatal.
—Oscar Wilde

Savannah's stomach rumbled as the scent of coffee woke her. "Mmm, you read my mind." Her eyelids fluttered open. "Hello?" Rays of sunlight streamed into the room, caressing a sofa and wooden table several feet from where she lay.

"Luke?" She smoothed the long-furred rug beneath her with a hand. Images of his muscled body covering hers heated her cheeks. Aware of her nudity, she pulled a blanket up over her shoulders. What was she thinking? Of course he wouldn't be lying next to her—not unless he wanted to go up in flames before daybreak.

A sudden wave of loneliness washed over her, and she reached for her undergarments. She tugged on her shirt, ignoring her bra. It was obviously too much to ask for one decent guy. No, she fell for pathological liars or egotistical pigs.

She paused, stepping into her jeans. Luke was neither but his need for blood and the fact he couldn't walk into daylight definitely put a damper on any potential for a relationship. Of course, she wasn't thinking about a relationship with him, not really. *Liar.*

"Oh, shit. Sorry. Call me when you're done." Broderick turned to walk back down the hallway.

"No, wait." She pulled her jeans over her hips and buttoned them closed. "I'm fine."

He faced her then headed toward the coffeemaker. "I swear I didn't see anything and thanks for being quick. I'm in desperate need of this stuff."

"You drink coffee?" She stood and left the blanket folded on the sofa.

"Sure." He poured himself a mug. "You didn't think Luke would drink this, did you?" He held the pot up. "Want some?"

"Yes, please. I didn't think he needed it. I assumed someone made it for me." Her lips twisted. "Silly thought, I guess."

Broderick shrugged and handed her a steaming mug. "Not really, but he needed to head out of daylight a few hours ago. Coffee would have been stale. I like mine real fresh." His gaze combed over her as she took a sip. "Did you sleep well?"

"Mm-hmm." Cradling the mug, she looked downward and drew a circle on the floor with the tip of her toe. "Do you know if Luke is going to stay in his room all day?"

"Not if he has his way." Broderick topped off his coffee. "He usually prefers I pull down the blinds and close the curtains but he's been a prickly bastard, so I think I'm going to let him stew a bit. Besides, he can handle a bit of sunlight if it's indirect or he stays to shadows. Not my fault, if he chooses to behave like a dick."

"Oh." She wasn't going to argue with his reasoning.

"Help yourself to whatever's in the fridge. I'll be down the hall if you need me." He strolled away.

Savannah took a sip and pulled open the refrigerator. Eggs, cheese, mushrooms...an omelet. Her stomach growled at the thought. She didn't do much eating last night. It hadn't exactly been a priority. She bit her lip and smiled to herself.

A knock at the door startled her. Putting down the half-carton of eggs, she stepped around the kitchen island and glanced down the hallway leading to the bedrooms. Neither Broderick nor Luke left their room, which either meant they didn't hear anything or didn't much care. "Fine."

She approached the door and peeked through the peephole. The guy on the other side wore a snowsuit. A stray tourist? And yet he seemed familiar. She backed away slowly. *Don't be paranoid.* If the guy was a vampire he wouldn't be out in broad daylight. Probably someone she recognized from their stop in town. And yet, as she pulled back the lock, a light wind swept across her cheeks. Down the hall, Broderick all but flew toward her. His short, unruly waves fluttered around his face and his eyes burned a pale blue.

He lifted an arm. "Savannah, no. Don't open it."

She didn't have time to contemplate the change in him or the reason for his warning. Someone shoved open the door and clamped a leather vise around her throat.

"Let go." She kicked, digging her fingernails into the man's gloved hand. Nothing helped; his grip was unrelenting.

"Don't even try it." Hauling her by the neck, the male dragged her across the cabin porch into the forest. Savannah's bare feet scraped against snow-covered ground, shoving aside a thick layer of icy powder as she scanned for some sort of fallen branch or root to hook onto. He moved fast.

"Let her go!" Broderick raced outside the cabin, sliding in the snow as he closed in on them.

Thank God. She tried to scream but a pitiful mewling replaced her words.

"Or what?" The man half-turned, spinning her as if she were a rag doll. His grip on her never loosened. His eyes burned the same otherworldly blue as Broderick's.

"Or I'll drain you dry and leave you to local wildlife," Luke said.

Her stomach flipped at the sight of him standing on the cabin stoop, dressed in black with shades on.

Broderick spun around. "Get the fuck back inside. I've got this. He's a halfling."

Luke ignored him and took a step forward. "Made a decision yet?" he snarled at her captor. "You will not take her and get away from both of us."

"And if I kill her?" the halfling spat, squeezing her neck tighter. Savannah coughed, wheezed for breath.

"You would be dead either way." Luke's voice was calm but his jaw clenched. "And whoever is paying you would be none too happy."

She blinked, struggling to stay awake as her captor seemed to contemplate his options. Daylight flickered.

"Damn it." Broderick leaped forward, tackling them to the ground. She rolled to the side as his fists pummeled her attacker's chest and face. Barely able to control her wheezing, she gripped her chest.

"Get up." Luke wrapped an arm around her torso and carried her up the short set of stairs into the cabin. For some reason, her feet wouldn't cooperate. "Can you breathe?" he asked.

She nodded, coughing an affirmative answer.

Setting her down on the sofa, he leaned on a large chair beside her. Broderick entered soon after, dragging her struggling attacker with him. "Would you like to do the honors before I tie him up for questioning?" he asked Luke, who turned and punched the halfling in the face. The man sagged in Broderick's arms.

"Who is he?" The burning in her throat made her voice hoarse.

"Not sure," Broderick said. "But we will find out."

Luke stood before the fireplace. He flexed his fists. She wanted to comfort him and assure him she was now okay, but his expression frightened her.

"Where do you want him?" Broderick held her attacker up.

"Put him in my room. No need to mess up your whole cabin."

Savannah glanced at Luke. "What are you going to do with him?"

"That is none of your concern." He wiped his brow then rubbed his eyes. "Shit."

Damn his stubbornness. "Not my concern? In case you didn't notice, it was my neck he strangled outside."

"Savannah, stop. I am not arguing right now."

"Neither am I. I want to know what you're going to do..." Her voice trailed off as his forehead and cheeks blistered. "Your skin—you've been burned."

"I know." Irritation laced his tone. He bent and supported himself against the wall next to the fireplace. "Please call Broderick."

"What do you need?" She stood, suddenly worried about his moist, yellowish complexion. Beads of water or sweat—she was not sure which—dripped down his brow. "What's happening?"

Luke stumbled, slid against the wall. "Fuck."

"Luke." She ran to where he'd collapsed.

* * * *

Luke came to in darkness. He turned his head and scanned the dark wood and plaid decor. Somehow he'd made it back to his room or rather, the room he stayed in at Broderick's cabin. Bloody bastard had not closed the blinds as he was supposed to. If Luke hadn't been so bewitched by Savannah the night before, he might have done it himself.

"I swear I can hear your mind snarl," Broderick drawled as he entered from the bathroom, carrying a warm glass of blood. "Breakfast, dear?" He held up the glass.

"Stupid ass stunt you pulled. What if we had not gotten there in time?" Luke tried to stand up from the bed and wavered, grasped one of the bed's posts. His exhaustion unnerved him even as it pleased him. For once in a long time, he felt a human's frailty. Savannah's blood inside his system probably did nothing to help his state.

"Damn it, you're weak. I'm sorry about the blinds. You're right. It was stupid, but she is okay, not even a bruise on her neck."

"For now," Luke replied.

"If we're dealing out blame, you pulled a piece of shit stunt yourself. You could have gone up in flames."

Exposing himself to sunlight had been idiotic but he would do it again if it meant making sure Savannah was okay. "Maybe. I still have no regrets."

"Here, take this." Broderick held out the glass of blood. "And wipe that accusatory look off your face. I may have been annoyed by your latest tantrum but I wouldn't ever put Savannah at risk."

Luke accepted the glass and sat down on the coverlet. Broderick probably could have handled the halfling but probably was not a guarantee.

"I wouldn't have let anything happen to her."

"I know—I know you would have tried everything." He bowed his head. "I am not sure I could have stopped myself even if I'd wanted to. She consumes my mind."

"Yeah, I can tell." Broderick sat beside him on the bed.

Luke sensed his curiosity but nothing came of it. "Where is the halfling?"

"He's restrained in my room. Not quite conscious but he'll be there soon. I punched him a few more times to make sure he wouldn't wake up."

"I want to question him before I do anything further."

"I figured," Broderick said. "What do you want to do with Savannah?"

Luke sighed. He was not ready for her to see him as the true monster he was. "Keep her occupied."

"Easier said than done."

"I imagine she is fairly shaken up." He stood. "Make her some food, keep her warm. Both ought to help."

"Seeing *you* would help. She wants to know you're okay."

He staggered into the bathroom. Even in the dim lighting, he could see blisters muddling his reflection. He now looked a grotesque part. "Tell her I am fine." He braced himself with his hands on the wash basin's counter.

"Luke."

"What?"

Broderick hesitated a moment before he said, "I know you love her."

Loved her? Luke took a deep breath, not because he needed to breathe but because he did not know how to respond. This was not how it felt with Victoria. Victoria had been innocent and sweet and what he wanted in his life. Perfect for him. Savannah was not perfect. Far from it. At times he felt fairly certain he wanted nothing to do with her, and yet, he needed her. A need ingrained so deep it threatened to squeeze the life from him. He turned away from the mirror. "I am no good for her."

"Why don't you let her decide what's good for her and what's not? Are you going to deny what I said?" Broderick neared.

"No."

"What are you going to do?"

He bent his head, rubbed his neck. "I am going to change her."

Chapter 24

Take time to deliberate; but when the time for action arrives, stop think-
ing and go in.
—*Napoleon Bonaparte*

Savannah paced the living room, flinching as a man howled at the other end of the cabin. The pain in his screeches made her skin crawl. She brought her hand to her neck and released a sigh. He couldn't touch her now.

"Hungry?" Broderick flipped an omelet and pulled a couple plates from a cupboard.

How could he eat after what had happened? Her stomach growled in protest but the thought of food brought nausea. "No."

He sliced the omelet down the center then shoveled the two halves onto plates. "Try to eat, you need the nutrients." He placed one of the plates before her. "Sit."

She sat on a stool, but pushed the plate away and frowned. "No thanks. I'm fine with coffee."

"Suit yourself." He shrugged, forking a mushroom into his mouth.

He acted so nonchalant, when Luke possibly killed a man less than fifty feet away. "Why do you need food? I mean, you're not completely a human. Shouldn't you be drinking blood or something?"

"I prefer the taste of food, but I need both." He sipped his coffee. "Blood's a bit sour for my tastes and unlike pure vampires, I don't crave it unless I'm desperate for its nutrients. It's like certain wines or spirits. Takes a bit of getting used to, you know?"

No, she didn't, nor did she care to know. Still, Broderick's description sounded more likely than strawberries and cream. Ugh. "I think I'm going to be sick." A sudden churning unsettled her stomach and she slid from her stool. Moisture beaded on her forehead.

Broderick stopped eating and stared. "Shit." Moving quickly, he rushed forward and slipped his arms around her. "Damn it." He carried her outside, propped her up, over the railing.

Savannah emptied her stomach of the coffee she'd drunk and dry heaved for another couple minutes. "I'm dying."

"I beg to differ," Broderick said as he helped her stand upright. "Right now I'd say you're very much alive." He took a step back. "Want to go inside?"

She shook her head, wiped sweat from her temples. "I can't stand to hear the screaming. What is he doing to him?"

He guided her to a chair and sat down beside her. "Don't ask questions you don't want to hear answers to. You know what Luke is. You can't accept part of him."

She shivered and bit her bottom lip. Broderick was right.

"Look, try not to think about it," he said. "And if you can't help yourself, remember the halfling is the bad guy. We need information from him." He stood. "You're cold. I should get you a blanket."

"No." She placed a hand over his. "Please don't leave me alone right now."

He settled back in his chair and rubbed his quadriceps. "What do you want, Savannah?"

"I want to sit here for a moment."

"I'm not asking what you want now. I'm asking what you want with Luke."

"What do you mean?" She held her breath. Maybe he'd drop the subject if she avoided it.

"Don't pretend you don't know what I'm talking about," he said, meeting her gaze. "He needs blood to survive and though he is selective about his victims, he has victims nonetheless. Can you live with that?"

Savannah released a long sigh. How she wanted to shout *yes*. But it would be a lie. Good or bad, nobody deserved to die, not in such a monstrous way. "I don't know." She shook her head. "No, I lie. I can't. I just can't."

"Have you told him this?"

She rubbed her brow. "He knows what I think of vampires."

"If it's any consolation, the man there is not a human. He's a halfling like me."

"It's not a consolation."

"Luke wants to help you, Savannah. He wants to discover who sent the halfling."

"I know." She wrapped her arms around herself.

"Come on, we need to go." He rose to his feet.

"Where are you going?"

"To check in on Luke, talk to him about this. Please come inside. You'll get sick out here and I don't want to take any chances in case they sent more than one man."

Shivering, she went with him. A hot shower would chase away the chill.

* * * *

Luke sat and stared at the lifeless body lying on the floor. He wiped his lips with the back of his hand. Blood streaked across his skin. Sloppy, but what did it matter? He was tired of trying to be something other than what he was.

"And so the pity party begins." Broderick entered, handed him a rag. "Get yourself together. And I'm not only referring to the blood."

"Where is Savannah?"

"She's fine. I left her to take a shower. She, uh, wasn't feeling good."

"She believes me to be a monster."

"Your behavior lately hasn't exactly shown her otherwise. Today was a bit much to take."

Luke wiped his hands, bent his head and rubbed the back of his neck. "This is reality. I am no Romeo."

"That's for sure."

"What do you expect me to do? Woo her with wine and chocolates? Love notes and flowers? Do not be absurd."

"And why not? You're a vampire, not a vegetable. Why don't you tell me what the hell you are planning? You certainly don't appear productive, leaving your scraps everywhere." Broderick waved a hand at the body on the floor. "You'll have to burn him."

As if he had forgotten. "Thanks, detective, for stating the obvious."

"Get anything worthwhile from him?" Broderick asked.

"More than I wanted to hear. His name was Giovanni. He worked for Lorenzo."

Broderick's eyes widened. "What did you say?"

Luke rubbed his eyes, suddenly more tired than he'd felt in decades. "Lorenzo wants Savannah. He has been playing me this entire time. The worst part is, I suspected something was wrong. He has been moody of late—even more so than usual."

"The halfling admitted Lorenzo wants Savannah?"

"No. He works for Lorenzo, but I recalled him from the night at the blood auction. He shot at us. I only saw him for a brief moment but his face shows up distinctly in my mind." Luke smoothed a hand over the stubble on his jaw. "I have seen him at Blood Bar. Lorenzo lied to my face."

"I've never liked Lorenzo."

What kind of bloody mess had he gotten Savannah involved in? "I do not understand why he spent this time under some sort of pretense. He had several opportunities to attack Savannah and yet he waits until now. Why?"

"Sounds like Lorenzo. Backhanded and cowardly, if you ask me."

"I did not *ask* you."

"Obviously, otherwise you wouldn't be in this mess."

Grinding his teeth, he met Broderick's gaze. "Need I remind you, your investigative abilities have contributed to our current predicament?"

"No, you needn't remind me," Broderick said. With a sigh, he sat on the edge of the bed. "I don't understand why Lorenzo would have hired someone to shoot at you. A stupid risk, especially if he was trying to get on Rafe's good side."

"Agreed. Whatever the reason, it will cost him. At least now I know how he got hold of the blood."

One of Broderick's brows shot upward. "What blood are you talking about?"

"My arm. You remember seeing what Savannah's blood did to it. At Rafe's auction, there was a vial of blood supposedly used to cure our kind. Lorenzo's men must have stolen it and used the attack as a distraction."

"Why?"

What did Lorenzo truly want? He had to be crazy if he actually believed he could take on the Ancients. "It was supposed to be an antidote." Quieter he whispered, "I think I was his bloody experiment." He recalled Lorenzo's expression of wonder as he'd said *vampire killer*.

"Lorenzo has been on the outs with Drago for a while." Broderick paused. "Do you think he wants Savannah to start some kind of street war with her blood?"

"I had not thought a street war, but since you mention it, the idea is plausible."

"Insane," Broderick said.

"Not from Lorenzo's viewpoint." Luke sighed. "He already feels cornered. Think about it. The possibilities are endless. He could use Savannah herself to draw others in." His muscles tensed at the thought of her as a sex slave. "Her blood could be given to enemies he wants to rid himself of. He might even come up with a way to use her blood in some kind of weapon form, killing vampires from a distance. Christ, he would be untouchable. Even more so, now that we know Rafe's so-called cure is a hoax."

"What do we do? They already know you're here and if Lorenzo has a lick of smarts, he'll soon know his man is dead. I have a friend who has a villa at Lake Como. We could head there."

"No." Luke shook his head. "We are going back to Rome."

"Rome, are you crazy? You'll walk right into the middle of a disaster."

Luke nodded. "We cannot keep running. We will attend the charity auction tomorrow. Vampire society will be there, including the Ancients."

"Um, I don't see how this is going to protect Savannah."

"I told you." Luke stood up and lit a match, then tossed it onto the dead halfling. Giovanni's body caught fire quickly. "I am going to turn her. As a vampire, her blood will lose its usefulness to Lorenzo and anyone else who decides to hunt her. As a vampire she will be meaningless to them."

"You better clean up the mess his body is going to create." Broderick threaded his hands through his hair. "I still think you're overlooking a few huge issues here. One, if this works and you somehow survive, Savannah will kill you for turning her. Or two, if this goes how I think it will go, her blood will kill you. How are you going be with her if you're dead?"

Luke sat on the bed, the orange and blue flames of Giovanni's burning body dancing before him. "I never said anything about being with her."

Chapter 25

One of the hardest things in life is having words in your heart that you can't utter.
—James Earl Jones

"Hello?" Savannah shivered despite the fact the scalding shower had heated her skin. No matter what she did, nothing made her feel clean, calm. She ran a hand over her arm, caressing the thick sweater Broderick had loaned her and tiptoed down the hallway to where she heard voices. Luke and Broderick were arguing.

"Luke?" She pushed open the bedroom door then screamed. The charred remains of whom she assumed was her attacker crumbled into a shapeless puddle in the middle of the floor.

"Bloody hell!" Luke shouted, shoving Broderick toward her. "Get her out of here."

Savannah took a step backward and tripped on the hall carpet. Broderick caught her and cradled her to his side. "You okay?"

No, she wasn't. "I-I..."

"Shit. Let's get you packed." He guided her into her room and sat her on the bed. Uncontrollable trembling wracked her. He folded back the comforter. "Get beneath the covers."

She did as he asked, too tired to protest.

He pulled her small suitcase from beneath the bed, opened the closet and folded a few articles of clothing into the open case. "Remember what I said. He was a bad guy. One of Lorenzo's goons. Understand?"

She sniffled and gazed up at him through tears, hating herself for feeling so weak and helpless. Something didn't make sense. "Lorenzo?"

"I guess for once, Luke is fortunate he doesn't trust easily."

She settled against her pillow, unable to block the sight of the charred halfling from her mind. "What's he going to do with the remains?"

"Clean them up. Despite certain parts of our nature, we aren't filthy creatures."

"I wasn't suggesting you were." She frowned. Broderick acted annoyed. How dare he? She hadn't asked for any of this and certainly didn't deserve his attitude.

"You don't have to say anything." He closed the lid to her case and zipped it up. "You're an open book, Savannah. Everything is displayed in your eyes. Luke didn't choose what he has become, nor did you or I choose much of what has happened to us. We are who we are. I would think someone who's been through what you've been through would understand being dealt an unfair hand."

"There's quite a difference between being a vampire and being hit by a car. I don't kill people by drinking them dry. That's what he did, isn't it?" She held her breath, anticipating an answer, hoping against what she already knew to be true.

"And if he did? You've never had to drink blood to survive." A little quieter, he said, "I misjudged you. I expected more. Too much, maybe."

What did she say now? She always disappointed others.

Let him judge her. She cleared her throat and wiped at her eyes. "Maybe."

Broderick bent his head and sat at the end of the bed, back to her. "We're going to Rome in a couple hours."

Rome? Nothing made sense. Lorenzo was there. She wanted to ask him why, but her mouth wouldn't form the words. Her throat knotted, and she buried her face in the pillow to avoid any further embarrassment.

"Get some rest. We'll wake you when it's time to leave." He came to his feet and left the room.

* * * *

Luke glanced sideways and took in Savannah's stoic expression. She sat as stiff as a statue in the passenger's seat. Gone were her smiles, affections, caresses. This would make parting easier. He had been naive to hope for more.

"Why is Broderick angry with you?" she asked.

He lifted his chin. "I could not say. He is a halfling and prone to erratic mood swings like you humans."

"I'd say irrationality is a trait universal to all species."

He'd asked for that one. "He has trouble accepting some of my decisions."

"Is he right?"

Not if she were to continue living. "He understands what I must do but his feelings allow him to get too attached."

She breathed in deeply, the sound loud amongst the silence. "Are feelings bad?"

"I should ask you." Luke glanced her way, momentarily met her gaze. "Are they?"

"Not if a pair is meant to be and their relationship is a feasible one."

Ah, so now it was clear. "And we are not feasible, is that it?" He could have kicked himself for pressing her but wanted to hear her say why they could not be.

She knotted her fingers together, breathing unevenly. "I changed for someone once before and it hurt deeply. With you it would be an even greater change, and I'm not sure I can risk the hurt."

"I see." Even now she would not admit her true thoughts about his kind. "Is that all that's holding you back?"

"Why do you push me?" Her voice rose. "Why do you want to hear me say something cruel?"

"Not cruel, the truth." His body shook as he tried to maintain calmness.

"Could you promise me you would never kill again?" Her voice broke on the last two words, as if it cost everything to say them.

"No." He would never make a promise he could not keep. Even now he made plans to save her. If those plans involved killing Lorenzo, he would do so without a second thought.

"Why not?"

"Death is a part of me. You stated you could not change for anyone ever again. I cannot change who I am, either. As much as I want to." He brushed her chin with his fingers. "I could not live with myself if anything were to happen to you, understand?"

"I wish I could," she said.

His chest seized at her words. The road curved ahead, slithering like a snake through verdant landscape. A heavy mist glowed silver beneath the moon's light, its arms stretched and wafting across the hills. The lonely scene spoke to him. Its rhythm would have matched his heart's beat, had he possessed one.

"Beautiful night," Savannah whispered as she faced the window.

"Yes." As a young man, he'd dreamed of traveling the world, seeing not only Italy but the Orient and the Americas. Nights like this one stunned him with their beauty and yet tonight possessed a sadness, as if his dreams would soon come to an end. "Tell me about your restaurant."

She frowned. "What do you mean?"

"Back in Boston before you were hit by the car, you must have made plans to open it. What were they?"

She smiled as if remembering something wonderful. "I wanted to be a chef. I was going to start trying my recipes on the bar crowd." She shrugged. "If everything panned out, I hoped to one day get my own place. Of course, I thought this before I ended up tens of thousands of dollars in debt."

"You will have your restaurant one day." Somehow, he would make sure of it.

"It's hard to believe now."

"I want to see you cook."

"What?" She frowned. "Why? You don't even eat food."

He wanted to see her happy but could not say the words. "Does not matter, I think it would be interesting. Victoria never learned to cook—times then were different."

"I can imagine." She bit her lip as if thinking about her response, and his stomach flip-flopped in the silence. "When do I cook?"

The charity auction was tomorrow but they could arrive later, after dinner. "Tomorrow."

"Okay," she said. "On one condition."

"What?"

"You invite Broderick."

He scowled. So much for his brilliant idea. "Why on earth would I invite him?"

"Because he can actually eat my food. And it seems to me you owe him an apology. I don't know what you two argued about, but I do know he is only watching out for your best interests."

"Fine." He did not like it, but she spoke the truth.

Savannah laid her head back. Her eyelids drooped, nearly meeting the dark circles beneath her eyes.

Reaching over, he brushed her leg then whipped his hand back. He did not intend to make her more uncomfortable than she was. "Rest."

With a quick nod, she let her lashes flutter closed.

Chapter 26

The best weapon against an enemy is another enemy.
—Friedrich Nietzsche

Lorenzo slid his hand over the deep indentation of the woman's waist then spanned the curve of her hip with his fingers. A masterpiece and yet, not what he searched for. She didn't possess ivory skin, ebony hair and cat-green eyes.

"I am done here." Annoyed and bored, he pushed the brunette off his lap. "Where is he, damn it? He should be back now." Each day, Savannah became more of an obsession. Was this it? Had he been relegated to a stereotypical drug pusher who spent his every free moment fucking whores?

Marcelo guided the woman from the spacious booth and turned to him. "My lord, are you referring to Giovanni or Paolo?"

"Does it matter?" Both in fact, but he was more concerned Giovanni had done something stupid and fallen prey to Luke. "I told Giovanni not to try anything without my go ahead. He said they reached the cabin last night. I spoke to him this morning. It is now nightfall and he has yet to call. This is my punishment for sending a boy. Foolish idiot probably got distracted."

"Paolo will find him, I am sure of it."

"He better." He laid back his head, closed his eyes and concentrated on keeping himself calm. He thirsted now and would need to drink soon.

"You look pale. Shall I bring you a fresh glass of blood?" Marcelo's voice quavered on the last word, giving Lorenzo pause. He opened his eyes, turned to Blood Bar's entrance. "What is it?" His throat went dry as Luke entered, weaving through the crowd toward him. "Bring me some blood. Now," he gritted out. "And make it warm."

Marcelo hurried off without a word.

"Luke." Lorenzo greeted Luke with a smile despite the strong urge to strangle the immortal life from him. Now was not the time. There were too many witnesses, both human and vampire.

Luke nodded in acknowledgement.

"I must say I'm surprised to see you here. Didn't you say you were leaving town?"

"The trip was cut short. I had some business to take care of here." Luke's dark eyes were devoid of emotion.

"I see." Damn Giovanni. If he weren't already dead, Lorenzo would finish him off once he saw him. "What brings you here on this fine night?" He accepted the glass of blood Marcelo brought to the table and sipped. "Would you like some blood?"

Luke ignored his question and leaned forward, his eyes burning the deep red of the blood in the glass. "Care to explain what you are trying to play at, sending your man to kill Savannah?"

"What?" He bolted up from his seat. "I'll kill the bastard. He wasn't to lay a hand on her." Fire burned through him at the realization Giovanni had nearly destroyed his plans.

"Do not bother, I already did the honors," Luke said.

He sat down. "I guess a thank you is in order."

Luke's impenetrable gaze bored into him. "You lied. He was the one I saw at the auction."

Lorenzo sipped, then pulled out a cigar. He had to tread carefully in answering his questions. At this point, Luke probably would not believe anything he said. "You're right. I lied. You wouldn't have let me close otherwise. I was concerned about you and sent Giovanni to watch you, but apparently he kept his own agenda. I am not so stupid as to go after Savannah, not knowing her value. Besides, I have bigger fish to deal with."

"Do you actually expect me to believe you? Since when have you had issues controlling your own men?"

"Happens more often than you think. He was an idiot." He lit his cigar and took a puff. "One who deserved the punishment he got. Come now and let's leave this alone. No matter what I say, you won't believe me. So it seems we are at an impasse."

Luke's chair scraped the floor as he rose. "I am giving you fair warning. Come after Savannah again and you will not live to see another moonrise. In fact, I will feed you to the Ancients myself."

If the prick wanted to play dirty, so be it. "Don't be absurd. I may be trapped in this hell of mine but my allies are many. You don't stand a chance against me."

"I do not care a bloody lick for your threats. Come after mine and you are a dead. Do I make myself clear?"

"Who do you expect to protect you from the Ancients?"

Luke turned and headed toward the exit.

"You'll regret this."

"I shall take my chances." He disappeared through the crowd.

Damn it. Lorenzo swiped his hand across the table, clearing it of glasses and a stone ashtray.

Marcelo approached. "Did you discover what happened with Giovanni?"

"He's dead."

"And you're letting his murderer go?" Marcelo bowed his head and stepped back. "Forgive me. I thought you wanted the woman."

"I do. And I'm through being patient." He stood and took another puff from his cigar. "Luke is a man distracted." And he was up to something. "Get ahold of Paolo and tell him to get back here. We need to move quickly."

* * * *

Savannah woke in the stillness of predawn. Tucked into the warmth of her bed, the chill of being alone seeped into her bones. She was back in Luke's apartment. Sitting up, she smoothed a hand over her chest and stomach. A silk slip covered her, stopping above her knees. She didn't remember exiting the car, which meant Luke must have carried her up and changed her clothes. The thought sent a current of heat coursing through her and she hated her body for its reaction. "Traitor."

She wanted him. As a human, as a vampire, she no longer cared which. Damn him. He made her a hypocrite. How could she ask him to change himself when she refused to do the same? Broderick was right. She should understand better than most the difficulty in being accepted for oneself.

Throwing the comforter aside, she slid off the bed and hurried to the door. She wanted some air, time to think. Outside her room, the hallway was dark, but her sight adjusted as she made her way toward the staircase leading to the roof. Time in the garden might relax her.

As she neared Luke's room, she slowed. His door was open. Curious, as he never left it open. She paused at the entrance. The bedroom was as spacious as she'd expected. A cozy sitting area opened up into a larger space where a four post bed stood against the middle of one wall. Beyond the bed, the gray light of night's transition traced Luke's silhouette against an enormous window. Shirtless, he leaned on the glass. Low-slung pants hugged the base of his back and hips. Slender rays of moonlight dusted his shoulders, emphasizing their broadness and the definition of the muscles in his arms and back.

She placed a hand on her stomach to calm the flurry of nerves whirling within her. This might be easier if she weren't so attracted to him.

"Only a couple hours until I must close the blinds," he said. "This is the closest I get to sunrise, as the sun is strongest for us then."

"Your door was open." She winced at her statement of the obvious. She'd never entered his room before. Why had he allowed her to tonight?

"Trouble going back sleep?" he asked

"Yes." She twisted her hands together and stepped forward.

"And yet you entered a monster's lair."

After the way she'd behaved yesterday, she deserved his bitter words. "I planned to sit in the roof garden."

He hung his head. "Enjoy yourself. Forgive my barbs, I grow tired."

"I didn't think vampires got tired."

"Not much physically, however, that does not exempt us from life's taxations." He lifted his head but his face remained in the shadows. "What is it you want, Savannah? I cannot read your jumbled emotions and quite frankly, I have no inclination to probe further."

"I know," she said, thinking about her next words. Maybe now wasn't a good time to talk to him and he was too fed up to hear her out.

"If you have come to fault me for your arousal—"

"No." Her cheeks heated at his words. "Not exactly." She breathed in deep. "I came to apologize for being so difficult."

"What brought this about?" He moved toward her. "Have you changed your mind about becoming a vampire?"

She bit her lip and shook her head. "No, but I do realize you have no control over what you've become. After all I've been through, I should have been more understanding."

He stopped, facing her. His gaze searched her face. "And now?" His voice was no more than a whisper.

"I don't care anymore." Savannah trembled, resisting the urge to cover her chest by crossing her arms. "I want to be with you, for as long as you'll have me."

His eyes drifted closed, lashes like midnight against the olive tone of his skin. When he opened them, they seemed nearer and when he cupped her neck in a hand, she didn't resist. "I feel I have waited an immortal lifetime to hear you say those words." He kissed her then, hard and unyielding, grasped the sides of her ribs and teased the tender undersides of her breasts with his thumbs. He pulled back slightly, leaned his forehead against hers. "Stay with me tonight, Savannah."

Unsure of her voice, she nodded.

He tugged her forward, twisted her so she faced his window. The rooftops of Rome spread out before her, sprinkled with intermittent cupolas. "The view is beautiful. I hadn't realized...I never looked outside my windows."

Luke kissed her jaw, worked his way down her neck and to her shoulders. "I never woke to see sunrise as a human. Now I long for the opportunity." He hooked his fingers beneath the thin straps of her slip, brushed them down her shoulders. The silk material peeled back, revealing the two rosy tips of her breasts. "Do you know what I want to do to you?" He breathed out the question against her ear as he rolled one nipple between a thumb and index finger.

The streets below were empty. Still, she couldn't stop the anxiety about her body. "My scars—"

"Are beautiful." Releasing her nipple, he slid the slip over her hips, letting it pool on the floor. She wore nothing beneath. "Close your eyes."

She did as he asked.

His touch was firm but gentle as he lifted her arms, pushed her forward against the glass. "Your skin looks like porcelain beneath the moon's light." He kissed her back, eased his hands along the indentation of her waist and over the flare of her hips. Groaning, he pressed his length against her backside.

When had he removed his pants? Goose bumps rose on her skin as her head fell back. She moaned, arching forward. Her nipples became like tight little beads and shocks of pleasure sparked from where they rubbed against the glass.

Hands on her hips, he lifted her, placing himself beneath her entrance. One thrust and he could enter.

Savannah whimpered. "Please."

Driving upward, he sheathed himself within her. In and out, he tortured her with slow, deep strokes. "Better?" She heard a smile in his voice.

"Hmmm." She nodded and lifted herself up on her forearms, leaned against the window. Her breath fogged the glass. With each thrust, her breasts swayed, hitting the smooth, clear surface in front of her. "Luke."

He pulled himself from her, but before she could cry out in despair, he turned her and plunged into her again. "I want to see your face when you come." He cradled her back as he dipped his head, caressed the pink tip of one breast with his lips. His body ground against her, spreading her legs further apart.

She threaded her hands through his hair, but he caught them and restrained them above her head. Crest upon crest built up within her as his gaze bored into hers. The friction between their bodies pushed her toward the edge. She shook her head, unable to deal with the growing angst. "I can't."

"Let yourself go." He kissed her. When she came, he deepened the kiss, swallowing her cry.

Pulling away, he cupped her chin and tipped it up so she faced him. His lips twitched as if resisting a smile. "Not quite as hard as you thought?"

Hard? If anything, it was way too easy to lose her head around him. "Not quite."

He stepped back from the window, taking her with him, legs still wrapped around him. His hardness pulsed within her. He hadn't yet found his release and the realization unsettled her. Did he not find her appealing?

"Shhh." He placed a finger along her lips. "Release whatever doubts are occupying your mind." He pulled himself from her and set her before him. "This night is yours."

She wanted to pleasure him, but the words to tell him so stuck to her tongue. She faltered in her step.

"Careful, pet. I have you," he said, steadying her.

With one hand, she encircled his length. Covered in her release, it glistened. Up and down, up and down, she caressed him.

Moaning, he stilled her hand and holding it, tugged her with him as he moved toward the bed. He lifted her, set her on the bed and covered her. Their bodies intertwined, and he wedged one knee between her thighs.

Tonight he became hers and she, his. She reached up and cupped his face, bringing him closer. His mouth melded to hers, his kiss impassioned but not rough. He broke the kiss. Moving down her, he poised himself above her entrance.

"What are you doing?" She lifted herself up on her elbows.

"You shall see." His dark eyes danced as he leaned close, flicked her clit with his tongue. Back and forth, faster then slower.

Hands fisted in the sheets, she arched upward, surprised at the tremors of ecstasy lancing through her. Could she find another release so soon? "Luke," she cried.

Gripping her rear, he lifted her closer, suckling her as her hips jerked against his lips. When the storm of pleasure had calmed, he rose. "Tonight you are mine. There is neither past nor future to think about." *Let your mind be free*, he whispered through her mind.

She nodded and helped him slide a condom down his length. He pushed into her. Her slick canal accepted him easily, and she lifted her pelvis to meet him, matching his hurried rhythm. One hand wrapped around the back of his neck, she pushed herself up and kissed him. Her breasts bounced with the movement, her nipples grazed his chest.

He reached down and cradled her back, rolled her so she sat atop him then thrust into her harder, faster. Pushed forward by the force, she braced herself against his shoulders as she looked down at him. Her curtain of hair shaded his face from the moonlight and she drew it back to see him. His every muscle tensed as he plunged into her. Waves of pleasure built inside her.

Releasing a deep growl, Luke drove into her one last time. One fang swept against her nipple, pushing her into release.

* * * *

Savannah slept peacefully beside Luke, her soft purrs alluring. He could not tell how long he'd stared at her, imagining an impossible life. A life that involved a house full of children and grandchildren. One where he woke each morning to see her curled into his side.

"Luke?"

He met her questioning gaze. "You are awake."

She nodded. "I called your name several times. Is everything okay?"

He breathed in her scent and wrapped an arm around her. "My mind drifted elsewhere. The truth is, I have not felt this incredible in a long time. I could not ask for more."

"Well, we shouldn't stop." Savannah licked her bottom lip and pulled on it with her top front teeth as she came up to her knees and straddled his hips.

Luke lifted his hands but she caught them, pushing them down to the bed. Her bare breasts swayed over his face and he longed to catch a nipple between his lips. "What are you doing?"

She tilted her head. "Taking control. Do you think you could handle surrendering yourself to me?"

No his mind screamed and yet his insides quivered with anticipation and excitement. He wanted to surrender himself. He wanted to show her he trusted her. "You would not be in your current position if I could not handle it."

"In that case..." She bent and nibbled the length of his jaw, made her way down his neck and across his chest. She scooted lower along his body. The friction between them drove him insane.

Luke groaned as she circled one of his nipples with her tongue and trailed her way over his stomach. His muscles went taut with restraint as he ached to grab her and return the attention.

"Not yet." She laughed as she smoothed her thumb along his length. She encircled him, pumping up and down. "I can feel you thrumming beneath me. Don't worry. You'll get your turn soon enough." Holding his gaze, she licked her lips and brushed their wet softness against his tip.

Luke growled. "Any man, human or otherwise, would have a difficult time handling you."

Savannah lifted her head and smiled. "I guess that makes you a lucky guy."

Lucky would not even begin to cover how he felt at this moment. He cupped her face, guiding her to him as he pushed himself into a sitting position. "Beyond lucky," he said and kissed her. He deepened the kiss as he caressed her arms, gently pulling her toward him.

She placed a hand on his chest and pulled away. "Not so fast, charmer. First things first." Reaching down, she gripped his shaft and rose up on her knees. She pressed his tip to her entrance then slid herself down the length of him. Whimpering, she ground herself against him, wrapped her arms around his neck. "Kiss me, Luke."

His pent up passion unraveling, he kissed her. As if it had a mind of its own, his body arched into her, driving him deeper into her wet sheath. He surrendered to her rhythm as she rode him, her hips building speed like a piston.

Head thrown back, she cried out first as she pressed herself to him.

His cry was deep and guttural as he released himself into her.

Silence hung heavy during the minutes that followed. Something had changed within him, yet he hesitated to say what.

Savannah seemed to sense the difference, but said nothing. Instead, she guided him back against the bed and curled into his side. Within minutes, her breaths softened into a slow and steady rhythm.

"Sweet dreams, love." Luke placed a kiss along her temple and curved his arm around her.

* * * *

Sensual. Luke almost laughed at the thought. As a human, he'd never experienced a woman with a passion for food. His mother, who'd deemed cooking beneath her, would not have known the difference between poultry and venison. And Victoria, like today's women, had eaten like a bird for fear of an expanding figure. Not Savannah.

Her hips danced slowly, their only apparent melody boiling water and the clink of a whisk along the sides of a pot.

He shook his head, making a poor attempt to avoid the innocent seduction. After last night, he found it difficult to keep his gaze from straying to her. "Where did you learn to cook?"

"I've always loved to experiment. Guess it's creating something others get so much pleasure from. I used to cook with my mother. Don't you have a favorite meal your mom made?"

"No." He laughed. "My mother never cooked. We employed a housekeeper who made incredible scones and blackberry preserves. At times, she indulged my cravings." He shrugged. "I fear my short human life left me lacking in exposure to culinary delights. I was not an adventurous sort in that aspect."

"And as a vampire?" Savannah asked.

"Those of us who are purebred neither need nor desire food as you humans do."

"Too bad. I don't know what I'd do if I couldn't cook. Can you smell the butter?" She turned, her eyes gleamed with delight. She looked beautiful in a white, off-the-shoulder sweater dress. Simple, yet understatedly sexy. "I don't even need to taste it to know this polenta is going to be amazing."

"I must take you at your word." He breathed in deep. Fontina and parmigiano reggiano permeated the atmosphere and yet the scent tantalizing him belonged to her. Vanilla and orange blossoms. He closed his eyes, slid from his stool to stand behind her. His hands lingered over her hips.

"Smells delicious, huh?" She spun around and yelped at his nearness. "Luke, what are you doing?"

He bent his head over her bare shoulder and opened his eyes. He did not need a mirror to know they glowed deep burgundy with hunger. He grasped the whisk from her hand and stirred the yellow puree behind her, embracing her between his body and the stove. "Must I wait until later for a taste?"

She laughed and shoved him back, but not before he felt a tremor wrack her. "Savannah." He groaned and buried his face against her chest.

The bell to his apartment buzzed.

"Bloody hell," Luke said. "He is early." He would kill Broderick.

"Don't be rude, he's your friend." She pushed him aside to answer the door.

"Wait." He slipped his hand around hers and spun her back to him. "Finish up here. I will greet him."

Her eyes narrowed then she reached for the pot of polenta and removed it from the burner. "Fine, but be nice."

Nice? The halfling deserved a lesson in etiquette. Luke walked to the door and opened it. "What happened to the key I lent you?"

Broderick grinned and stepped inside. "Wouldn't want to interrupt anything." He held out a bottle of red wine. "I brought *vino* for the lady."

"You are fifteen minutes early."

He scoffed, removing his leather jacket. "If you hadn't started with her already, fifteen minutes is hardly going to make a difference."

"I disagree," Luke replied. "Still, we shall postpone that discussion until I have time to school you in the art of giving pleasure."

"Ouch." Broderick laughed. "Guess I did get you at a bad time."

"You're here." Savannah entered the foyer, arms spread for an embrace. The sight stole the words from Luke's lips, forcing him to turn away. "Since you're here, you can help Luke finish setting the table. He's been a distracting assistant, to say the least."

"I bet he has, but I see you're learning fast. Haven't even been here five minutes and you're putting me to work."

"No work, no food," Savannah said in a sing song voice as she headed back toward the kitchen.

"You good, man? You talk to Lorenzo?" Broderick's hand came to rest on Luke's shoulder.

"I spoke to him."

"And?"

"It is as I expected," Luke replied. "He has been behind everything this entire time. Of course, he would never admit this."

"What are you going to do? Will you tell her what she is?"

"Not yet. I do not want her frightened." Luke turned, nodded toward where Savannah had disappeared. "We can talk later. Ready to make yourself useful?"

"Sure, let's do this."

Chapter 27

Jealousy is that pain which a man feels from the apprehension that he is not equally beloved by the person whom he entirely loves.
—*Joseph Addison*

Luke clasped his hands beneath the dining room table for fear he would snap the solid slab of wood in half. Considering the trouble Savannah had gone through to lay out tonight's meal, the move would hardly get him in her good graces.

Jealousy was a vicious sentiment. And an unpleasant, new one for him. Born into privilege and wealth, he'd expanded his holdings through buying and selling real estate.

As a human, station alone had earned him friends and garnered the affections of society's heiresses. Not so with Savannah.

"Wow." Broderick made a show of rubbing his flat stomach as he slid further down in his high backed chair. "I've been around long enough to know a great meal when I've eaten one and that was most definitely a great meal. You would make a wonderful chef."

Savannah smiled and sipped her wine.

Luke had lost count of how many smiles she'd shared with Broderick. This was her fourth glass of wine, though, and the Chianti had worked its magic. Or so he preferred to believe.

"Oh, tonight was nothing," she gushed, grasping Broderick's wrist. "You've got to try some of my classics. I don't claim to be Italian but I make a mean cannelloni."

"Dish time." Luke stood, picked up the almost empty wine bottle and shoved it at Broderick's chest. "Guest's honor. You can help."

"But I'm not done with my drink." Savannah pouted, her face etched with confusion. "And we're having such good conversation."

Maybe so, but if she smiled at Broderick one more time, he would end up doing something he would later regret. "It is late. We must leave for the charity auction soon."

"Another auction. What kind of charities could vampires possible have? Why must we go?"

Luke caught Broderick's gaze. "We have already established we are not an uncivilized people. Please get dressed. We will wait for you here." He turned to Broderick. "I will lend you a blazer."

Savannah rose from her chair, her expression one of restrained anger. "I can see you've gone into your closed-mouth mode again." With a polite nod at Broderick, she turned and left the room.

"You've only angered her," Broderick said. "Why not tell her the truth? You plan to kill Lorenzo and turn her."

"Do not be daft. She would leave here running for her life or whatever short time remains of it." Luke walked to the foyer closet and pulled out a black blazer. "Besides, if I can avoid changing her, I will." He lifted the blazer. "Here, this matches your pants."

Broderick accepted the jacket. "I don't see another way to get her out of this alive or without being tortured. Still, she would forego a lot as a vampire."

"I know." Luke rolled his shoulders. "I want you to ensure she has everything she needs to open her restaurant. Life as a vampire would be different but she can still achieve her dreams."

"What about you?"

"What about me? You know what needs to happen for me to turn her."

"You can have someone else turn her," Broderick said. "Not everyone knows what her blood is capable of."

"No. I do not want anyone else touching her. I cannot trust anyone else."

"Have you thought about the fact that she loves you? I see it in her face whenever she glances your way." Broderick stood and faced him. "It mirrors the look you have when you see her."

"Do not be absurd." He glanced away, unable to meet his friend's gaze, when he knew he spoke the truth. "And even if what you say is the case, what difference should it make?"

"Oh, I don't know. Maybe you deserve a chance at happily ever after and that mushy crap?"

Luke bit out a sarcastic laugh and shook his head. "There is a reason they call it mushy crap."

Broderick sighed. "Any other plan in the works?"

Nothing, unless a deal could be established with the Ancients. "I shall speak with Rafe tonight."

"A death wish, considering you used his stolen vial of blood."

"My arm is also proof it did not work."

"How do you know he'll be there, anyway?" Broderick threaded his hands through his hair. "And if he is, there are so many things that can go wrong. He might try to kill or capture Savannah himself once he knows there is no cure against her."

"The Ancients always attend these charity events. Makes them appear generous. I do not believe Rafe would capture her." Luke shook his head. "He had his opportunity. My instincts lead me to believe him different."

"You've got a lot riding on mere instincts," Broderick said.

Luke nodded. The risk he took was beyond dangerous. What if Rafe did not accept Lorenzo's death in exchange for protection? What would he request?

"I'm ready." Savannah walked out in a simple, navy gown with an asymmetrical neckline. The dress hugged her curves and as she approached, side slits swung open, revealing a creamy expanse of shapely legs. "How do I look?" She spun and the dress fluttered up, showing off dainty diamond-encrusted shoes. A collar of diamonds and sapphires covered her most visible scars.

Broderick gained his ability to speak first. "Absolutely stunning."

She smiled then turned and glared at Luke.

"Breathtaking." His voice came out gruff and he lifted his good arm. "Shall we go?"

* * * *

The charity auction appeared much like the garden event Savannah attended the first night, only tonight rain forced them in doors. Trying hard to behave civilly instead of strangling Luke, she smiled and plucked a glass of champagne off a passing tray.

"There are a lot of people here tonight," she said as a group of elegantly dressed vampires passed by, laughing amongst themselves. "And I feel underdressed, even with this necklace."

Next to the graceful immortals, that was probably the understatement of the century. She wished Luke had given her more information about their plans, but pushing him earlier when he was annoyed would have gotten her nowhere.

"A larger ballroom would have been preferable." Broderick squeezed her arm gently. "And you look lovely. Don't worry about your dress."

"Poor planning on our host's part. It has been threatening rain for several days now." Luke pulled Savannah in front of him as they wove around the maze of vampires and blood slaves filling the room. "This is an immense torture. I detest crowds. They make me feel claustrophobic."

"What a surprise," Broderick drawled.

"Wait with Savannah a moment, I will return shortly."

Savannah's back went cold as Luke removed his hand and disappeared through a cluster of people. "Doesn't he drive you crazy?"

"With Luke, you have to learn to take both the good and the bad. After a time though, you learn there is much more good than bad."

In her aggravated state, she was reluctant to agree. "Where is he going now?"

"I believe he spotted Rafe," Broderick said.

"He is going to talk to the Ancients? Why?" An icy coldness settled deep in the pit of her stomach.

"He wants to talk to them about Lorenzo."

"And if they won't listen to him? He should have given them a vial of my blood."

"Yes, and then you'd be chained in some basement being drained for experimental purposes and we'd be dead."

Trapped amongst packs of vampires didn't seem any better. "If life deals me such a fate, so be it."

Broderick tugged on her arm, pulled her to face him. "You don't mean that. Whether you speak from fear or concern, I don't know. Perhaps both, but I assure you Luke wouldn't do this for just anyone. If he didn't care for you, you would have been dead long ago. Stop behaving like a naive human. I know you're capable of more."

She bowed her head, suddenly embarrassed at her spoiled retort. He was right. Wine had gone to her head, creating a pounding headache. "I'm sorry."

"Impeccable timing." Broderick's eyes widened as Lorenzo approached him from behind and lifted a knife to his neck, gliding it along his tight, pale skin. "Enchanting as always, Ms. Michaels."

"Leave, Savannah," Broderick said.

"How noble, but I'm afraid she has no place to go. Or maybe she doesn't want to leave you stranded." Lorenzo smiled. "Am I right?"

Savannah stepped back, only to find a steely arm had snaked around her midsection. She shoved at the arm clothed in black cotton. "What do you want?"

Three large vampires came to stand on either side of Broderick as Lorenzo approached her, caressed her ear with his lips. "I've got plans for you."

An icy shiver skipped down her spine.

Broderick's expression had turned stormy. "Let her go. Your quarrel isn't with her. What is it you want?"

"Nothing you or that prick Evans could give me." Lorenzo trailed a finger along her jaw, turning her gaze upward so she looked into his angular face. His eyes flared a deep pomegranate. "Sleep, dearest."

"No." Fear coiled within as her eyelids drifted shut.

Chapter 28

Fear cannot take what you do not give it.
—Christopher Coan

Fear and rage clenched Luke's chest as he headed down the long hallway in hopes of cutting Lorenzo off. The house seemed more like a labyrinth with its rooms and hallways. He should have expected the other vampire's interference. He had not reached Rafe across the room when he'd seen Lorenzo and his minions surround Broderick and Savannah. Lorenzo must have grown desperate, to attack this publicly, especially with Ancients in attendance. If Rafe was there, it stood likely Drago and Cybele were also.

A shadow crossed the intersection before Luke. "There is nowhere you can go," he said. "I do not know what kind of businesses you have got running but she alone will not hold off the Ancients forever. You cannot truly believe she is the answer to your problems."

Lorenzo turned and laughed, shook his head. "No, I don't believe her to be the answer to all of my problems. But she sure as hell will make my life a bit easier. Besides, I hear there is a lot of money to be made in the underground blood market." Savannah hung limp in his arms, her hair a midnight veil over her face.

"Hand her over."

"I don't think so." Lorenzo smiled uneasily. "You made your stance clear. Don't worry though, I won't abuse her too intensely. Wouldn't want my weapon of destruction to run empty." He shifted her in his arms, shaking the hair from her face. The wine from earlier tinted her lips a deep red. "So still, as she sleeps. Pure innocence." He laughed.

"She does not deserve to be used this way." Luke edged closer, his gaze trained forward even as he sensed Broderick's emotions. "Think about what you are doing. You are lying to yourself if you believe you will walk away unscathed." With each step, he honed his body for action, knowing Lorenzo must have sensed the company.

"Any closer and you'll regret it." Lorenzo spun, but too late. Broderick launched himself from behind. Lorenzo loosened his grip to fight him off and Savannah fell to the wooden plank floor.

"Take her and go," Broderick said, struggling to keep a hold on the elder vampire.

Luke took in his friend's bloodied face, courtesy of Lorenzo's halfling goons. Lorenzo remained an aged pureblood, stronger and faster than them both. This time, Broderick most likely would not leave the fight standing. Nodding a silent *thank you*, Luke scooped up Savannah and ran. Chandeliers and people whipped by, but he did not slow as he broke through the crowded ballroom into the night.

Christ. What had he been thinking, taking such a chance? He should have been preparing for the inevitable instead of dreaming like a lovesick human. Only a day ago, he'd ridiculed Broderick and Savannah for possessing such weakness as to be driven by emotions. And yet he wanted nothing more than to pretend he was human.

Time ticked by. He stole a glance at Savannah. Her lashes fanned along pale cheeks. So peaceful in her slumber. Such irony, that he'd found her when the death he'd desired for so long grew close. Lorenzo would never stop chasing her and without the protection of the Ancients, others would follow. Luke's only hope was to buy enough time to turn her.

In no time, he reached the city. The impossibly fast click of his shoes along the cobblestones echoed as Savannah shifted in his arms. She moaned as Lorenzo's sleep command wore off, and he slowed pace so as not to make her sick.

"So sleepy. Luke?"

"I am here, pet."

"I dreamed we went to an auction and Lorenzo was there." She shivered and he squeezed her close. He would miss her scent of citrus and vanilla. As if she suddenly realized they were moving, she lifted her head and blinked at the racing scenery. "Where, what's going on?"

"Shh, love. Trust me. I will take care of you." He would not, could not fail her.

* * * *

Broderick swiped an arm across his mouth, breathing hard. Blood, dirt and sweat stained the ripped sleeve of his borrowed blazer.

"You're waning and I haven't even gotten started." Lorenzo laughed, casually rolling up his cuffs. "Did you actually think you could pin me? Idiotic fool."

"Don't you worry about me, I've got plenty of fight left," he lied. He might have been better off if Lorenzo's goons hadn't played a number on him, but considering he'd won out in three to one odds, he couldn't complain. Still, this time around didn't look or feel promising.

"You never were a good liar."

Broderick barked a laugh he didn't quite feel. "I guess I lack your talent in that arena."

Lorenzo swiped at him with a fist and Broderick leapt to the side a nanosecond too late. Bone crunched along bone, setting his face afire. He pulled back. Every second he stole gave him a chance to heal.

"No use buying time, halfling. You don't heal fast enough." Lorenzo lunged again, catching Broderick in the side. Breath left his body in a rush. "How do you like the feel of it?"

Damn Lorenzo and his bullshit taunting. He thrust forward with his right fist, grazing air as he missed his target by a couple inches. Too slow. Moving too slow. "Like the feel of what?"

"Death, of course. Don't you feel it creeping up on you?"

"You wish."

"Don't be stubborn. I can still use you."

"I'd rather die." Broderick spat.

Lorenzo rushed toward him, buried his forearm against Broderick's neck. "Something I can easily arrange." He pressed forward.

Broderick's throat burned and his breaths wheezed. Pushing back at Lorenzo, he lifted his chin higher. "Go ahead." If it was his time, he would go with pride. "When you find Luke it will be too late."

"He can't possibly fight off all my men." Lorenzo laughed. "Your efforts have been for nothing."

"Never." Broderick took a gulp of air and pushed back. Despite his attempt, his breaths grew shallower, his throat more painful. And then it stopped and he gulped in a mouthful of air before coughing uncontrollably. What the hell? Even with the relief of being able to breathe, his vision blurred and he doubled over.

"What have we here?" Drago entered the small space, making the air hum around them.

Broderick attempted to stand. If he thought himself done for before, there was no hope for him now. What was the Ancient doing here? Did he want Savannah too?

"Drago." Lorenzo's shirt hung off one shoulder and his mouth was bloodied.

Rafe stood behind Drago, arms crossed in front of his chest. "I warned you not to cross me. If it weren't for the score that needs to be settled, you wouldn't have lived to come to this auction tonight."

Lorenzo's gaze flipped from Drago to Rafe. "Savannah is with Luke and my men are after them. If we go now, I can show you everything I said is true. She can kill us all."

Drago tilted his head. "A bit of deja vu? Do you take me for a fool? Will you assure me the same way you swore you never touched my sister, never exposed her to danger?" Drago closed in, facing off with Lorenzo.

Lorenzo shook his head. "I can explain."

Drago laughed. "I've looked the other way with you for far too long. I only spared your life because you kept to the shadows and my sister thought she loved you. But now she's overcome that ridiculous notion and you've made the stupid decision to come out of hiding. I believe it's time I do what I should have done decades ago."

Lorenzo hissed and the two vampires dove at each other, wrestling in a blur of movement between the walls of the hallway. Snarls echoed as they bared their fangs. Lorenzo moved fast but he didn't stand a chance against the Ancient. When the shuffling stopped, Lorenzo hung limp in Drago's arms.

"You killed him," Broderick said, disbelieving what he'd seen. The Ancient had made it seem effortless. He rubbed his throat, knowing otherwise.

"So I did."

As if on cue, a couple of vampires entered the hallway. One took Lorenzo's lifeless body from Drago's arms. He then turned to Rafe and said, "You're needed for the opening auction speech, my lord."

"Fine." Rafe straightened his jacket. "I'll be right there."

Drago brushed a hand down his jacket and pants, which had remained impeccable despite the fight. "I believe I'm going to have a drink. Run-ins with riffraff always leave me thirsty. Besides, I'd rather avoid Cybele if possible. As soon as she learns I killed her ex-lover, she won't be too happy."

"I'll do my best to keep it secret for as long as possible," Rafe said.

Drago nodded and left them standing in the hallway.

Rafe spoke to the man who still held Lorenzo. "Remove his head and burn it along with the body." He turned to Broderick. "Where is Luke?"

"He left with Savannah." Broderick ran a hand through his hair. "Lorenzo's men went after him."

"He's going to try and change her, isn't he?"

"I believe so, yes."

Rafe turned to his men. "I must go. Have Cybele give the welcome speech."

"Yes, my lord." They turned and left.

"Let's go." Rafe grabbed the back of Broderick's left arm and guided him to a back entrance.

"I don't understand. Why are you helping us?" Broderick asked.

"Let's say, I don't like to let debts go unpaid."

Chapter 29

Each night, when I go to sleep, I die. And the next morning, when I wake up, I am reborn.
—Mahatma Gandhi

Luke sensed Lorenzo's men before he saw them standing at a vacant cross street ahead. Several more would follow them. He slowed to a walk. "Listen to me," he whispered in Savannah's ear. She nodded, eyes wide. The fright he saw in their emerald depths turned his insides. "There is much I still need to tell you but we are short on time. I am going to give you my blood to drink. You understand, right? There is no other way. These or other vampires will find you. They will use you."

"I know."

He set her down, unbuttoned the cuff of the sleeve covering his good arm and rolled it up. Bringing the underside of his wrist to his mouth, he met her gaze and bit down. Blood, sweet and tangy, oozed from a vein. "Here." He lifted his arm to her mouth.

She gripped his hand and forearm, swallowing as she stared at the broken skin. "I put my mouth there and drink?"

"Yes." He held back his wrist a bit as she tried to pull it close.

"What is it?" Savannah asked.

"I want you to know I am sorry, for everything," he said. "And I love you."

She tightened her hands around his arm, tears pooling in her eyes.

"You need not say anything. I wanted you to understand." He went quiet as a knot formed in his throat. He was not sure he knew the words to convince her any further.

She pulled his wrist close and rested her lips around the edges of his puncture points. Her eyelids drooped as she drank, a sight more erotic than any he had ever known. A ripple of heat speared through him.

"Enough." His voice came out gruff, hungry. He did not want her to stop. She pulled away and a blush stole up her neck. Her full lips dripped red.

"What the hell do you think you are doing?" One of Lorenzo's halflings approached, leading five vampires. The dark waves of his hair skimmed his shoulders and his pale blue gaze glowed beneath the dim street lamps. "Don't do anything stupid."

Luke laughed and pulled Savannah against him. "What would you classify as stupid?"

"You're outnumbered. Let her come with us and we'll let you live." The halfling turned, looked at his companions then grinned at him. "At least for a little longer."

"And if I refuse?" With a hand, he smoothed over Savannah's back then around her shoulder, lifting her hair away from her neck.

"We'll kill you and take her anyway. So what's it going to be?"

"What are you doing, Luke?" Savannah trembled beneath his touch and he hated the fact they frightened her.

The vampires and halfling surrounded them, their thirst for death suffocating. Luke gripped Savannah's neck and forced her to face him. "Fight, Savannah. Never give up on your dreams."

She bit her bottom lip in an attempt to stop its quivering. "Where are you going?"

"So brave. Even now, my pet." He caressed her cheek.

"Touching." The wavy-haired halfling closed in, his muscles contracting as he readied himself to pounce. "But it's got to come to an end."

Luke stood ready for him as he dove toward them. Tucking Savannah into his side, he spun and caught the halfling by his neck, propelling him with his own momentum into a store front. The male crashed into a metal grill, denting it and cracking the glass behind it. Two vampires attacked and he evaded their punches, buying several feet of distance.

Savannah's heartbeat galloped, her blood swished. Bending his head, he found her jugular with his mouth and let his fangs sink in. She gasped and stiffened within his arms then slowly relaxed. And for one infinitely small moment, she tasted sweet. Pure. Amazing. But soon the burning began.

The others froze in their tracks, watching and waiting, curiosity etched into their faces. Luke drank until the slicing pain radiating from the center of his chest made him dizzy. When he pulled away, his knees crumbled and he hit the cobblestone. Even the cool night air did not provide relief from the searing heat engulfing him. Reaching forward, he collapsed onto his front, and rolled to his back.

"Luke, oh my God. Luke." Savannah's face filled his vision as she kneeled beside him, hands roving over his face and body. Tears streamed down her cheeks.

He wanted to tell her not to cry, but could not speak. Blood soaked her hands, and he feared she had somehow been hurt, but as red crept across his vision, he realized he bled.

"You stupid vampire." She shook her head and bent to kiss him. Blood from his mouth stained her lips. "Why?"

With all his strength, he lifted a hand and caressed her jaw. He did not have strength enough to push thoughts into her mind. He could only hope she saw the answer in his eyes, understood he loved her with his entire heart and whatever piece of his damned soul he still retained.

Dropping his hand, he laid his head back. Her change would start soon and with it, hate would come. Pain numbed him, bringing a glorious cold. He felt light and almost human. His eyelids grew heavy. It would soon be over.

"Luke."

His name caught his attention and he searched out the voice. Broderick bent over him. "You fucking idiot."

Forever with the insults. Luke coughed an answer but Broderick shook his head and said, "I understand. I'll take care of her."

Relief settled in his chest and he let go.

* * * *

"No." Savannah lay on the cold, wet cobblestones, unable to believe she watched the man she loved disappear into thin air. How cruel, destiny didn't even leave her a body to mourn.

"It's okay." Broderick's hands gripped her shoulders and she shook them off.

"No, it's not." Deep anguish bubbled up within her, rocking her body. Sobs came in a gush, painful in their intensity. "I loved him." And in the chaos of the moment she hadn't even remembered to tell him.

"I know. I did too. He was like a brother to me."

She turned and met Broderick's gaze. In the gray blue depths of his eyes she could see he meant it.

"I promised him I would take care of you," he said. "You will go through the change soon and it's going to be painful."

"No, she won't," Rafe said.

Savannah pushed herself into a sitting position. The Ancient stood beside them. Anger burned through her chest. "You. What are you doing here?" She rose to her feet and pushed at his chest. "This is your fault."

"No, Savannah." Broderick shook his head, still squatting over the area where Luke had disintegrated. "If it weren't for him and Drago, I wouldn't be here. I wouldn't have had the chance to say goodbye."

"No, she's right," Rafe said. "I didn't know Luke's intentions, otherwise I would have warned him. The Blessed don't change. They can't." He turned to face Lorenzo's men. "Your leader is dead. Leave, unless you want to join him." As if to further prove his point, he whipped out his arm and all six hit the wall. They scrambled to their feet and ran.

"Wait a minute." Broderick stood. "What do you mean, they can't change?"

"Who doesn't change?" Her head pounded and none of what they said made sense.

"They're pure and sacred. For those reasons, their blood harms us." Rafe bent down beside her. "I am sorry for your loss."

She turned away from him. "What is he talking about, Broderick?"

Broderick placed a hand on her shoulder. "I should have forced Luke to tell you."

"Tell me what? What does Rafe mean, when he says I can't change?" she asked him but turned to Rafe for an answer.

"Three hundred and thirty-three seconds." Rafe leaned against a wall, arms crossed. "Your body ceased to live at one point in your life for this length of time. Enough time for you to reach heaven and return."

"Your accident changed your blood. Made you a sacred being capable of destroying our race," Broderick said. "That's why Lorenzo wanted you."

Savannah blinked. "My blood." She recalled the morning her blood burned Luke's arm. Heat seared her, deep in her chest. "You both knew this entire time? And Luke? He did this on purpose." Why hadn't they said anything? Why had Rafe let this happen?

"He thought this the only way," replied Broderick. "He didn't know you wouldn't change. He wanted to tell you but worried about your reaction."

She looked down, unable to think of a reply

"I must go," Rafe said as he bent close. "I don't expect or care for your forgiveness and trust, but I will tell you I didn't want Luke's death. He saved my life at the auction and his spirit has given me a renewed sense of purpose. I know what he meant to you. I am sorry this happened." He walked over to Broderick. "Drago does not concern himself with her, for now. Best to keep it that way for as long as we can. Take her back to Boston. I will ensure her safety. No one will make an attempt on her life. It's the least I can do."

Broderick nodded and Rafe left.

Savannah stared at his retreating back. He and another Ancient had saved Broderick from Lorenzo. She was grateful but the hurt from her loss overshadowed everything. What would become of her now?

"In time you may forgive him...you may forgive us." Broderick lifted an arm and she looked down at her hands. They were still covered in blood. "It's okay," he said.

She wiped her palms on the slinky material of her dress then hooked her arm through his, letting him support her. "I want to leave as soon as possible. I don't want anything to do with vampires or the Blessed or any of this."

"I understand. There are a few affairs of Luke's I need to take care of. Can you handle going back to his place?"

She nodded. She wasn't sure she could handle anything at this point but she needed to shower and the more efficiently she let Broderick work, the faster she'd leave Rome.

At Luke's apartment, she sat on his living room couch as Broderick combed through a box of Luke's belongings.

"Luke would have wanted you to take this money. It was part of your contract."

Savannah shook her head at the check Broderick held. "A contract I never completed. I don't want any of his money." She rubbed her arms, unable to chase away the cold. She'd sat under the hot rush of water for nearly an hour and yet the chill still seeped deep into her bones. "I want to go home." And bury herself beneath a pile of blankets.

Broderick approached and touched her chin, lifted her gaze to his. She didn't want to face him. Didn't want to see the sadness that lingered there. "Look at me, Savannah."

She did as he asked. The knot in her throat threatened to come undone and her stomach flexed. She needed to hold herself together.

"Luke did what he did because you gave him life. He lived through your dreams and hopes." He lifted the check. "Without this, you might as well throw those dreams away."

Savannah began to turn away then paused. What a fool she'd been. He had known what would happen. She remembered Luke's words, his request she fight for her dreams. Damn him. With a sigh she took the check, slipped it into the purse slung across her chest.

The side of Broderick's mouth lifted in some semblance of a smile. "Good. I know it is difficult now but with time you will learn to dream again."

She nodded but only because she didn't have strength to argue.

Broderick drove her to the airport. He didn't say anything further because there wasn't anything left to say—at least that's what she told herself. They parted ways at security and she couldn't help but feel a load lifted from her shoulders. He was her last connection to the past couple weeks, to Luke.

As she sat in the plane and gazed at her faded reflection in the window, she smoothed the shadows beneath her eyes with a finger. Her face appeared drawn and much older than her twenty-nine years. Flight attendants droned on about life vests and emergency exits but she hardly heard them, nor did she care to. She wished the plane would fall out of the sky or skid off the runway, and those thoughts made her feel guilty. Those around her deserved better than the suicidal ponderings of a wannabe chef. If only a black hole would open up beneath her and suck her in.

"Excuse me, miss. Can I get you a drink?" A bright-eyed blonde smiled at her, showing a row of straight, perfectly white teeth.

Savannah wondered what the woman would say if she asked for blood. She resisted the urge. "I'm fine. Thank you." Without giving the flight attendant a chance to ask anything else, she turned toward the window and let exhaustion have its way.

Chapter 30

With my ninth mind I resurrect my first and dance slow to the music of my soul made new.
—Aberjhani

Luke sank into the comforting warmth enveloping him. It seeped into his body, infusing him with an energy he had not felt in decades or more. Somehow he understood it protected him and he imagined he could be quite happy spending an eternity in this pleasant nowhere. He could not see anything around him, nor did he care to look. He felt good, soothed and at peace, and only that mattered.

Too soon, the coat of comfort dissipated, leaving the cold, hard reality of a cobblestone street. Suddenly, his body ached everywhere. He could not recall ever feeling this sore, not even as a human. "Christ."

Rolling onto his back, he groaned and shivered as his skin dipped into a tire-sized puddle of water. He pushed himself into a sitting position to avoid the chilling wetness and rubbed his forehead. His head throbbed as if someone had taken a jackhammer to it. Bloody hell. When was the last time he'd had a headache? His completely nude state did not help, especially since he sat in the middle of a narrow Roman street. And he had no recollection of how he'd arrived there.

"Savannah." Where was she? He turned, scanning his surroundings, and recognized the area. A side street of Piazza del Popolo. He had been with Savannah here, cornered by Lorenzo's men. He swore he'd drunk from her but it blurred in his mind.

Either way, it would not do to sit naked in the middle of the street. Francesca. Her *pensione* was nearby and she would know what to do. He needed to find Savannah.

Scrambling to his feet, he half stumbled and half walked on wobbly legs. He stuck to shadows and used the wall to brace himself as his body grew weak. Something was wrong. Had he been exposed to some sort of sunlight? He had not felt this nauseous in over two centuries. His stomach lurched with every step.

By the time he had reached the door to Francesca's inn, sweat had beaded on his forehead, above his lip and around his neck. If it were not so cold outside, he might have passed out. As it was, standing seemed to take an immense amount of effort. Fortunately, the door swung wide with his first knock.

"My goodness, Dante." Francesca stepped forward and dug her small hands into his skin as she attempted to support his weight. "What happened to you?"

What had happened to him? If only he could answer that question for himself. "Pardon my state of undress. I am not sure where my clothes have disappeared to. And Savannah, she is gone. I have to find her."

The older woman shook her head as she lowered him into a chair and brought him a blanket to place over himself. "You aren't going anywhere in this condition." Francesca bent low, gripped his chin and tilted his face up to hers. Her burnt toffee gaze narrowed as she searched his face. "Incredible. I never thought this would be possible. I even hesitated despite my visions, but seeing it confirmed it is something of a miracle."

"What is possible?" He had not the slightest idea to what she referred. She looked him up and down, studying him as if he were something or someone she had never seen. "Please, Francesca. You must help me find Savannah."

"The girl, did you turn her?"

He nodded. "I had to. Lorenzo's men did not leave me much choice."

Francesca pursed her lips then released a long sigh. "The most I can hope to do is prepare you. You can't go find her without understanding the change you've undergone. And if she truly has gone through any kind of transformation...let's wait and see."

"Prepare me for what?" Luke asked, exasperated. "I have not undergone any changes. I am merely exhausted and out of options. For all I know, Broderick could be dead. Perhaps I can contact Rafe but every passing minute, my chances of finding her lessen."

Francesca shook her head and left the room.

Luke put the heel of his hand to his forehead and massaged in a circular motion. His headache acted up again. Who knew if Lorenzo's men would leave Savannah alone even if he had succeeded in turning her? He could only hope they would give up on the idea of her as a weapon. She would be strong as a new vampire, but not strong enough to fight off Lorenzo.

"Here." Francesca entered the room and placed a plate of bread and a glass of milk on a table in front of him. "I baked this bread today. I think we should hold off on extra butter or jam for now."

What the devil was she talking about? "I cannot possibly eat this. You know my diet requires something a bit more substantial." Even as he said the words, his mouth watered at the sight of bread and milk.

"Eat it. If you are still craving something more *substantial* afterward, I will see what I can scrounge up."

Luke eyed the bread. A small bit of it would not benefit him but neither would it hurt him. And for some reason the thought of biting into bread held great appeal. He snagged the slice and bit into one of the sides. Buttery softness melted onto his tongue, and he moaned. "This is amazing," he said as he bit off a large piece of the slice. He reached for the milk and gulped it down. He lifted the glass out to her. "Have you any more?"

"Of course," answered Francesca. "But I think it best if you slow down. This is new to you."

"I need strength. I need to find Savannah." He broke off another piece of the bread and shoved it into his mouth. His stomach lurched, and he dropped the small portion remaining. "Bloody hell." He pushed up from the chair and stumbled to her lobby area, tripping over the blanket he held covering himself. After heaving several times, he'd emptied the contents of his stomach into a small trash bin. He swiped his arm across his face and groaned. "I told you I could not eat bread."

"No, you're wrong." She walked over to him, hands on her hips, her face twisted into a frown. "You ate too fast."

Francesca was off her rocker. "Need I remind you I am a vampire? We do not feed off freshly baked bread. I need blood." Although the thought of eating anything now rolled his stomach. He leaned back against the wall. "I think I need to lie down."

She shook her head. "You don't need blood. Sleep? Perhaps yes. Humans need lots of sleep."

What was she talking about? "Francesca, I have not a clue of what you mean, but at this point, it may have to wait until later. Sleep sounds good."

"Fine," she said and slipped her hand into her skirt pocket, pulled out a small knife. "But after I make a point because you obviously aren't listening to me." She sliced the knife across the skin of his shoulder.

Luke jumped, instinctively placing a hand over his cut, which stung like fire. "Why did you do that?" He pulled his hand away and frowned at the blood dripping down his upper arm. It was not healing. "What is going on? Why is this happening to me?" He raised his gaze.

Francesca smiled, eyes shining with tears.

"Do not cry, Francesca. Please do not fret. Everything will be fine." Or so he hoped.

Francesca shook her head and laughed lightly. "Oh, Dante. I do not cry out of sadness. I am happy. Don't you see? You are human, Dante. Welcome to purgatory."

* * * *

In the light of dusk, Rafe sat outside Cafe San Eustachio and watched tourists thumb through their brochures and maps. Lost and absorbed in their trivial lives. Still, he loved to watch and pretend himself a part of it all, if only for a small space in time. A weakness he would never admit.

His cell phone rang and he pulled it off his belt clip, flipped it open. "*Buonasera.*"

"Uh, good evening, Rafe. It's Broderick."

"Is she awake?"

"She just left for work. Each day has been a struggle but she's trying."

"Good. Small steps." He remembered vaguely what it was like to be possessed by such strong sentiments, but a couple millennia or so of masking them would cure anyone's emotional vulnerability. "How long before you have to be on your next case?"

"I'm going to New Orleans next week. I've gotten word from a friend she'll be there."

"I'll have my men in place before then. Don't worry, Savannah will be safe."

"I know."

Rafe hesitated, feeling he should say more, but also out of his element. "You're a good friend. Luke believed that too."

"Thanks." Broderick exhaled heavily. "I'll catch up with you later, okay?"

"*Ciao.*" Rafe ended the call. Broderick was a halfling and still young. If he lived long enough, he'd soon learn there was no room for emotions. Still, after Luke's death a change had occurred in the halfling, and he could sense one in himself, which left him uneasy.

A familiar scent wafted past him and he lifted his head. Savannah? He scanned the crowds but didn't spot the human. "Impossible." She couldn't be in Rome, anyway. According to Broderick, she'd left for work. He smoothed a hand over his stubble and sipped an espresso. A ripple of warning lifted the light dusting of hairs on his arms.

Drago was right, he needed a vacation. The last one he'd taken had been several decades ago and long forgotten. Asia? No, he went there often enough on business. A lot of their rarer blood producers came from the Orient. This time he wanted somewhere more secluded and of course, shady. Although he could withstand much more sunlight as an older vampire, he preferred not to push his luck. South America? He smiled. The rainforests would be perfect over the next few months.

"I hoped I would find you eventually, although it has taken several months." The man speaking stood a foot from Rafe's table. Gray slacks hugged his slim hips and trim waist. A blue, collared shirt skimmed his broad chest and arms.

"Evans?" Impossible. He'd seen the vampire disappear with his own eyes. "How?"

The man sat down across from him. "The truth is, I cannot say. I passed." He hesitated. "I cannot explain how, but I awoke sometime later, naked and alone."

"Your body disintegrated." The man looked like Luke, sounded like him, dressed like him. The only difference was his scent. It was human. Rafe leaned back in his chair. "Fascinating. A Blessed's blood doesn't kill. It transforms. You took a risk coming to find me." No human had ever willingly searched him out. Another first, meeting a human who'd previously existed as a vampire.

Luke shifted in his seat, nodding. "I had no choice. I need your help." He looked up, meeting his gaze. "These past few weeks, I have been searching for Savannah. I thought she might be with Lorenzo but he seems to have disappeared completely. Considering my current state as a human, I cannot exactly come out and ask."

Of course. "She isn't with Lorenzo and she didn't turn."

"What do you mean? She drank from me and I drank from her."

"The Blessed cannot be turned. If I had known your intentions, I would have stopped you. Broderick told me you came looking for me, only, it was too late when we found you."

"Where is she?" Luke's hands fisted on the table. "I must have left her to Lorenzo. I do not even know what became of Broderick. I need to—"

"You haven't heard?" Rafe asked. "Lorenzo is dead."

"No, I had not heard. I have lain low. Enemies abound."

"And yet you came to me."

Luke's fists loosened as he relaxed back in his chair. "Yes. If you had wanted me dead, I would have been long ago. And if I am wrong on that account, it would not have mattered. Without Savannah, even a mortal life is not worth living."

"I see," said Rafe. And yet he wasn't truly sure he did understand Luke. "Why now? Why not when you were first changed? A lot has happened over these few months."

Luke took a deep breath. "A fair question, and I shall give you an honest answer. My transformation, as you called it, was not an easy one. I walked well enough but my legs gave out far too often. My stomach could not keep down food. I slept the majority of the days away."

"You relearned to be human to some degree."

Luke nodded. "Exactly. May I ask you a question about the night I last saw Savannah?"

"Ask away," Rafe said.

"Did you kill Lorenzo?"

"No, I didn't have that pleasure. Drago staked his claim long ago. I merely handed Lorenzo over after he did a number on Broderick. Broderick is alive and well."

"I am glad to hear he is okay, and I owe you my thanks," Luke said.

"After what you did at the blood auction, I'd say we're even." Rafe signaled to a waiter for his check. "Savannah is back in Boston. You needn't worry, as Broderick checks in on her and I have sent my men to protect her. No harm will come to her."

Luke's chest rose and fell, and his expression was blank.

The temptation to touch his hand and read his mind was strong, but Rafe resisted. "So what will you do now? Fly to Boston? The past few months have been a struggle. You'll want to avoid scaring her."

"Not yet. I need to procure a property in Boston. A central location for a restaurant."

"You're going to make her dreams come true."

Luke sat quietly for several moments. "I am going to try."

Rafe frowned. What must it feel like to love someone so much you'd risk everything for them? He'd never know.

"And you?" Luke asked. "You see our love as a weakness."

"No." Rafe leaned forward. "I see your humanity as a weakness."

"A pity. Weeks ago, I saw my first sunrise in centuries. It left me speechless. I have woken every day since to catch a glimpse of it." Luke rose as the waiter came to the table with the check. "Thank you for your help." He paused in turning. "Forgive my audacity, but wherever you were when I interrupted you, that is where you should go. You had a relaxed expression, pleasant almost."

"Ah," he replied. Luke was observant as a human. "I considered taking a vacation."

"I see." Luke shrugged. "Perhaps you should do more than consider it."

Rafe nodded and watched as Luke strode away, disappearing into the crowd of tourists.

Chapter 31

Every beginning comes from some other beginning's end.
—Seneca

"Order's ready," Savannah called as she exited the kitchen of Murphy's Irish Pub. "Country fried sweet potatoes with mango chutney. Hummus with balsamic vinaigrette and garlic toast." She handed the large appetizers to Shannon. "These both go to table seven."

Shannon accepted the platters and deftly wove her way through the crowded bar to deliver them safely.

"The new waitress is good, Max." Savannah smiled. "I like her."

"She's okay." Max leaned along the solid wood bar, chin jutting in what she'd term a masculine pout. From the way his blue eyes settled on Shannon, Savannah knew the waitress was more than *okay*, but she kept the thought to herself. She'd spent enough time around Max to pick up on when he was in a fighting mood.

"These past few months you've gone and spoiled my customers, Savannah. How am I supposed to come up with mango chutney and balsamic whatever when you're gone?"

She shook her head and handed another couple plates to Shannon. "Don't start with me. Rosie knows the recipes and she will train someone else in case she needs a backup. Besides, if I get the place I want, it will only be down the street from you. Within walking distance. Speaking of which—" She pulled off her apron and hung it on a hook outside the kitchen door. "I need to leave soon to go meet the seller. I know the location is great but I haven't had a chance to check inside. It's been closed for years. For all I know, the place might require months of work." And lots of money, which was more than likely since the offer seemed way too good to be true.

A tinge of guilt and sadness settled inside her. Four months since Luke's death, and she still found each day a challenge. For the first couple months, she'd resisted depositing the one hundred thousand dollar check Broderick had written her, but Broderick was right. Without the money, she would never have paid off her debt and kept Luke's request. Even with savings and the remainder of the money, she still might have only enough to run the restaurant for four months. She'd have to hit the ground running.

"Do you need me to come with you?"

"No, but thanks. This is the first time I'm seeing it so I'd rather take my time and picture how I want it to look."

"Gotcha." He sighed and pulled her rain coat from beneath the bar. "The heavens look like they're about to open so you'd better take this."

"Rain means good luck." She took her jacket and slipped it on. "Thanks, Max. I'll be back before the evening rush. I promise."

"Yeah, yeah." He waved a hand at her. "Go on and get out of here. The sooner you go, the sooner you come back."

Savannah waved goodbye and stole out the front door. The day was mild for Boston in winter and as Max predicted, rain started within minutes of exiting the pub. By the time she reached the restaurant location a few blocks down, her hood had fallen back, leaving her hair and face soaked. Droplets clung to her cheeks and chin, dripping down her neck into her wool v-neck sweater. The water chilled yet refreshed her at the same time. She shivered and pulled off a soggy piece of paper taped to the door.

Savannah,
Running a bit late. Go ahead and take a look around. See you soon.

She turned the paper over, careful not to rip it. Simple enough instructions, although they could have texted or called her. Oh well.

Twisting the knob, she pushed the door open and stopped. Hardwood floors covered the large space. Maybe oak or pine? Stone walls and a large fireplace. The ceiling gave the space a log cabin feel and despite its size, the restaurant exuded coziness. Afraid to drip all over the place, she pulled off her coat and laid it next to the door then scooped her hair off her face and neck. Obviously, the seller went to great lengths to keep the place in great condition.

Heading toward the back, she pushed open a large wooden door and gasped. The kitchen was huge with stainless steel countertops and appliances. Copper pots hung from a ceiling rack and knives lined a good portion of the back wall.

"What?" She dug into her bag for the information she'd printed on the location. She could have sworn it was a yoga studio prior to being put on the market. Nothing mentioned a restaurant. Not that she'd complain. It was more perfect than she could ever have imagined.

"Is the space to your liking? I did most of the upgrades myself but admittedly had to get some help installing the rack. It weighs a ton, or at least it felt like it after holding it over my head for twenty minutes."

Deep and smooth, the sound of the male's voice froze her. Closing her eyes, she took small, slow breaths. *Don't lose it now. You've done so well.* God help her, he sounded exactly like Luke.

* * * *

Luke's heart thudded intensely as he gripped the wall. Two hundred or so years as an immortal and he had forgotten how weak the human body was. Savannah had not turned and the last thing he wanted was to die of a heart attack before seeing her. Perhaps he'd said too much? Not enough?

Suddenly nervous at her stillness, he pushed off the wall and took a step toward her. "The space is fairly bare. If anything is not to your taste, we can negotiate it in the contract."

She turned. Her eyes shone like pools of emeralds in her pale face. "Am I dreaming?"

His chest ached at the sadness in her voice and expression. He shook his head.

"Then you're alive." She released a shuddery breath and eased down to the floor. Tears slid slowly at first but her breath caught on a sob, turning them into full-blown waterfalls.

"Do not cry, love." He moved forward and kneeled beside her, hugged her against him. "I am here now. Nothing will come between us ever again."

"No." She punched at his chest, the impact surprisingly hard. "How could you? How could you leave me? How could you not tell me what I… what I am?" Pushing away his arms, she tried to crawl away.

He grabbed her arm. "Savannah, wait. I know I behaved a complete idiot."

"No," she bawled, slapping at his hands. "Leave me alone." She created some distance and rocked in a fetal position. "Please, leave me."

"Listen to me, pet." Panic he would not be able to convince her to listen settled in.

"I'm not your love. I'm not your pet."

He scrambled to his feet and moved to the windows along the back wall of the kitchen. The rain had slowed to a drizzle and the sun's rays streamed through. "I did not know how you would take it. I died that day. Look at me."

She shook her head, her moans muffled as she buried her face against her knees.

"Savannah." He bent and pulled her to her feet, uncaring he was rough with her. Desperate for his chance. "Look at me." He shook her.

Her chin lifted before her eyelids drifted open but when they did, the tears had stopped. She frowned at first then her eyes widened as she observed the sunlight shining on his face. "How is this possible?"

"I told you, I died."

"I don't understand." She touched his face, smoothing a finger over his stubble. "Are you—"

"Human?" He finished for her. "Quite." He smiled.

"I don't understand. How?"

He shook his head. "Your blood didn't harm me, it blessed me, changed me."

She bit her bottom lip as if considering her next move.

He unclipped her hair and tucked several strands behind one ear. "Did I ever tell you your habit of biting your bottom lip drives me crazy?" He did not give her a chance to answer as he cupped her chin and kissed her. She tasted of fresh rain and salty tears. Her hand rested on his chest, timid in its exploration over his shoulder and around his neck. "Bloody hell, I missed you." Deepening the kiss, he scooped her into his arms and pushed open the kitchen door with a foot. Setting her on her feet, he took off his wool coat and laid it on the floor. Next, he pulled off his turtle neck.

Her gaze settled on his chest and the hunger he saw there made his heart skip a beat.

"What about the windows?" she asked.

"I have a second chance to be with the woman I love. The windows are hardly a priority. Besides, it is raining. Peeping Toms avoid the rain." He tugged the long-sleeved sweater over her head. Her pink lace bra made his mouth water.

"They do?" She arched a brow.

He grinned and lifted her, letting her legs wrap around his waist as he lowered her with him onto his wool coat. "If they know what is good for them, they do." He kissed her neck and pulled back. "Of course, if it bothers you we can go elsewhere."

She shook her head. "I've come to an understanding with my scars."

"*Every* part of you is beautiful."

She reached for his belt.

"Just a moment." Before she could tug down his pants, he undid the clasp of her bra and hauled her onto his lap. "Patience, love. Let me treasure you."

She placed a hand against his chest. "Has it been you all along? Did you upgrade this entire space?"

He closed his eyes and took a deep breath. "Even the floor you're lying on." He opened his eyes and met her gaze. "For you, for your dreams. And if you'd let me, I would do that and more every day for the rest of my life."

"I need you, Luke."

Bending his head, he found one pert, rosy tip of a breast and suckled. He released a loud, long groan.

Savannah moaned and dropped her head back, pushing her breasts forward. "I've dreamed of this so many nights. I never thought to see you again."

"I know. Forgive me." He squeezed her wet nipple and suckled her other one. "I thought I lost you too. I did not know how else to keep you safe." He buried his head against her stomach, cradling her back as she arched into him. "I say it is time we removed these." He unbuttoned the clasp of her jeans and peeled them over her hips and down her thighs, exposing pink lace underwear. He took a deep breath and coughed.

"Are you okay?" She stilled beneath him.

Remembering a time he'd felt better would have been a feat. "I have yet to accustom myself to the changes in breathing." Wearing her pink lace underwear, she was a sight. Her skin supple, the creamy mounds of her breasts open to his touch. How he had missed her. He swallowed, suddenly recalling he had not loved a woman as a human in over two hundred years.

"Luke?"

He cupped one perfect, creamy mound. "You always wear matching undergarments," he said.

Savannah rose on her elbows, her breast becoming heavier as she leaned into his hand. "Do you really want to discuss my lingerie?"

Luke closed his eyes. Her skin wore the familiar scent of orange blossoms. "I have not loved a woman as a human in a long time." He opened his eyes and met her gaze, amazed at the understanding he recognized there.

"I love you, Luke. And I would accept you in any form. I now realize that." She covered his hand with hers, pushed it against her. "Touch me, be with me."

Fighting the urge to take her right then, he kissed her mouth. His fingers slipped beneath the thin lace and reached her clit, flicked the nub back and forth. "Hell. Forgive me." With one hard yank, he tore the lace from her body and pushed two fingers into her slick sheath.

Savannah climaxed immediately, crying out and gripping his head as her body rolled with waves from her orgasm.

"You were waiting for me." He smiled, enjoying the tranquility of her expression, her half-closed eyes and parted lips. Climbing over her, he settled his hips in line with hers and waited for her to look at him.

Slowly her eyes opened, and impatience lay within their depths. "Are you not going to come inside me?"

"Would you like me to, minx?" Luke came to his knees and unbuttoned his trousers. He slid them off, hovering over her.

Savannah nodded.

"Tell me so," he said. "I want to hear you say the words."

"I want you to come inside me, Luke."

He brought his tip to her entrance and met her gaze.

"I love you," she said.

Her words were all he needed to move forward, thrusting himself inside her, and he growled with the intensity of his emotions. She felt amazing. Like a silk-lined glove, she hugged his length, rolling her hips with each drive into her. "I am never going to let you go." He drove forward. "Never. Do you hear me?" He worked like a piston, moving harder and faster with each plunge into her.

Savannah nodded and let out a soft mewling sound before she catapulted upward and wrapped her arms around his neck. He thrust one last time and poured his seed into her, cradling her to him.

Smoothing her cheek along his, she kissed his ear. "Ditto."

He pulled back. He'd heard the word before and yet its meaning eluded him. It seemed becoming human had not made him any more modern. "And ditto means?"

She sighed and kissed him, lingering on his bottom lip. "It means unless you have another buyer, renter or whatever for this restaurant space, you're going to have a hard time getting rid of me."

Chapter 32

Love is the condition in which the happiness of another person is essential to your own
—Robert Heinlein

Almost eight months later...

"Hmmm." Savannah stood back from the large pot and tasted a spoonful of what appeared to be a yellow creamy puree. "This is the best creamy polenta I've ever made. I think being pregnant definitely has its perks when it comes to supersensitive senses. I've got to rewrite the recipe."

Luke bent beside her and placed his hand on her slightly rounded stomach. Only recently had it begun protruding and he could not resist touching her every chance he got. "You mean, now since you have moved beyond the morning sickness stage?"

She frowned and shoved him gently. "Of course. Stand back or you'll get burned. Need I remind you again you no longer cure instantly?" She tsk-tsked at the scars on his arms. "I should ban you from my kitchen altogether."

Instead of obeying, he moved around behind her and wrapped his arms around her waist. "Do your worst. Every moment of being with my wife is worth the risk." He kissed her temple, earlobe then neck.

"Charmer." She laughed, lifted a hand and caressed his cheek and lips.

"Enough, love birds. There's already one loaf in the oven." Broderick nodded at her belly. "And the restaurant is opening in a few hours. I said I'd help wait tables this weekend, not run the restaurant."

"See what you did?" Savannah elbowed Luke. "No worries, Broderick. Most of the staff should be in soon. I don't expect tonight to be too bad, as it's a Tuesday."

Luke rubbed his ribs and grinned. "My modest wife for you. Works miracles, but at some point she is going to have to start delegating more to the wonderful people she hired."

Broderick shook his head. "Kiss ass."

Luke shrugged. Maybe so, but at least he knew whose ass to kiss. He smiled and lovingly rubbed Savannah's hip.

"Not yet." Broderick met his gaze. "You two can get back to loving later. We've got a visitor."

Luke straightened. "But we are closed."

As if on cue, Rafe entered the kitchen, his impenetrable mask in place. "Savannah, Luke." He nodded. "I hope you don't mind my dropping in."

Luke straightened. What was the Ancient doing so far from home? "Rafe."

"No, we don't," Savannah said, patting Luke's arm. "You know you are always welcome here." She hugged Rafe, who received her awkwardly.

"No worries, Luke," Rafe said. "I'm only here to wish you a happy birthday and congratulations."

Happy birthday? "But you are mistaken. I was not born on this date."

Rafe reached into his backpack and pulled out two packages. "I'm talking about your *second* birth as a human."

Luke nodded in understanding.

Rafe handed the packages to Savannah. "The box is from Francesca. I don't believe you've met her. She's a good friend of Luke's who took him in after his transformation." Rafe met Luke's gaze. "Is that not right?"

"It is. I have told Savannah about Francesca. Our hope is to bring the baby to Rome once she is old enough to travel. I would like for Francesca to meet her."

"Oh, these are stunning." Savannah held up several glass napkin holders. They sparkled beneath the light, their metallic colors rich and vibrant.

"They're made of Murano glass. I believe Francesca said each had a unique design. Collector items. The second package is from me."

"Please tell her thank you from us." Savannah pulled the paper wrapping aside from the second package. "Oh, Rafe."

"Handmade lace tablecloths," he said. "I thought they would be useful for your restaurant."

"Thank you, they're beautiful." She stood on her tiptoes and kissed his cheek. Setting the tablecloths down, she turned to Broderick. "Would you mind helping me get some napkins from behind the bar? I need to fold a few more for tonight."

"Sure," Broderick said as he followed her out of the kitchen.

Luke released a sigh of relief his wife was no longer in the room. "Thank you for everything."

"I'm not sure you mean that." Rafe set down his backpack and peered into the large pot on the stove.

"I assure you, I do. You may excuse my nervousness. Previously, I stood a slight chance protecting my wife and unborn child. Now I am a mere human again."

"But you enjoy it, don't you?" Rafe cleared his throat. "Francesca also said to ask you about your paradise."

"She is something else." Luke smiled. "You can let her know paradise is treating me just fine and that I hope there are no further parallels with my life and his. And in answer to your question, I would not change what happened for the world. I would die first before reclaiming immortality."

"Powerful words." Rafe picked up his bag. "I'll pass along your message to Francesca when I see or talk to her next."

"Where are you off to now?"

"South America. For a couple months or more. I've decided to heed your advice and do more than consider a vacation."

Luke lifted a brow. "I am glad you decided to move forward with it. The other Ancients permitted you to leave?"

Rafe smirked. "Drago suggested it." He tilted his head. "Enjoy your day and take care of your family."

"I will."

* * * *

Savannah walked in to find Luke leaning against a counter, deep in thought. "What did Rafe want?"

He looked up, smiling as he saw her. She placed a hand on her stomach as their child fluttered within her, then smiled. "Was he not going to stay for dinner?"

"No, he is on his way to South America."

"Are you serious?"

"Yes." Luke tugged her to him. "Says he needs a vacation."

"Oh." About time. He seemed a great guy, beyond the edgy exterior and serious demeanor. The fact he was one of the most powerful vampires living might scare some women off, though.

"Savannah, what's going on in your mischievous mind?"

"I'm thinking maybe Rafe will meet someone meant for him."

Luke stepped back. "It is not easy. You do realize what happened to us was extremely rare, perhaps even unheard of?"

"I do, but I still wish him the best. Over a year ago you never would have imagined you'd be standing here as a human, making out with your wife."

"No." He kissed her. "As always, you make me see sense."

"Tease." She gently shoved his arm. "Have I told you how much I love you?"

"Yes." Luke smiled. "But I shall never tire of hearing it."

Meet the Author

Toni Kelly first discovered a passion for writing at the tender age of six when her mother would "publish" her scribbled tales using trusty old Word Perfect. Gradually, stories of geese and golden eggs became poems and essays, until one fateful night nearly a decade later when Toni snuck a romance novel from her mother's room. The cover's backdrop was scenic, with mountains and a lake, but the couple of focus really caught her attention—a beautiful woman with long, wavy red hair and a stunningly handsome male enveloping her in his arms. Needless to say, several nights of reading later, Toni was in love with the characters as well as the romance genre itself.
So, after years of reading thousands of novels—romance as well as other genres—and several attempts to write "stories" for leisure, Toni decided to make a go of her passion and write her first manuscript.

When Toni is not writing or thinking up new plot ideas, she loves traveling and experiencing different cultures, languages and traditions. Many times these experiences provide inspiration for her writing. In addition to this, Toni is bilingual in English and Spanish and currently working on teaching herself Italian whenever time permits.

Acknowledgements

A special thanks to…

My family and friends, who have supported and inspired me.

Mary, my editor, whose encouragement only pushes me to further grow
as an author.

Turn the page for a special excerpt of Toni Kelly's

Irish Dreams

It's one thing to resist an Irish dream, quite another to resist a dreamy Irishman.

After being traded for another woman by her fiancé, Maggie decides she's had it with men. Good thing she's far away from him, in Ireland fulfilling her best friend's request to be maid-of-honor. Wicklow and the Emerald Isle are more than she expects…green, lush, and exactly what she needs. What she doesn't need is rescuing by some emerald-eyed charmer.

Newly divorced, Ethan Moore is ready to enjoy bachelorhood. Only one problem…the fiery-haired Maggie Christy. Unlike any woman he's ever met, Maggie draws him close and turns him inside out. The attraction is unexpected and inconvenient, but nobody ever said true love was easy.

On sale now!

Chapter 1

"Only smiles, Margaret Christy." Elsie Rogers grabbed Maggie's hands and squeezed tight, smiling with the cloud-floating happiness of a woman in love. "This is Ireland, land of rainbows, legends. It's beautiful here and there are tons of gorgeous Irishmen all over the island. Last thing I want you thinking about is a jerk whose name I won't even mention, as he doesn't deserve such an honor."

"I'm not," she lied, pushing thoughts of Rick away. Elsie was right. Maggie took a deep breath of Irish country air and released it slowly. Ireland was like a dream. The Georgian styled Rose Hill House, Elsie's soon-to-be permanent home, sat atop a hill amongst a crescent of trees. A blanket of ivy crawled midway up the house's stone facade, reminding Maggie of the homes in the historical romances she loved to read. "It's strange because I always thought of myself as a city girl."

"Why is that strange?" Elsie asked as she turned to watch her fiance pull around the front of the house on the gravel drive.

"Well, we're out in the Irish countryside and the nearest city is actually a tiny village."

"Enniskerry is a very complete village. There are shops, restaurants, a barbershop, oh, and Dublin is only thirty or so minutes away from there. Dublin is quite a large city."

"I know," Maggie said. "You don't need to convince me. What I'm trying to say very poorly is that I somehow feel at home here." And despite the hollowness in her chest, she would be happy because her best friend married the love of her life--not because of some Irishman, or any man for that matter.

"I really am happy." Maggie forced an upward curve to her lips despite the fact her cheeks seemed cemented in place. "For you though, not some Irish stranger. Now come on." She tugged her friend's hand, leading her toward the waiting car. "Before your wonderful, handsome fiance gets mad at me for keeping you."

"Bryan isn't like that. He's great." Her lips parted in a dreamy grin. "Are you sure you don't want to come to Dublin Airport?"

"I'm positive. It's important you and Bryan be there to greet your parents. Besides, where would I sit, on your dad's lap? I'm a bit heavier now than at age five."

"Hardly." Elsie blinked her large hyacinth blue eyes. Those same eyes could be deceivingly innocent at times. Maggie knew better. "You sure you're okay with this?"

"Yes. Ask me one more time, I just might strangle you. Please don't worry. I've only been here a couple of hours. I wanted to tour the grounds. Before I know it, you'll be back and we'll be having dinner. Now go." She gave her a gentle shove.

Elsie turned and hugged her, kissing her cheek lightly. "Thank you. I'm so glad you're here."

Maggie walked through an enchanting garden, along a wall of bushes which appeared to be part of a maze. She brushed her hand against tidy, trimmed hedges. The Kelley estate might as well have been described on an Austen novel's pages. Different country perhaps, but stunning nonetheless.

A horse's frantic whinny came from near the forest beyond the hedges. She strayed toward it, recalling Elsie had mentioned the stables' location on the opposite side of the estate. Strange, the sound would come from the forest. Unlike Phoenix, no skinny, spiny-looking stumps grew here. No, these were rich, thick, knobby-looking trees. Those you read about in fairytales or legends.

As she rounded an edge of trees, a horse stood in the open, white, magnificent and somehow wedged between sharp boards of a broken fence. Maggie approached, wary. How had the horse gotten across the estate without being seen? The animal shoved its body to and fro, eyes rolling backward. "Whoa." She glanced beneath the horse. A mare. "Whoa, girl."

The mare tossed her head, lifting then slamming her front hooves on the ground.

"Careful, girl. You're going to hurt yourself." Maggie didn't have much experience with horses but it didn't take an expert equestrian to see the animal would end up stabbing itself unless it calmed down. She took several quick breaths, and lifted shaky hands toward the mare. A little bit closer. "All right, I'm moving these boards in front of you. Please don't panic." She spoke to herself as much as to the horse and climbed the fence.

Maggie found her opening and reached out, keeping her body back as she tugged on an upper plank. With several yanks, the stubborn piece of wood broke loose. "There you go, girl. One more."

The mare stopped shoving and backed up as if to give some room.

"Atta girl. You're a good lady, aren't you?" Maggie cooed. The thundering within her chest slowed. One more piece. It sat lower, requiring a jump off the short fence. The horse didn't mind. Bending low, Maggie moved closer and reached for the second plank. A shrill ring of her cellphone disturbed the morning stillness.

In response, the mare rose on two hind legs and came down, breaking the second plank away. Maggie avoided her hooves but not the board flying toward her. A burst of sharp pain radiated across her forehead. Her vision went black.

* * * *

"We're done, Miriam. If you love me as you say you do, you should have thought first before jumping into bed with that bastard co-worker." Ethan Moore held the phone away from his ear as his soon-to-be ex-wife ranted about how he never loved her enough. Perhaps what she said fell closer to truth than he'd admit. Didn't change his mind or mood. He didn't care to hear a recital of his life's mistakes at this time. "Enough. Sign the blasted papers and be done with it. You never loved me, you loved my money. Take the estate in Georgia. Don't call me again until you've signed everything."

She started to protest, when a high-pitched scream echoed across the hills. Christ, what now?

"I've got to go." He pushed the End Call button on his Blackberry. Hooves beat against the earth, and his most recently purchased mare cantered toward him. "Whoa." She barely slowed as he stepped alongside her. Grabbing her mane as he'd done with many different horses since childhood, he swung himself onto her bare back and squeezed lightly with his thighs. She eased her pace.

"Aye, there's a beauty." He reached down, gave her flank a few gentle pats. "What has you running, Misty Eyes?" And where was his damn groom? Curious as to how she ended up at the edge of his property, he guided her forward, over the hill's crest. Below, along fence separating Moore property from the Kelley estate, a body lay sprawled on verdant lawn. The scream he'd heard. "Shit."

His gut seized and with one hip thrust, he pushed the mare into a gallop. He slowed near the body. A woman, by the shape. Holding the horse's mane, he swung down from her back. "Stay here."

Dressed in jeans and a simple white collared shirt, the woman lay immobile. A mass of burnt-red curls covered her face, locks he would have admired under other circumstances.

"Miss." Careful not to move her, he lifted her hair, unveiling a quarter-sized cut on the upper right of her forehead. Blood streamed down her brow, contrasting sharply with her pale skin. With a couple fingers along her neck, he picked up a steady pulse beneath her skin. "Miss."

She stirred. Twisting her head, she attempted to sit up, and made it halfway to rest on her elbows. A crease formed between her brows. "Ouch. Horse?"

Christ. Had Misty Eyes caused this? Now he would kill his groom. Slipping his hands beneath her, he lifted her up. Her weight felt slight, her curves subtle. "You're going to be okay."

"Horse," she murmured.

"Don't you worry about Misty Eyes. She's fine."

Dark skies above them rumbled, threatening a storm. He slid her onto the mare first before mounting behind her. Fat drops smacked his face and hands. Pulling her back, he settled her against his chest. Scents of vanilla and rain enveloped him, soothing yet fresh. Definitely not what he needed, but no gentleman worth his name would leave an injured woman abandoned. He'd only heard a couple words. Her accent wasn't Irish. Most likely a tourist who'd strayed from the road.

Heavy-looking clouds rolled across the gray sky. Rain fell harder, seeping through the thin cotton of his shirt. At this rate, they'd find themselves sopping wet before reaching the cottage. Squeezing his thighs, he pushed Misty Eyes from a trot into a canter. Nothing need be complicated. He'd take the woman to his cottage, get her cleaned up then send her on her way.